CAVERNS OF THE CROSS

CAVERNS OF THE CROSS

HAL SISSON

Edited
by
Linda Field

ARSENAL PULP PRESS
Vancouver

CAVERNS OF THE CROSS

ARSENAL PULP PRESS
103-1014 Homer Street
Vancouver, B.C.
Canada V6B 2W9

The publisher gratefully acknowledges the support of the Canada Council for the Arts for its publishing program, and the support of the Book Publishing Industry Development Program, and the B.C. Arts Council.

Typeset by the Vancouver Desktop Publishing Centre
Printed and bound in Canada by Printcrafters

CANADIAN CATALOGUING IN PUBLICATION DATA:
Sisson, Hal C., 1921-
Caverns of the cross

ISBN 1-55152-049-4

I. Title.
PS8587.I79C38 1997 C813'.54 C97-910922-1
PR9199.3.S57C3 1997

Acknowledgements

My thanks to Doug Cherry and Ed McCourt (gone but not forgotten)—University of Saskatchewan English professors to whom I promised I would one day write some novels. And to Pearl Baldwin, Bill Fowler, Pat Macdonald, Dwayne Rowe, and Glen Acorn, fellow wordsmiths; Bob Tyrrell and Linda Field, editors; Brian Young and Carolyn Swayze, literary agents. And to anyone else who gave me encouragement, with special thanks to those who tried to discourage me, thus making me more determined to do so.

The organizations, cults, and theories in the novel do exist and form an essential backdrop to the fictional events and characters, with the exception of Azusipa Dionusos Inc., which is a fictitious drug company.

PROLOGUE

Whenever God erects a house of prayer,
The Devil always builds a chapel there;
And 'twill be found, upon examination,
The latter has the largest congregation.

Vatican City, Christmas Day, 1999 A.D.

HIS MOTHER HAD GIVEN him the tripartite talisman when he joined the priesthood. Pagan tainted, it hung unobtrusively among the beads of his rosary. Called a *figaschmuk* in some parts of the world, the golden good luck charm took the form of a clenched fist with thumb thrust upward at the world between the first and second fingers. The other two items on the amulet were a tiny gold nail and the cuspid tooth of his great-grandfather. Together they made up his worry beads, whose meaning was, "Fight Tooth and Nail—Against the Devil." And that he did.

As one hand stroked the figa, he watched Monsignor Sebastian complete the final check before the annual "Urbi et Orbi" speech to the City of Rome and the world. He sat as if sculpted by Rodin, his body leaning forward, his other hand on his chin, remembering that no Pope had ever beaten the system that stretched back two thousand years. He listened to the bands performing outside in St. Peter's Square. Under the long white robe, a huarache-clad foot tapped time to the strains of the Papal Anthem. It didn't seem to play well—the music had sounded better in South America, with more bounce, more beat. He missed Rio de Janeiro, where he had been an archbishop until the net results of the assassination of Pope John Paul I, Albino Luciani, and of another such attempt on the life of Pope John Paul II, had eventually placed him on the throne of St. Peter.

He waited behind the tall windows backing the central balcony and looked out over the fifty thousand people who jammed the immense curving plaza. At morning mass in the Basilica, while the Sistine Choir chanted the Pontifical High mass "Thou Art Peter," he had proceeded down the aisle to the Altar of Confession above the burial place of Peter, the Prince of Apostles. There he had sworn that this Christmas Day he would make an announcement important to the future of all parishioners of the Holy See on Earth.

He was aware that challenging the traditional dogma had long been considered heresy by the civil service of the Vatican. Authority is power: the power to decide the issues in dispute, whether they are questions of doctrine or practice, and whether they are approved by the Curia or not. So what should he do, what should he decide?

But that doesn't matter any longer, he thought, for it is I who have to make up my mind now. I am the Pontiff, and therefore the authoritative instrument that interprets Christ's mind on this issue. That's what I am, and God knows it has to be decided. There are some things upon which I never did agree with Karol Wojtyla. He wasn't always right and the same will apply to me. A good man, Pope John Paul II, he thought, and although Ali Agca hadn't killed him, he had certainly shortened the Pope's life.

And now I, the two hundred and sixty-fourth successor to Peter the Fisherman, the elected lineal descendant of the Vicar of Christ . . . Pope Cesare Romereo I . . . I am in the hot seat.

He had chosen the name because there were so many Popes named Pius, Peter, John, Paul, and Innocent in the past few centuries that an ecclesiastical program was needed to tell them apart. The Pope can be a man of any nationality, but ideally he would be a man of no nationality. Impossible, of course. He was the first Pope from South America, chosen, like his predecessors, by a small group of electors. Wojtyla from Poland had started a trend. Prior to his election most Popes had been Italian, although there had been a few Syrians, Greeks, Spaniards, and Frenchmen, one Englishman and one Dutchman. The Roman team dominated the league, because they controlled the scheduling, and always played on their home turf, with very few, if any, games on the road. In any event, thought Romereo, the Pope's office appears to be the lineal descendant of the

Caesars, which is why I used my own name. It also contains the name "Rome." The Curia had been favourably surprised by his choice.

The bells of St. Peter's began to toll the hour. He stood up, adjusted his underwear under the pretense of fiddling with his robe, and then, flanked by his new Secretary of State and the Vice-General of Rome, he stepped through the glass doors opening onto the third floor balcony of the Apostolic Palace, high above the oval of St. Peter's Square enclosed by Bernini's colonnades. Stepping into the winter Roman sunshine like so many Popes before him, he heard the roar of the crowd burst over his head and ricochet between the building and the Leonine Wall, filling the square with noise. Involuntarily he thrust his hands over his head in a cheerful salute to their friendly welcome, a reflex from his soccer-playing days. Almost knocked off my mitre, he thought. He adjusted his hat and stepped up to the microphones. His peripheral vision registered the equipment of both Vatican Radio and Television, which would relay his Christmas message to nearly two hundred countries in many languages, an estimated audience of six hundred million. The vast crowd in the piazza crossed themselves as one, shouted "Viva el Papa!" His voice sounded strange to his own ears as it boomed out over the banks of loudspeakers positioned around the square.

Dear God, he prayed silently, don't let me bungle this.

CHAPTER ONE

MEKRAN MKENDIO

WITH HIS EYES FIXED firmly on the pot-bellied figure of the Native guide ahead of him, Nestor LaPretre followed Pacheco through the Acquarico River rainforest. They followed no discernible trail, just Pacheco's sense of direction. With one hand Nestor alternately wiped rivulets of sweat from his face and brushed off the spiders that kept falling on his head and shoulders. His guide was a member of the Huarorani tribe of Ecuador, known as Aucas, which means "killers." Pacheco, however, lived in the village of Paroto Yaco, which in turn was an outpost of the town of Coca, which was an outpost of the City of Quito, the capital of Ecuador, which some consider an outpost of the world. Nestor's guide was what could loosely be called a "friendly" Indian, as opposed to what Pacheco described as "free" Aucas, who are hostile and live throughout the Upper Amazon, often referred to by the inhabitants as *sacha mama hermosa*—beautiful mother jungle.

In the forest, Nestor and Pacheco came upon a small stream in a low gully, which suddenly opened into a clearing and revealed a plantation of yucca. This was definite evidence of the presence of the Aucas in the jungle. Nestor bent down to examine the crop more closely. Seeing him do so, Pacheco hurried back and grasped his arm.

The guide nervously admonished him not to pick the plant, not to steal from the Red Feet. Nestor peered about apprehensively, but all that he could see was a thick wall of plantain and coconut trees rising like towers, in various shades of green; all that he could hear was the chattering of monkeys—the other main source of food for the Indians.

They moved off again into the rainforest, continuing their search for an elusive plant, rumoured to contain a drug of mysterious powers. Eventually they circled back toward the oil camp of the Ecuador State Petroleum Corporation, where they would again spend the night.

The Aucas were a tribe of South American Indians, feared throughout the hinterland for their vicious attacks on other tribes and their women. They were called Red Feet because the men wore little more than a string around their waists, and painted their bodies and legs with the red dye from the seeds of the Anita tree. These Aucas lived primarily from the hunt, but also grew crops of yucca. Living in communities of up to forty people and separated from other settlements by many miles, they moved every two years because the Ecuadorian soil could not support successive crops, nor could the surrounding jungle continue to sustain them.

Considered one of the most remote tribes on earth, many of the Aucas had never met outsiders. They wanted no contact with civilization and often took drastic measures to prevent the encroachment of strangers on what they regarded as their private preserve. The Red Feet were rumoured to be able to prevent pregnancy and control the population of their various nomadic bands by ingesting quantities of a certain plant which grew in the rainforests of the Amazon basin. The effects of the plant were said to last for long periods of time.

Nestor LaPretre, a Canadian plant geneticist, had come to Ecuador hoping to find the powerful plant. He had been working on experiments for new contraceptives for a long time, and hoped that the plant would be the final ingredient he needed to make a breakthrough.

Nestor had gone to the Ecuadorian authorities in Quito to explain his mission. The United Nations Population Control Program might also be interested, he'd told them, because they sought to keep populations within the bounds of food supply and a healthy environment.

Skeptical at first, Carlos del Toro, the government official, asked many questions. Nestor answered each thoroughly, his enthusiasm building. Slowly del Toro began to warm to the subject, mentally listing the positive consequences of such a find. In the end he offered as much help as was available.

Carlos del Toro had hired Pacheco, who in turn introduced Nestor to a Native woman. She was ancient, with a lined and weathered face. As they squatted in a circle inside her hut, she told them, yes, there was a vine called *mekran mkendio.* To prepare it for use, the buds and reproductive portion of the plant were gathered and set aside. Then the rhizomes, or underground stems, were dug up, washed, and chewed to a pulpy mass, usually by girls with strong jaws and teeth. The pulp was spat into a wooden bowl, mixed with coconut milk, then kneaded by hand. Next the buds were mixed in, and the whole mess left to ferment for several hours. After straining the solids out, the liquid was ready. The drink, called *kaiapo*, was consumed for up to a week by girls who had reached puberty, which kept them from getting pregnant.

Getting the old woman's description of the plant was a slow and uncertain process, but get it he did. It was a deciduous perennial climbing vine growing to perhaps the height of two men. The roots were yellow; the leaves cordate or heart-shaped. Mulberry in colour, the hairiness on the under surface of the plant extended to the topside but only at the edges, giving them a reddish tinge. The top surface of the thick leaf was light green with prominent veins, notched in a peculiar manner at the apex. This plant could be related to the yam family. The medicine woman had also told them that the leaves, when chewed, were considered a remedy for flatulence because of tonic and digestive properties. It was, all in all, a versatile plant, but one whose main benefit was the prevention of pregnancy.

Traditionally, in many of the local areas, females married while still in childhood. Given this plant cocktail at puberty, they became infertile for many years, some claimed up to six. The older women even claimed it prevented discomfort in menopause.

A scientist had to be skeptical, to be a disbeliever until something was proven, but having come this far, Nestor would follow the lead to its end, whatever came to pass. After all, he was a professional plant hunter, travelling light and usually alone, and if he had to hack his way through a wall of living jungle with a machete, dragging his canoe behind him, he'd do it to accomplish his goal. Now was the time, especially before even the rainforest itself disappeared in the onslaught of civilizations' formidable army of oil companies, ranchers, gold miners, settlers, and Christian missionaries.

Nestor conferred with del Toro after talking with the medicine woman, and together they mulled over the information on the plant. Depending on how many doses were taken, the potency of the particular plant, and the age of the person ingesting it, the end result was prevention of conception for a year or longer. In spite of a niggling suspicion that the old crone was having him on, Nestor's enthusiasm was growing.

Father Athol Levesque, a missionary of the Capuchin Brothers, viewed the rainforest from a helicopter which skimmed the surface of the impenetrable foliage below. Nothing else was visible, except for an occasional village, camp, clearing or river, or where a track had been cut through the jungle by the oil companies. Their seismic crews were constantly detonating dynamite charges as part of the search for petroleum. Bulldozers and chain saws had ploughed a few narrow roads through this thick jungle.

Levesque knew that the Indians didn't like the jungle to be disturbed by loud noises. They worried that the sound would frighten away the monkeys, resulting in poor hunting. They must think they are being invaded, thought Levesque.

Indeed, a war had been going on in that portion of the Amazon since about 1956. On the side of civilization were about fifteen U.S. and European oil firms, invited by the Ecuadorian government to help exploit the riches of the nation's region. Once roads were established, settlers were bound to follow into the virgin rainforests. At one time, only three thousand people lived on six million acres, but now there were more than one hundred thousand. This wasn't a lot by modern standards, Levesque knew, but still too many. Civilization had allies—influenza, measles, virulent malaria, and chicken pox—to which scourges the bodies of Indians had no immunity or resistance.

On the other side were the Indians—the Red Foot Aucas and other indigenous tribes, nomadic and small in numbers, who fought to defend the land upon which they had always lived. Their only weapons were spears, arrows, sticks, and stones. Facing extinction, although perhaps not perceiving that fact, they clashed more often with the cowboy-type settlers—and more blood was being spilled between the Indians and the oil company employees, just as had happened in Brazil.

Father Levesque gazed down on the home of the Natives and the countless named and unnamed species of animals, insects, and plants, all of them endangered. “They seek to do good,” he roared out the helicopter door into the wind. There were none to hear him over the high decibel whine of the rotor blades and the motor. “But they know not what they do!”

“But I know what they do,” he muttered more quietly to himself. “They spend billions on these goddamned—you'll pardon the expression, Lord, but I mean it—projects, which destroy everything. It is all for naught!”

Having got that off his mind, Athol once again began his spotting of the land below. They were now flying over an area where several deadly attacks had felled palm and lumber company workers, and where several years previously the Red Feet had speared five American evangelists to death.

Evangelists, yes, but they wouldn't kill a priest, a true man of God, Father Levesque reminded himself. At least they hadn't done it yet, and there had been several contacts between priests and the Aucas. Levesque himself had met them a few times both in and near the outpost of Lago Agrio, where some of them occasionally came to trade. He felt that his robes, cross, and friendly demeanour were his armour, and would make them realize that he came in peace. He always wore his cassock—after all, he didn't wish to be mistaken for a Protestant. Recently he had made several flights in the helicopter in the hope of finding an accessible camp of Aucas so that he could attempt a visit. At sixty-seven years of age, during his long career as a missionary priest, he had conquered many tribes for Christ, and had every hope of doing so with the Aucas. If he could befriend and convert one band, the Holy Church could use it as a base to bring true Christianity to the Huaroranis, thus stopping the violence and the killings. He, Father Levesque, would be the instrumental factor in preventing their extinction.

The pilot signaled to the left. Athol swung his binoculars in that direction while the chopper circled to get a better view. A small plantation came into sight—a group of six thatched huts around the edge of a clearing, some palm leaf mats, a cooking fire. Half a dozen men were huddled near the fire; several shades of red flashed through his glasses. There were some women, three children, a baby being fed, some dogs and chickens.

“That's it,” Levesque yelled into the pilot's ear, “this is the place. Don't spook them by circling again. Mark the location.”

The chopper, rapidly gaining altitude, flew back to Coca and the Mission.

CHAPTER TWO

REDFOOT AUCAS

MEN CHECKED THEIR RIFLES and equipment in preparation for another day of guarding the convoys of trucks that travelled from one rainforest location to another. The men controlled the roads, the Aucas controlled the bush. "Where do you want to go after breakfast?" the camp foreman asked Nestor.

"I just search," Nestor replied, looking at the map. "Since I don't know exactly where to look, there is no need to go any long distance. There's lots of jungle, so if you drop us off at the middle of this straight stretch of road, we can get a directional fix to hit on the way back."

"Good enough," said the foreman, "just so we don't have to go looking for you. That's not part of the deal. My men don't like it. You better take this gun with you." He handed Nestor a Colt .45 revolver in a shoulder holster and a few rounds of ammunition. "I've got enough problems without having to look for your body in the bush."

Again Nestor and Pacheco moved into the hinterland surrounding the oil camp, Nestor carrying the collecting press and wearing knee-high rubber boots as protection against big pincer ants and other biting bugs. It was just past dawn as they watched the mist slowly evaporating through the trees. Their eyes searched the jungle floor, looking for the heart-leafed plant. As this was a search for a particular species, Nestor did not follow his usual practice of gathering varied plant parts that seemed worthy of attention, or any species that he considered new and different. This time he only wanted what he had come for—the entire *mekran mkendio* plant: roots, vine, seeds. He would also take cuttings for propagation and some soil samples for antibiotic screening. Later the plant would be grown in a greenhouse on his experimental station, serving as a germ-plasm repository in his genetic research into its chromosomes.

Luckily the rains held off. Although the sun scorched the treetops, it was cool in the underbrush, even chilly in the early morning. They saw monkeys, anteaters, and birds, heard some distant explosions, and once an unseen helicopter flew overhead. For Nestor the place was a positive mental joy, if not a physical one. From a scientific view, it was stimulating despite the discomfort. Botanists and zoologists estimate that there are maybe five million plants, insects, and animals in the rainforests of the world—constituting half of all the plant and animal species on earth, a gene pool that could provide humanity with improved crops, medicines, and the potential for scientific discoveries of incalculable benefit.

Pacheco, with a backpack containing rags, bags of peat moss, and small provisions, and carrying his .303 rifle, walked at Nestor's side. They seldom spoke, except for Pacheco's complaints about his heavy load. They looked over at each other often; Nestor had no wish to become separated.

Nestor looked up and stopped dead in his tracks. In front of him was a cool and misty grove of tall trees covered with a tangle of lianas and other vines, in the centre of which a giant ceiba tree sliced the sky. As he edged closer to the tree he saw the most exquisite orchid he had ever seen. It hung like a rare jewel, with a dozen enormous blossoms of a colour not usually associated with *orchidacae.* It riveted his attention as he sprang quickly forward to observe its beauty more closely. In his enthusiasm he didn't see the crooked root that tripped him and arched his body head first into the thick tangle of vines and underbrush beneath the big tree.

Surprisingly, Nestor felt no pain upon landing. Instead he became aware that he'd fallen on something soft and unfamiliar. It took some moments before the object registered in Nestor's mind. This also came as a surprise to the twenty-nine-foot anaconda that had chosen that spot for a full-bellied siesta while digesting a monkey.

"Jesus Christ!" he shrieked. "Snake! Snake!"

Like lightning, the cool, muscled flesh of the giant reptile coiled instinctively around Nestor's fear-stricken body and started to crush him into insensibility, only slightly hampered by the simian remains in his belly. Nestor reacted quickly, reminding himself not to exhale, to keep his chest expanded as much as possible. He struggled mightily, but not in an attempt to extricate himself from the serpent's coils, for he knew no human would have the strength to do so. He was trying to get the Colt out of the shoulder holster. He got his right hand on the butt of the gun and jerked at it with all his might. The revolver came free just as he thought it was all over. He would never get a better look at a boa constrictor—the tough iridescent dark green skin with black spots, the large head and gaping jaws looming over him as he felt his ribs strain under the frightful pressure. Was the safety catch on or off? Damned if he could remember. Son of a bitch! He would just have to shoot and hope, try to aim into that god-awful mouth.

He pulled the trigger. Nothing happened. His fingers searched frantically for the safety. As he blacked out, his dimming eyes saw a spear go into one side of the boa's head and out the other.

The coils around Nestor's body jerked, tightening and relaxing alternately as the boa thrashed around in the agony of death. Luckily Nestor could not see or feel himself being flung about on the forest floor. The only observers of that little wrestling match were Pacheco and two Aucas, one of whom ran forward to retrieve his spear. They pulled the coils of the monstrous dead snake from Nestor's body and stretched them both out on the ground.

He lay in the thicket for several minutes before his eyes began to focus on his surroundings. Three figures stood at a distance, watching him. Gradually Nestor realized that two of them were of a reddish hue and naked. But nothing could scare him now, not after the boa constrictor, part of which he could see lying motionless nearby. Slowly Nestor's attention was drawn to something in the immediate vicinity of his face. It was a heart-shaped leaf with a notch at the top, a reddish edge, and prominent veins. In a moment, his heart began to race. *Mekran mkendio!*

Nestor's excitement about both being alive and finding the *mekran mkendio* translated into excessive gratitude toward the Aucas. It was hard to tell which they liked better—the gift of his Bic lighter or the windfall of the large snake, which would provide good eating for the whole tribe. Nestor noted with some trepidation the eyes of his rescuers—they were as cold and expressionless as a rock face.

Guarding the *mekran mkendio* carefully, Nestor rested on the ground as he watched the Red Feet work over the giant snake. The big bulge in its belly was many times larger than the boa's ordinary circumference. One of the Aucas slit the bulge with a machete, revealing the already decomposing body of the monkey, which seemed to please them mightily. Nestor knew enough not to demonstrate fear or weakness as he choked back his nausea. He wondered how a snake whose mouth was only inches wide could swallow a monkey whose body measured more than a foot in diameter. Still dazed, Nestor watched as the Aucas said a few words to Pacheco in Huarorani, packed up the snake and the monkey and faded away into the jungle.

"I want to come with you, Father." The speaker was Sister Angelica Toucan, a Catholic nun based at the Capuchin Brothers Mission, who had been of great assistance to Levesque in his proselytizing amongst the South American Indians. They were in the Coca Mission building office discussing Father Levesque's ambitious plans, which he had formulated upon his return from the air reconnaissance when he had spotted the Red Feet. "I know I could be of use and I want to be there from the beginning," Angelica pleaded with him.

"It's against my better judgment. I don't want you to get hurt, Angie. I'd feel so badly if anything went wrong. We've been together too long."

"That's just it, Athol, I'm sure nothing will go wrong. But if anything did happen, I'd want to be there with you. Please," she said, staring straight into his eyes.

"Oh, all right then. Now let's get on with it." Father Levesque could never resist her forthright ways. They continued with their preparations for a return helicopter flight the next morning, to the site where, at long last, Levesque hoped to establish contact with the Huaroranis.

Levesque was worried about the oil, lumber, cattle, and gold interests in the area. Their incursions were causing irrevocable harm through pollution and destruction of the rainforest, not to mention the more immediate threats of violence and death to both the indigenous population and the invaders. Men with machetes and rifles walked the bad roads between the isolated shacks of the settlers, and the Indians roamed the rainforest with spears and arrows. The Red Feet were hunters who never ran after their enemies, brandishing weapons. They attacked only when their prey was off-guard—sleeping or otherwise occupied.

Levesque's liberal view, although controversial within the organized Holy Church, was that he should work through faith and Jesus for the poor and powerless using any means possible. Gifts and promises no longer sufficed as they had in the past. The first step was to establish dialogue and friendship. The next would be to develop effective ways of responding to the violence, trying to promote lasting peace based on human rights and a more just social order. Levesque was well aware that heaven couldn't be built by slitting throats, nor could evil be undone by materialistic affluence.

Very early the next morning, Levesque and Toucan, full of enthusiasm for their mission, took off in the helicopter, which was loaded with presents and supplies. On reaching the site, the pilot circled over the Aucas' village. Levesque did not notice the red stripe on the roof of one of the thatched huts. Instead he saw the upturned faces of the Indians, who were waving their arms and gesturing in a demonstration of friendliness toward the huge mechanical bird. The clerics began to drop presents from the chopper—useful items such as cooking pots, machetes, and packages of salt. The man of God decided to make his big move. With food rations already packed in knapsacks for just this endeavour, he told the pilot to return in two days' time, and with Sister Angelica in her nun's habit and he in his robes, they descended the rope ladder from the helicopter toward the ground below.

Nestor's entire body was one big bruise. He was tired from shock and his leg hurt like hell as he followed Pacheco, dragging himself through the hot, humid jungle. Both were burdened with samples of botanical material from the *mekran mkendio* and the orchid plants, encased in damp jungle soil and peat moss, and wrapped carefully in rags. In custom-made bags of mosquito netting Nestor carried the roots, vine, seeds, and budding fruits of the *mekran mkendio.*

It was now the middle of the day, when the equatorial heat silences most birds and animals. The only sounds Nestor heard were their own footsteps and breathing. They had started back toward the oil camp road, and wanted to make it before the dark descent of the tropical night. Only time and experimentation would indicate whether their botanical burden had the genes necessary for the special qualities that had been attributed to the vine by the Aucas, but Nestor was hopeful.

An hour passed, and the pain in Nestor's leg was unabated. Pacheco now held up his hand in a signal to halt. The steaming jungle was silent except for the faint murmur of water over shallow rapids from a nearby stream. Moving slowly forward, they peered through the gloom into a small clearing in the matted tropical growth. The sun spilled myriad splinters of golden light over the small thatched huts. Palms spiked the sky with their verdant blades, and from the surrounding undergrowth grew hundreds of luxuriant tropical flowers. The scent of recent cooking mingled with that of the flowers. There was no sign of human life, yet the place looked inhabited and tranquil. A lone mongrel dog appeared, moving away from a point in the centre of the clearing not yet visible to them. The canine dropped what he was eating and, snarling, slunk off into the underbrush.

Pacheco pointed with concern to a tall stick with a bone tied to its top, and the red stripe on the top of one of the huts. "This means they are at war against outsiders," he whispered.

Nestor and Pacheco quietly decided that either no one was there, or if there were they were in hiding. The best plan, therefore, would be to make some noise, not appear to be stealthy, and walk in a friendly fashion into the clearing.

They then discovered that they weren't the first visitors to the village that day.

The corpses had been left on the open ground in the centre of the huts. Twenty-one large and heavy ceremonial spears pierced the bodies of a priest and a nun. Each spear measured nearly four metres and was decorated with rope ornaments.

This time Nestor couldn't contain his nausea. Pacheco turned white, crouched and quickly scanned in all directions while cocking his rifle. Nestor pulled his revolver from its holster. Nothing moved, no sound was heard. With a grimace, Nestor tried to pull one of the spears from the priest's body. The thick shaft was heavy and had passed through the body and been driven into the ground beneath.

Pacheco jumped to his side. "No! We must leave. They are watching; they know we have guns. We must leave, quick!"

"But we should . . . we can't leave. . . ."

"This is an ancient Aucas ritual," Pacheco explained in a low voice.

"Spears are important, just like the white man's flag. It is bad medicine to take the spear out. The Red Feet see it as a challenge."

"Say no more, Pacheco," replied Nestor, his voice high-pitched. "But why are there so bloody many spears in their bodies?"

"Each Auca sticks one in."

"My God . . . and look at the other wounds on their bodies. There are dozens of them, and some are stuffed with something."

"Leaves to stop the blood flow. So they suffer longer," Pacheco explained.

Nestor couldn't stop shuddering. "They must have died in agony. Is there nothing we can do?" he asked, his eyes riveted to the dead bodies.

"Get out quick, and alive, Señor. But they may not come because we have guns." Pacheco tapped his rifle. "Holy people do not have guns," he said, nodding at the mutilated corpses.

"How did they get here?" Nestor paused. "And why did they come?"

"Helly-bird, Señor. I heard it early this morning."

"For Christ-sake, they didn't deserve this!" Nestor pondered what he had just said. I'm not as good a Catholic as I should be, he thought; but then who is, compared to these two who lay dead on the ground. Giving up their lives for their faith. Rightly or wrongly trying to convert the Indians to a foreign religion.

Pacheco seemed to read his mind. Looking at the bodies, he said, "The Red Feet have no need to be Christians. They just want to be left alone."

CHAPTER THREE

OPUS DEI

LATIN FOR "WORK OF GOD," *Opus Dei was founded in 1928 in Madrid by Josemaria Escriva de Belaguer y Albas, a lawyer, ordained as a priest in 1927, who was closely associated with the fascist regime of Francisco Franco. Promoted to the rank of Monsignor, Escriva de Belaguer, with formal approval from the Vatican, moved the organization's headquarters to Rome in 1947.*

Opus Deistas profess to be the only individuals who hold firm to the true Christian faith. They believe themselves to be a spiritual elite and religious elect who can save the Church with their faithfulness to the Holy Spirit and God the Father.

Although Opus Dei's membership is dominated by priests and a large percentage are from the wealthy classes, it also includes ordinary lay men and women, both married and single, from all walks of life. At the time of Escriva de Belaguer's death in 1975, membership numbered 60,000 in eighty countries; in 1987, the United States had some 2,500 members, both men and women; the Canadian membership included approximately 600 in twelve centres, the majority in Quebec. Three times larger than the Jesuit Order, Opus Deistas will admit only to belonging to "God's Work," and nothing more.

Although detractors charge Opus Dei with wielding undue economic and political power in the Catholic Church, in 1982, Pope John Paul II granted it the status of "personal prelature," making it a unique global diocese and an autonomous entity headed by Monsignor Alvaro del Portillo y Diez de Soltano. In 1992, Escriva del Belaguer was beatified by John Paul II, who overlooked criticism of both his character and of the organization.

The great river of Roman Catholicism is having difficulty concealing a secret. Beneath the smooth surface two conflicting streams flow, one of which threatens to break through its banks and go a separate route. Anything that might prevent such a division is worth consideration by the leader of the world's pre-eminent religion. Riding the current in the

Vatican boat, the Pope must seek solitary guidance, listening carefully for the secrets of life and of infinite wisdom.

That is why the fate of an obscure parish priest, murdered by Peruvian pagans, concerned Pope John Paul II.

The Curia finally received the report of the deaths of Father Athol Levesque and Sister Angelica Toucan of the Capuchin Brothers Mission in Peru. The Holy Church was shocked, for the Father was well-known to the missionary branch, having performed stalwart work in the field for many years, bringing many converts to the true faith.

When Pope John Paul II, before his demise, heard the news, he was disconsolate, for he had been impressed by the reports of hardiness and zeal that had been displayed by the elderly priest. Father Levesque had never received the accolades or promotion which might have been his due in a more civilized area; he had remained content to serve on the frontiers of the world and of Christianity.

Pope John Paul was dimly aware of a problem. He had personally led the ultra-conservative elements who had fast-tracked, to an unprecedented degree, the early sainthood of the right-wing extremist Josemaria Escriva de Belaguer y Albas of Spain—the spiritual leader and founder of the new and influential cult of Opus Dei. In doing so he had set a precedent.

John Paul sensed that pressure might be brought by Liberation Theology proponents to make Father Athol Levesque a saint. If so, and if that process was not seen to have been at least instigated, John Paul might find himself facing another exacerbation of the growing schism between the two camps in the Church, which threatened to split Roman Catholicism into separate warring factions for the first time since Henry VIII and the creation of the Anglican Church of England.

Ordinarily the process of sainthood takes centuries to complete. Not so in the case of Monsignor Josemaria Escriva, who died in 1975. Called "our father" within his *Opus Dei*—the cult called "Octopus Dei" by some—he liked to be confused with "Our Father who Art in Heaven." On May 17, 1992, in a solemn ceremony in St. Peter's Square, John Paul II beatified the Spanish churchman, an important step toward sainthood. The Pope knew that he had previously helped Opus Dei win legal recognition from the curial bureaucracy as a "personal prelacy"—a kind of global super-diocese. Belatedly he'd begun to realize that he had made the Opus Society a church within a church, had made them an organization which considered themselves a spiritual elite and a religious elect, and had thus bestowed great power upon them. They had amassed their own wealth and membership, and as a result might be another reason for the Church to divide against itself. Was the monolith about to crumble? The possibility of yet another schism must be avoided. The status quo must be maintained at all costs.

But perhaps everyone could be placated, particularly the malcontents, if some outcome of a salubrious nature were to be commenced posthumously on behalf of Father Levesque. And after all, he had died a martyr to the faith, and recognition of some sort should be forthcoming.

John Paul summoned the Prefect of the Sacred Congregation for the Cause of Saints, the person in charge of such matters as canonization, beatification, sainthood, miracles, the saving of souls, and the preservation of relics. The department was founded in 1588 for such purposes as the Inquisition.

"I would like to nominate Athol Levesque," said John Paul, "for beatification as a first step toward canonization." The Prefect called a meeting.

Cardinal Bettini held the office of Vatican Secretary of State, exceedingly well placed to influence the Curia. As such, he was also an ex-officio, and the most powerful member of the Prefect of the Sacred Congregation's committee.

Monsignor Brian Kelleher was Cardinal Bettini's secretary. He was instructed by the Cardinal to attend meetings and make sure that there was adequate expression of the opinion that Father Levesque was a man committed to the poor people of God and their liberation from injustice, widespread poverty, subhuman conditions, and repressive regimes. Father Levesque had gone where there were no doctors to take care of ailing bodies, no priests to take care of ailing souls. His beatification could well represent a symbol of peace and reconciliation in turbulent regions.

Simultaneously, a powerful Opus member of the Peruvian Church was brought to Rome by lay friends of Cardinal Bettini to represent the opposite traditionalist position on matters theological. They wondered if perhaps Levesque had not been too political in nature. Had he not been a Third World activist, at worst a practicing Marxist, espousing social and economic change at local, national, and international levels? Further, didn't South America spawn and espouse mongrel forms of Catholicism combined with aspects of paganism, many of which were secretly a form of Native liberation movement, attempts to avoid the white man's rule? Levesque had therefore encouraged a note of rebellion against government, against the Establishment, of which the Church was a big part. To recruit this speaker, Cardinal Bettini used his secretary at the headquarters of Opus Dei, where he also held high office and was a respected member. It was a closed organization, its members there by special invitation only.

Thus Bettini covered all the bases. He would decide who was to be a saint in this Church, not Pope John Paul II or Opus Dei. And in his book, Levesque was no saint. Priests, he thought, should confine their endeavours to spiritual yearning and redemption and stay out of politics. For himself, Bettini strongly believed in having a foot in all camps. All the better to control the action.

The committee summoned the resident Vatican expert on South and Central American Church politics, who pulled the file on Father Levesque from the Curia archives. All sources proved that Levesque had worked amongst Blacks, Natives, and Mestizos in some very dangerous situations, especially the war-like Chiriguano, Campas, and Quecha Indian tribes. He had also worked with the Tupis of the eastern interior, who believed in a "Divine Hero" who would lead them to a "Land without Evil," to which shamans, warriors, and even common people might go if they had shown proof of courage and endurance during their lifetimes. Father Levesque had convinced them that this divine hero was Jesus Christ.

What Rome looks for in such cases is fairly simple. They want miracles, with whatever proof the "postulator of the cause" can drum up. The postulator acts as a sort of attorney for the defence, gathering evidence and presenting it to Rome to persuade the Vatican that some Church figure is indeed worthy of sainthood. Usually Rome waits a couple of centuries, so such evidence can be either hard to find, or easily found, as the case may be. And the resultant decision is not easily refuted by anyone.

In Levesque's case, the postulator recognized only one possible miracle. A young blind girl was alleged to have recovered her sight after eight days of praying. Waking from a dream, a priest suddenly appeared before her and healed her eyes. Later, when she found she could see, she identified the priest as Father Levesque. With testimony that such a recovery was medically possible, this sudden healing could be ruled miraculous by the Sacred Congregation. But it takes two miracles to make a saint, so the postulator's recommendation to the Committee was that there must be proof that Father Levesque had performed some other minor wonder, had healed other sick, or foretold some future event, such as a death.

The entire file was then referred to Bettini, who read the contents with interest. Levesque had crossed one bridge too far, he thought, when he took on those Red Foot Aucas. It was a horrible death, but at least it had made him a martyr. Bettini neared the end of the file. On the last page was an account of how the news of the deaths of Levesque and Toucan had been reported, first to Parota Yaco, then to Coca, then to Quito, and finally to Rome. The report stated that the bodies had been discovered and reported by one Nestor LaPretre, a Canadian botanist-geneticist. The reason for his having been in such a remote place was only given a few words: "DNA biotechnology in relation to plants said to contain drugs useful in contraceptive birth control and sterility."

Another heretical meddler, thought Bettini. It was the first time he had heard of Nestor LaPretre, whom he would see only once in the flesh, but whose name would reverberate many times through his mind.

CHAPTER FOUR

NATURCEPT

NESTOR'S CHILDHOOD HAD NOT been very happy, but he always shrugged this fact off as best he could. He wasn't much to look at, and he knew he had to rely on hard work and brain power to get ahead. Which was why he was tired. Well, why not? Sometimes he worked sixteen hours a day. Now it was Friday and the weekend stretched a long way before him.

He felt the sudden urge for a drink and some company. There was a British style pub nearby where they made their own malt draft. The locals still called it The Flying Pig, although the name had recently been changed to The Ale Cart, after worshippers in the mosque opposite said they found the name distasteful. A few pints of beer and some talk of far-away places was what he needed to relax. He wanted to let his imagination soar, to stop worrying over the lack of research money, to forget the frustrating problems of the past week. He might even meet someone, he kidded himself. Women seldom took him seriously, which is why he was now over forty and alone.

Nestor was small and neat, weighing one hundred and thirty pounds and standing five-foot-three. In times of depression he described himself as a shortass, just as many a schoolmate had done. His buttocks were too close to the ground, his short legs somehow out of proportion with his torso. If there had been a litter he would have been the runt, but he was an only son. His mother had died young and, strangely, no great warmth had developed between himself and his father, who was as cold as the winters on his family's Alberta ranch. Nestor was acutely aware of his father's lack of affection, but he could not seem to break down the barriers between them. He knew, though, that his old man was impressed by Nestor's high grades at school, so academic achievement was the best route to gaining his father's attention. Nestor wore horn-rimmed glasses over pale blue, deep-set eyes, which as a youth earned him the nickname Egghead. He'd been too smart and too different to be at all popular with his peers.

Nestor checked his appearance in the mirror before leaving for the pub. His new beard was flecked with grey, unlike his dark brown hair. Kept short and well-trimmed, the beard gave him the sort of professorial mien he wanted to cultivate. As he walked toward the pub, his thoughts turned to the subject he'd been obsessed with most of his life.

Agricultural molecular biotechnology was the game, and his aim was to join certain characteristics that don't ordinarily cross in nature. Scientists could now identify specific genes and their location in the chromosomes that determine the hereditary traits of any living organism. As a plant geneticist, he could, and had, determined which genes held the traits he had looked for in *mekran mkendio.* Once that was done, he had taken a sample of the DNA and transferred it to the chromosomes of plants having other desired characteristics. This process was called gene mapping.

How incredible, Nestor thought, that insects, tiger lilies, polar bears, bacteria, and people were organized in the same way, humans being the apex of evolution based on chance mutations in DNA. Scientists were now vying to dispose of chance from the process, an irresistible temptation to maintain man's alleged superiority over the rest of life, and use the new knowledge for his own benefit.

Nestor reflected on the 1980s, a period when scientists had begun to perform tasks along a wide research front. In a potentially volatile area of study, technology had advanced to the point where genes could be injected into animal cells, producing animals that later imparted new characteristics.

As a frontrunner in the research of plant genes and DNA, Nestor knew that the ability to tamper with genes was the ability to tamper with life itself. The weapons of the Second Green Revolution, Nestor thought as he limped toward the pub, included varieties of plants that resisted both disease and drought, grew quickly in short seasons, and produced crops that could be stored for long periods without spoiling. Through genetic techniques, scientists had hoped to feed the 10,000 or so people per hour who were being born into the world.

Early in his studies, Nestor had switched the direction of his thinking.

Biotechnology had for some time been heading toward the wrong destination, it seemed to him. His forte as a plant geneticist had been in the traits and qualities that might be contraceptive by nature or in end result. He'd discovered, however, that in the past there had been little interest in contraceptives. His research indicated that hundreds of plants had been used as aphrodisiacs and for procreation; for example, the root of the male orchis plant, from the Far East, could, when dissolved in goat's milk, purportedly stimulate as many as seventy acts of intercourse with one dose. Another favoured aphrodisiac had been the mandrake plant, a member of the potato family with dark leaves, purple flowers, and a yellow fruit with an acrid smell. In ancient times, the search was for roots, like ginseng, that most looked like human genitalia, which were considered to make the best love potions.

Nestor, deep in thought about the various love potions and philtres, looked up to see that he'd overshot the pub by several hundred metres. Feeling foolish, he turned and headed back to The Flying Pig. Inside, he found a corner table and ordered a pint. Once again, his thoughts turned to his work.

Nestor had recognized plants which were used by various peoples because of certain sex-oriented properties attributed to them. He'd read about one concoction of water lilies and syrup of poppies drunk by monks and nuns to curtail their libidos. Apparently, the more unpleasant the taste, the better—no doubt in order to associate sex with something disagreeable, thus fostering the Christian abhorrence of the sex act for any purpose other than procreation within marriage. Indian fakirs said that daily eating of the leaves of the *mirkousi* would cause impotence. Folklore for the most part, but Nestor knew that DNA biotechnology now promised the real thing.

The beer arrived and he buried his nose in the foam, taking a long swallow to quench his thirst. He contemplated the steps in his research as he continued to sip.

Lord knows how many plants and their various genes and derivatives he'd run through the computer to assess such qualities as hallucinations, impotence, aphrodisia, miscarriage, laxative reaction, glandular irritation, euphoria, stimulation of body fluids, rejuvenation, whatever. He had tested a myriad of combinations that might produce a substance that would help to create, when ingested, either inactive sperm in the male, or prevent the female egg from permitting fertilization. In the many experiments he'd carried out on such plants as cacti, belladonna, wild rue, olibanum, and coca, some results indicated potential.

The years of hard work gathering and crossing plants and their genes had yielded dividends. He had fostered his data base, followed his hunches, and paid attention to the vibrations he got from both plants and people. He was sure now that his particular combination of meticulous science and intuition was about to pay off.

Nestor took another swig of his ale and realized that he'd been making random notes in his book. The words jimson, chicory, slippery elm seemed to jump from the page into his head, repeating like a mantra. He shut his eyes tight for a long moment, then opened them and signaled the waiter for another beer.

To the combination of genes he had eventually integrated, combined, and refined, he'd added his intuition, infusing a substance derived from the DNA of a plant tissue source known only to himself. Those who ate, drank, or smoked the resulting concoction weren't able to impregnate or to become pregnant. Nestor was elated by the result, although a little cautious because the product tasted terrible and left a vague ill feeling. There were, however, additives that could improve the taste and thus the popularity.

His product needed a name. After some thought rearranging various word combinations, he decided on Naturcept. He took a gulp of his drink and flipped to a clean page of his notebook, where he printed NATURCEPT in block letters.

Perfect, thought Nestor. The name Naturcept sounded clinical, but would remind people that the substance was derived from a natural source. And the contraceptive properties, also implied, were almost an afterthought. The effects of Naturcept, ingested in any way, lasted for several months and, rather than diminishing the libido, actually seemed to enhance sexual arousal.

Other scientists were working on similar projects. It was best, and certainly more lucrative, to be the first to bring the product to market. It took time, good working conditions, and a lot of money to develop a new contraceptive and move it from the laboratory to store shelves. Nestor had a small stockpile of seed, technical records were all but complete, and only a few refinements needed consideration. He was very close. But he needed more money, and he couldn't depend on the government bureaucrats, too few of whom seemed to recognize the urgent need to make Naturcept available throughout the world. He had already used up his own finances; his father would spin in his grave if he knew what Nestor had done with the Alberta ranch that had been his inheritance.

Nestor sipped as he pondered the obstacles ahead. There was sure to be criticism from religious groups, right-to-life societies, and rival scientists who would question his research methods, as well as social activists who would question the ethics of international population control.

But the biggest obstacle, he knew, would be the Vatican, the single most influential force when it came to birth control, with nearly a billion adherents worldwide. Nestor resolved to attempt his own epistle to the Romans, to the Pope, with a view to persuading the Catholic Church to change its official stance on the subject. It would be nearly impossible, but if he could pull it off, it would constitute a giant leap forward in bringing his goal to fruition. Feeling much taller than his diminutive five-foot-three, Nestor drew himself up straight and smiled as he began to formulate a plan.

He was aware that other worthy people had tried to persuade the Holy See along the same lines, with no success. But he knew that Naturcept could be classified as "natural" because it came from plants which, in the religious view, had been placed on Earth by God for use by mankind. Perhaps the nitpickers among the bishops and cardinals, together with the pro-lifers and anti-abortionists, would concede this time.

So, as Nestor sipped his brew, he composed a letter to the Pontiff in Rome, care of the Secretary of State, in the hope that the question of the use of Naturcept by Church members as a birth control method would be discussed and considered at the first convenient opportunity, perhaps at the next Synod of Bishops.

CHAPTER FIVE

THE PRIORY OF SION

FORMED IN 1099, *the* Prieure de Sion *is a secret order and guardian of the Holy Grail, the genealogical record of the sacred bloodline of Jesus Christ, which originally existed in the south of France and is traceable to the present day. The declared objective of the Priory is the recognition of the bloodline of the Merovingian dynasty of the Franks, the legitimate descendants of Jesus Christ.*

Constituting a Christian royalty parallel to the Roman Catholic Church, members of the Priory are committed to preserving a secret about a bloodline deemed to be sacred and invested with magical and miraculous powers. The succession of Priory Grandmasters clearly implies an esoteric and hermetic Papacy based on John the Evangelist, beloved disciple in the Fourth Gospel, in opposition to the esoteric Papacy in Rome based on Peter. Like a shadow Papacy, the Priory was a counterpart to Rome.

As far back as 1738, Pope Clement XII issued a secret papal bull condemning and excommunicating all Freemasons, whom he pronounced "enemies of the Catholic Church." Published for the first time in 1962, the bull does not clarify why Freemasons were regarded as heretics, since many of them were Catholic.

The Knights Templar were formed as the military and administrative arm of the Priory, but the two severed ties in 1188. Although the Knights Templar were dissolved between 1307 and 1314, the Priory of Sion remained unscathed and continues to function in international affairs today. Acting behind the scenes, the organization has orchestrated several critical events in western history.

Among the alleged Grandmasters of the elusive secret society were Jean de Gisors (the first independent Grandmaster), Leonardo da Vinci, Isaac Newton, Maximilian von Hapsburg, Victor Hugo, Claude Debussy, and Jean Cocteau.

"How many of the Curia of the Roman Catholic Church know we actually exist? What do you think, Max?"

"You can rest assured that very few of the Curia are privy to that information at any given time," Secretary Maximilian replied. "But the Church knows we exist and have always existed. They know who we were and who we are. And we know how tricky they can be, so if we are going to send someone into their bailiwick to negotiate, then he had better be good."

Together with the many elusive men who had preceded him, the speaker was allied by blood and lineage to the ducal House of Lorraine and the Merovingian dynasty. He was the Grandmaster of the *Prieure de Sion*, one of the world's most ancient organizations. Any newly elected leader chooses his own name, but the Grandmasters all chose Jean, John, Joan, or Jeanne.

"You asked my opinion, Jean, and I gave it to you," Max continued.

"Ah, no need to get touchy. I simply mentioned that since he hadn't been on an important assignment for quite some time, he may be rusty. Hugo was always a loner. You never know what he'll do on a mission."

"But he always got the job done," Max stated emphatically.

"Yes, that he did. Would I be facetious to ask if you think he has the balls for this one?"

They both laughed. "There are some things he can't do anymore, Jean. He hasn't got much left to lose, but that means he completely disregards personal danger."

"And he has a bit of the royal blood—the *sang raal*—has he not?"

"He certainly has. Hugues de Payen, the original Grandmaster of the Poor Knights of Christ and the Temple of Solomon, back in 1118. You can't get much better ancestry than the poor fellow-soldiers of Jesus, the Knights Templar."

"An arrogant group of warrior monks to be sure, I'm proud to say," responded Jean. Their zeal had amounted to fanaticism, he thought, but that was understandable in those times. We created them, our own flesh, blood, and spirit, as it were, so I do have a bias in their favour. "Hugo Payne could be the right emissary, Max, unless he dislikes the Vatican so much that it affects his judgment. But then, it is not going to be an easy task for anyone. So get in touch with our North American friend and be sure he's ready and available."

"You'll want me to call a meeting also, Grandmaster?" asked Max.

"Of course. Convene a meeting of the Arche of the thirteen Rose-Croix of the Temple as soon as possible."

In a warm dark library of a French castle in the district of Lorraine, in the vicinity of the Ardennes, once the heart of the Merovingian dynasty, firelight flickered against the walls; one reading lamp on a desk relieved the gloom, its light not quite reaching the far corners of the room. A large chesterfield in front of the fireplace was flanked by soft leather reading chairs. The polished mahogany walls were punctuated with bookcases from floor to ceiling. A rich Persian rug stretched into the shadows and somber velvet curtains were drawn across the windows which faced the fireplace, above whose mantle appeared a coat of arms—a red cross with arms supported on each side by figures of Ursus, the Great Bear. On either side was a swarm of golden bees. In the dim light, closer scrutiny revealed the credo *Et in Arcadia Ego.*

Twelve people sat about the room in small groups, engaged in quiet conversation. Three were second-ranking members called *Croise,* and nine were the highest-ranked *Commandeurs* of the Grandmaster, or *Nautonnier.* Jean was seated in the depths of a leather armchair. Shadows dancing from the fireplace revealed his lined and weary face.

"Thank you all for coming," he said in a soft voice. "Let's get the meeting started. Max, please speak regarding the agenda."

As Max bent over the table, his head came into the pool of light cast by the lamp. The rest of him remained in darkness, giving a disembodied appearance to the liver spots and thinning hairline of the small, determined face and lively eyes behind rimless glasses.

"I'm going to get to the heart of the matter. You know the state of the world as well as I. Even though the position papers have not been disseminated, you all know what is in them. The time has come to take some form of action." His eyes scanned the room.

A voice spoke from a dark corner. "Mr. Secretary, what, if anything, can the Priory of Sion do?"

Jean's hand rose from the leather armchair. "We are here to execute policy, vis-à-vis the Vatican. To sum up recent history, let's go back to the fifties. The Curia have always opposed birth control in any form. But in 1951, Pius XII approved the rhythm method. And later," Max looked up, "you all remember *Humanae Vitae*? That passed in 1968. It outlawed contraception and artificial birth control. More recently, in October 1993, Pope John Paul II's *Veritatis Splendour* was published. . . ."

"That had to be the last straw," interrupted one member. "Not even John the Baptist would have been happy with that one."

"That's for sure," Max replied, "since it particularly singled out artificial insemination, homosexuality, abortion, contraception, and premarital sex as intrinsically evil."

"If you recall," said a woman member, "in the case of *Humanae Vitae*, sixty-four of the bishops, cardinals, and experts at the Pontifical Commission voted to approve birth control. But they were ignored."

"You are right," said the Grandmaster. "The Pope missed the chance to eliminate the hypocrisy of the Church position on birth control. He was neutralized by a strong faction in the Church hierarchy. Our job is to find that faction and neutralize them." He turned in his chair to face the members of the Priory High Council. Before he could speak, a pudgy hand at the rear of the room raised a snifter of cognac.

"Wojtyla certainly understood the power of the media. A lot of talk, but business as usual is the attitude of the Church. He and Opus Dei didn't do anything about the changes that should have been made."

"There are organizations and individuals in the Church who exert pressure on the Pope," Max joined in. "Look what happened to John Paul I. He was planning some dramatic changes . . . myocardial infarction was the official cause of death. Poor Albino Luciano. Popes were usually murdered for better reasons," he said, shaking his head.

"But more to the point," Max continued, "I'm given to understand that one of the reasons this meeting was called is to discuss a birth control product referred to as"—he glanced down at his notes—"Naturcept. With so many forms of contraception available, why are we concerning ourselves with this one?"

"Good question," answered Jean. "Naturcept is what the Vatican could easily call 'natural' rather than 'artificial,' thus giving them a face-saving reason for adopting it as an official method for use by the faithful. Our information suggests that Naturcept is the most efficacious method and the easiest to use. In all countries of the world. Keep in mind that there are now almost a billion Catholics—nearly twenty percent of the world's population—most of whom are in Africa and other Third World countries. And one in four in the west is Catholic."

"This meeting was convened," said the Grandmaster, "to try to effect solutions for the biggest problem we face today. Over the next fifty years, the earth's population is expected to exceed nine billion if something isn't done to slow it down. It has already surpassed the upper limits of sustainability. As Jacques Cousteau said, 'We ourselves are in danger, not only the fish.' The problem is real and urgent. What is this new Pope going to do about it? We of the Priory of Sion have always been in a position to influence the Vatican, although we haven't always used our position as capably as we might." He looked around the room as a murmur of assent rose from the twelve disciples.

"Could you review the information on Naturcept before we vote?" someone asked.

"Yes," Max spoke again. "Reliable sources state that experiments in agricultural-genetic-biotechnology, conducted by one Nestor LaPretre, a Canadian, have proven successful. The birth control product he calls Naturcept is natural and has been shown to be effective, safe, and long-lasting."

"I would say that LaPretre is going to need some protection," a voice suggested.

"So is his product and its formula. There are many sharks out there, and LaPretre is swimming with them."

Several of the group spoke at once.

The Grandmaster raised his hands for silence. "Certain people have to be persuaded that it is in their best interests to support Naturcept. We can't have a repeat of what happened to Paul VI or John Paul I. The reactionary forces in the Vatican will do anything to protect their power and the status quo. We know who these people are. Now is the time to act, to use the power we possess. The question is, how far do we go? We have a short list of possible agents and methods. We have experienced people in our organization."

"Are we going to need a hit-man?" asked one voice.

"We hope not," Jean answered.

"They are afraid of us," said Max. "We have always acted only when there was a crisis of such proportions we could no longer hesitate."

"Let's hear the motion," called a chorus of voices.

Max read: "In the event the Vatican refuses to co-operate in the world's efforts to prevent over-population through the use of birth control, the Priory of Sion moves to at first threaten, then implement if necessary, the release of proof that the Crucifixion of Jesus Christ was a fraud, and that Jesus himself was alive as late as 45 A.D., and that his progeny can be traced to this day."

"All in favour?" asked Jean the Nautonnier, then, peering through the gloom, "*nemine dissentiente?*" A pause. "Nil. Then it is decided. No more kid gloves. Persuasion and negotiation. And if that fails. . . ."

CHAPTER SIX

ANGOSTURA BITTERS

CARDINAL BETTINI ATE and drank sparingly. He didn't smoke and had a perfect record of celibacy. He regarded women as the vessels of Satan's temptation—their mission in life to give sacred sperm a nest, after which they were certainly dispensable. To preserve the teachings of the Church against radical change, Bettini believed that all methods and measures were legitimate.

Once a week in a cold shower, he recited a special prayer while flogging himself with a whip. For several hours a day he wore a barbed metal band on his upper thigh. For him, penance and mortification of the flesh for the sake of the Lord Jesus Christ were things which should be common among Catholics. In the Cardinal's view, there was only one proper way to make the sign of the cross. Not for him the principle of *vox populi vox dei.*

Jesus said to Peter one day on Mount Hermon: "I give you the keys to the Kingdom of Heaven. Whatever you allow on earth will be what Heaven allows. Whatever you forbid on earth will be what Heaven forbids." And that is the way it should be, thought Cardinal Bettini—if we decide it shall be so, then thy will is done—even if we have to help things along a little bit. There was precedent. He was reminded of "The Donation of Constantine," in which it was alleged that the grateful Roman emperor had given the Pope jurisdiction over the East and Constantinople. It was a document which was later revealed as a fake, but it had worked for many centuries.

When Bettini used the term "we," he meant the Pontiff and the Church, as well as himself; for he felt in his own mind and soul that he understood what was best for the Holy See. Bettini, a self-made man, would always exercise as much authority as he could muster, all in the cause of the Holy Roman Catholic Church.

So, when Monsignor Brian Kelleher had given him a letter from Nestor

LaPretre, Cardinal Bettini immediately recognized another attempt by a misguided scientist to abrogate the tenets of the Catholic faith. Why were their infernal inventions aimed at preventing life, when destruction of the supremely holy seed of God was a grievous sin? The sanctity of semen is the ultimate justification of the Roman Catholic strictures on birth control, and it must not be rendered ineffective.

What could be done if the plant contraceptive proved to be reliable, Bettini worried. The usual exercise of absolute and supreme power was, of course, his immediate thought. But how, since it must be done in a Christian fashion? Bettini fostered his own network within the Church, while maintaining membership and office in as many other religious entities as possible—of which the most important was Opus Dei.

The Cardinal was an imposingly tall, thin, ascetic man, with the narrow shoulders of one reared in the library, church, and papal court. His appearance belied his physical fitness. He combed his black hair sideways atop his high forehead and his deep blue-black eyes, matching the dark colour of his tonsure, were set in a well-lined face with hawkish features. Smiles seldom appeared on his thin, pale lips. When one did, together with his fixed stare, it brought a sense of uneasiness to any observer.

"Who has seen this epistle besides myself?" he asked.

"No one, Holy Father. Except for me, of course," answered Monsignor Kelleher. Bettini liked Kelleher because he was loyal and never asked irrelevant questions—traits to be treasured in a tight-knit organization.

Although Pope John Paul II had disliked theological and liturgical dissenters, he had been inclined to let them ferment. This led to items being discussed for too long before being resolved. Although a Pope is ultimately responsible for what will be decided by the Church, he is not the only one shaping its policies. This new Pope Cesare Romereo I was still an enigma. How difficult would he be to handle?

Bettini nodded his satisfaction as he looked around Kelleher's outer office in the Vatican building. Neat stacks of current files lay on the large desk and upon the cabinet against one wall. Kelleher was a careful and meticulous worker who read everything that came to the department. One of his office's duties was to intercept and treat as their own any mail or material which was considered to be of a sensitive Church nature, and anything that was felt to be of interest to Secretary of State Bettini or Opus

Dei. Kelleher colour-coded the material in accordance with its priority. He had a good instinct for what the Cardinal should or would want to read in his inner sanctum.

"Have you had enough time to work up any background on this LaPretre and his alleged new panacea?" Bettini asked quietly.

"It's all in this file," replied Kelleher, handing Bettini a folder marked up with red ink. "His work and experimentation appear to be legitimate and credible. But you will be the judge of that. Let me know if you wish anything else done, Eminence."

"Thank you, Father," Bettini answered. "I'll study it and apprise you as to what our course of action will be." He rose from his chair and retreated toward his office. "I don't wish to be disturbed unless it is very urgent."

CHAPTER SEVEN

NESTOR LAPRETRE

THE PLANE FLEW FROM the West Coast toward Ottawa, passing over one of Earth's most sparsely populated areas. An inhabitable area, true, but how many people would that bush support in a Canadian winter? Probably few and damn little more in the summer, thought Nestor, as he loosened his tie and belt, adjusted his shorts, then pressed the button on the arm of the economy-class seat, leaning it back a paltry few inches into the so-called reclining position.

He settled back as best he could to ponder his problems. His seat companion didn't seem to be the gregarious type, like some who felt inclined to relate their life history to total strangers. At least he hadn't been seated next to some mother with mewling babe in arms. If he had been it would have served as a reminder of his present preoccupation. In his window seat, he burrowed his head deeper into the two small pillows he had jammed against the body of the plane, eschewing the airline meal in favour of attempted sleep. Thoughts of his religious background, upbringing, and education flitted in and out of his mind before slumber intervened.

Much later the intercom seeped into his consciousness. He heard the tail-end of the expected announcement of their imminent arrival in Ottawa. Nestor hoped that his trip to the Canadian capital would alleviate the financial problems which were now the major block in the promotion of Naturcept.

Once at the hotel, he bought a newspaper in the lobby newsstand. As he filled in the card at the registration desk, the clerk said, "There's something here for you already, Mr. LaPretre," and handed over a sealed envelope.

"Strange," Nestor replied, as he peered at the envelope upon which his name had been written in longhand. "Is this your writing?"

"No," replied the clerk politely. "A woman came in earlier, just after I started my shift. She asked that this be delivered to you."

Putting the envelope in his pocket, Nestor wondered what it was about. Who knew of his arrival? The Canadian International Development Agency? Perhaps a secretary had delivered a message from them. Once in his room, he threw his luggage onto the bed and went down the hall in search of ice cubes.

Back in his room with ice and club soda in hand, he extracted a mickey of Chivas Regal from his bag and poured himself a stiff drink, then began running a bath. After undressing, he fetched the envelope, his drink, and the newspaper, and brought them into the bathroom. Easing himself gently into the water, he sighed.

This is just what I need after the long trip, he thought. He reached for the envelope. It contained a single sheet of vellum. He glanced at the signature first to see who it was from: Charlotte Lockwood—no one of his acquaintance.

> Mr. LaPretre:
> Would you care to do me the kindness of meeting me personally at the National Arts Centre, main information desk, at ten-thirty a.m. I will phone you at your hotel at nine a.m. to ascertain if this is convenient; if not, another time can be arranged. You do not know me, but I know who you are and will recognize you. The people I represent are interested in opening discussions with you in regard to your scientific discoveries in plant genetics and biotechnology, possibly for mutual benefit.
>
> Yours Sincerely,
> Charlotte Lockwood

Interesting and encouraging, thought Nestor as he sipped his drink. It could be good news, but why the unusual approach? Nestor lay back soaking up both the heat and the scotch. After some moments he reached for the newspaper and began to read. "Jesus wept," he said as he read the headlines. It was an exclamation rather than an oath. "Things never change." But I'm doing what I can, he thought. Reading once again about the world's problems only reaffirmed his decision to go as far as he could with Naturcept.

Nestor had left himself a full day to fine-tune his pitch to Canada's foreign aid agency, CIDA He had an appointment to meet their representative in two days at the federal building in Hull. He urgently needed financing to complete his project, but he'd never had any success with government grants or loans. He had thought he could count on the incompetence of federal bureaucrats, who routinely failed to spot trouble when entrepreneurs came calling for money. Ordinarily rosy business and marketing plans were not challenged, warnings from experts were ignored, and ventures were not monitored to ensure tax dollars were well spent. Maybe CIDA was now subject to over-cautious politicians who were ambivalent about investing in a technology that might give rise to moral objections on the part of the government. No, thought Nestor, I can't buy that, although they might be concerned about the right-to-life vote.

Nestor knew that Canada's International Development Research Centre held the patent on a birth control vaccine invented by an Indian immunologist, Dr. Gursaran Talwar, but it was at least six years from market. The vaccine worked by destroying the hormones that were essential to pregnancy. The woman would continue to menstruate and the embryo would not be able to anchor in the uterus—a contraceptive method not likely to satisfy the Church. But really, Nestor thought, the vaccine could not be said to cause abortion since intervention would take place before the egg is implanted.

Other immunologists, notably Australian, were trying to discredit the Indian vaccine, on the grounds that a product with less than an eighty percent success rate was not acceptable and that insufficient attention had been paid to toxicological concerns and potential side effects. Supported by the World Health Organization in Geneva, the CIDA scientists were also trying to develop a single-shot delivery system for the vaccine, but apparently were a long way off. The long-term effects of these methods were not yet known, and therefore had become of great concern to women's organizations, who saw birth control vaccines as technical solutions aimed at the social problem of over-population only, ignoring the status and health of women.

Then again, Nestor pondered, there was the controversial French abortion pill, RU-486, now being touted as an oral contraceptive for men, who took it before sexual intercourse. RU-486 blocked calcium, which sperm require for motility, from entering the sperm. Recent experiments suggested that RU-486 might work as a kind of "hormonal condom" for varying lengths of time—for one hour to one week to one month. Preliminary testing on rats and monkeys had begun and human trials were expected in several years time. RU-486, Nestor knew, was particularly odious to the Catholic Church.

Everyone, especially the giant pharmaceutical companies, had a problem to solve and an axe to grind while they tried to out-manoeuvre each other in order to be first on the world-wide market with the *ne-plus-ultra* of birth-control products. But Naturcept was of a different nature altogether, Nestor figured as he lathered his bony body. He had the jump on the competition, but still wasn't getting the funding he needed. Politicians were overly cautious. He could understand that when he read about the running battle in Canada which Dr. Morgentaler had to wage with right-to-life organizations and various Attorneys-General.

The pragmatist in Nestor concluded that the bureaucrats couldn't see how contraception and population control might fit into the plans or budgets of their departments, or they didn't have money for research in poor economic times, or—even more likely—they thought Nestor was some kind of lunatic.

Some of them didn't think there was a problem, and those who did couldn't believe that Nestor, virtually unknown outside the scientific community, could possibly have the solution. It was particularly annoying that the government awarded grants to so many people and groups who had no legitimate research plans or goals and who absconded with the money. However, thought Nestor, maybe CIDA could be persuaded to see how Naturcept might benefit the underdeveloped but over-populated countries who needed the most help. Or maybe CIDA could use their influence with Unesco or their own lending counterparts in Europe and the Caribbean.

Nestor finished his bath, toweled himself off, got into bed, and began reading the sports pages, which were less stressful than the real world. He dozed off wondering who Charlotte Lockwood was, who she represented, and just exactly what it was they wanted of him.

CHAPTER EIGHT

CHARLOTTE RUSE

CHARLOTTE LOCKWOOD SAW Nestor LaPretre leaning against the information counter of the National Gallery just after ten-thirty in the morning. Although she knew who she was looking for, his appearance didn't fit her picture of the scientist he was supposed to be; this man was short and ordinary. She approached and introduced herself.

Nestor saw an attractive woman of medium height, dressed in a dark Chanel suit over a high-collared silk blouse, a light raincoat over her arm. He noted rimless glasses, and eyes a strange colour of grey, or were they violet? She was a brunette, but on closer inspection her simple hair style revealed a touch of salt and pepper at the temples. The word demure occurred to him. Or perhaps she was deliberately attempting to appear plain.

"Welcome to Ottawa, Mr. LaPretre," she said. "I hope you had a good night's rest after your flight."

"I did, as a matter of fact—after a couple of scotches. I read your note, and here I am."

"So you are. And of course, you're curious."

"Yes."

"Shall we walk around the gallery?" she queried.

"Of course," Nestor answered, wondering if she was an art connoisseur, or if there was some other reason she wanted to keep moving. As they headed toward the collection, Nestor suddenly sensed something was wrong, and stopped in his tracks. "Who *are* you anyway, may I ask?"

Ms. Lockwood turned to face him. "I am informed by the people I represent . . . I have reason to believe. . . ." Seeing the consternation on his face, she smiled broadly. "Look, I'm not really in the mood for viewing Group of Seven paintings this morning. Can we go to the coffee shop? I could use one while we talk."

Nestor's shoulders relaxed. "By all means. So could I."

Coffees in hand, Charlotte led Nestor to a corner table away from other customers. Placing her coat over the back of a chair, she sat down, took a sip, then said, "I was asked to contact you and see that you received certain confidential information which may be of importance."

"They, whoever they are, picked a nice way to deliver their message," said Nestor.

"There's no need to compliment me, Mr. LaPretre, but thank you just the same," she smiled. "The letter you wrote to the Pontiff in Rome. Didn't you expect a reply?"

Nestor's half-raised cup dropped with a clatter to the saucer. He quickly reached for some napkins to mop up the spill. "Well . . . I expected *some* sort of answer. But I didn't expect personal contact." He reached for another napkin to wipe his brow. "I take it you are a Church emissary of some sort?"

Charlotte looked into his bespectacled eyes as she drank her coffee. Putting the cup down, she reached for her bag, retrieved a brown envelope and slid it across the marble table top.

"Thank you," Nestor said, still flustered as he turned the envelope over in his hands several times.

"I'm not privy to the contents," Charlotte said, "but I'm instructed to await your reply, whenever you care to make one. If your answer is yes, I'm to make arrangements. I presume it's explained in the letter. Do you want to read it now, or later in private?"

Nestor thought for a moment. "Now. Why not?"

"Then I'll get something to eat while you do."

Nestor ripped the letter open and pulled forth the stationery. It was expensive paper, obviously from the Vatican. Nestor proceeded to read.

> To: Mr. Nestor LaPretre
> Re: NATURCEPT
>
> In reply to your missive of recent date, I write to you on behalf of the Vatican.
>
> The Holy Church faces internal restiveness from some of its members, who register discontent about the position of the Church and the late Pope John Paul II toward birth control and world population.
>
> You, too, appear to express a desire to challenge the Church's

long-standing edicts and doctrines, which has long been considered heresy by the Holy See. At this point, however, Mr. LaPretre, the Church chooses not to deem you a heretic. Instead, we call you to Rome to discuss this matter in person and in detail, well before the fall meeting of the Synod of World Bishops. We have read your material thoroughly; your motivation appears to be noble.

You will understand the necessity for the utmost discretion in this matter. It is best no other parties receive advance notice of this proposal for discussion.

Please wait until you are contacted further. An emissary, with whom you will have already been in contact, will procure plane tickets and accompany you to Rome. Please hold yourself in readiness for the journey.

Yours in Christ in this year of Our Lord, 1999,

Angostura Bettini
Secretary of the Vatican State

Charlotte had returned to the table as he read, but Nestor had been so engrossed in digesting the contents of the letter that he didn't notice she had all but finished her danish and coffee.

"You are to contact me with your decision, Mr. LaPretre. I have written my address and phone number on this card. Call me when you have decided. Now, if you'll excuse me, I have a meeting to attend."

Nestor remained at the table after her departure, re-reading the letter and thinking about the present state of Naturcept, which was now at a remote experimental farm and greenhouse on Vancouver Island. He and his assistants had added to the new plant one refinement, a mixture of genes from the Yohimbe tree. This was intended for use by those who had a proven low libido to start with, for those with a tendency to impotence. The Yohimbe genes created yohimbane, which he suspected would act as an aphrodisiac.

Naturcept had progressed to the final stages, and could gradually go into increased production. Now he sensed a boost from a hoped-for but unexpected source of financial backing, although the letter wasn't clear. He decided he'd better keep his appointment with the Canadian International Development Agency.

CHAPTER NINE

BUMBLE-DOM

A FORMIDABLE AIR EMANATED from the building on the Promenade du Portage which housed the Canadian International Development Agency in Hull, across the river from Ottawa. Nestor wondered if it was the cold impersonality of the architecture that made him shiver as he stood in the street regarding the faceless structure. Why did he feel so queasy? Maybe he'd had too much to drink the night before. Perhaps it was his fear that the CIDA bureaucrats would be as unmoving as the building in which they were housed. Nevertheless, he squared his shoulders and entered the ominous structure.

He was met by an aging security guard wearing the blue Canadian Commissionaires uniform. Nestor asked the guard the location of Humphrey Baumgartner's office.

After completing a token check, another sentinel escorted Nestor to the elevator, which swiftly deposited him onto the eleventh floor. He stepped into a large foyer. From here he could observe numerous corridors and doors, in front of which was an elegant blonde woman. Nestor waded through the deep green carpet toward the receptionist's desk, wondering if they had any money left after spending so much on the decor.

"I'm here to see Mr. Baumgartner," Nestor said.

"Name?" she asked with glacial mien.

"Nestor LaPretre."

She consulted an appointment book, then, smiling, said, "Yes, have a seat, Mr. LaPretre. Mr. Baumgartner will be with you in a few moments. Can I get you some coffee?"

"No, thank you." Nestor seated himself on a large mauve divan, placing his briefcase between his feet. He was still contemplating his opening remarks when the receptionist said, "Mr. Baumgartner will see you now." Nestor rose and was guided through a door on his right into a large office whose predominant feature was an oversized, uncluttered desk. Behind it sat an equally large man, in a grey pin-stripe suit, with a trim moustache, receding hairline, and steel-rimmed glasses. After a firm handshake, Nestor was offered one of the straight-backed chairs that faced the desk.

"I'll come straight to the point, Mr. LaPretre," said Baumgartner. "I have your correspondence here on file." He indicated the folder that was placed squarely in the centre of the slick expanse of polished wood. "Very interesting subject matter. Seems to constitute a developmental situation in which the utilization of resources has not yet reached its optimum."

"Ah . . . yes, I suppose you could say that," Nestor hesitated as he tried to decipher the exact meaning of the remark.

"May I ask you for an update on anything that is related to the project's infrastructure?"

"Certainly," replied Nestor. "We have had continued success with Naturcept since I wrote to you six months ago."

"We have been conducting a thorough examination of your proposal, Mr. LaPretre." Baumgartner's furrowed brow belied his studied tone for a moment. "Particularly for cost-effectiveness. That is very important. Can't be done in a hurry, you know." His lips briefly formed a smile. "Perhaps you should just phase zero it for me."

He probably hasn't read it, Nestor thought. "Well . . . all right. There is only one way to initiate a new hybrid, multi-cross-bred plant like Naturcept. It takes time to grow the succession of crops that are necessary to get enough seed stock to test the end product. It can be sped up by hydroponic methods, but it is still slow. . . ."

"Just synopsize the process," interrupted Baumgartner.

"We cross-bred a great many different combinations of plant genes in the same growing time-frames. That way we got a lot of different products at the same time."

"And then?"

"After that comes intensive testing to see if any positive results have been obtained."

"That's the developmental stage. What about implementation? We are talking birth control here. Just how did you operationalize that aspect? It would necessarily involve optimum human involvement, would it not?"

Nestor nodded.

"And I doubt that can be sped up with hydroponics. Was the implementation personal on your part," asked Humphrey, a twinkle creeping into his stony eyes, "or did you outreach for end-users of this contraceptive?"

"We used volunteers, actually. Is that what you want to know?"

"I ask because there may be critical socio-cultural parameters with regard to utilization of intercourse for scientific purposes. Disinclusion of that factor could render the project non-viable in the target community. You never know what the public will object to these days."

"Did we have difficulty in getting volunteers? Is that the gist of that question?" asked Nestor, who was becoming irritated at having to struggle to understand the man.

"Near enough."

"No. If anything, the reverse."

"How is Naturcept administered? I would like to know that." It was a strangely concise and clear question.

"As I said, the subjects volunteered after we explained what we were attempting to prove. Of course some who were approached refused for various reasons—usually religious; but those who agreed to take part in the studies were prepared and ready to accept pregnancy if it happened to occur."

"Just as well; we wouldn't want to be accused of scientific experimentation in the production of unwanted babies. The Nazis tried that in the thirties. The government might have to take care of them."

Relatively understandable, thought Nestor, likely because he's getting interested. "From the various plants we engineered we prepared a palatable food substance—birth control pancakes, if you like. These have the consistency of granola bars. Sometimes we mixed it into a drink. If time and money were available we could likely produce Naturcept in capsule form, which could be taken either by females or males. Our volunteers were, for the most part, couples, but there does tend to be a lot of singles with this type of experiment."

"I wouldn't doubt it," Humphrey interjected.

"These people took part in what you might call 'acquaintance missions,' always trying to assess whether or not ingesting Naturcept effectively reduced reproductive capacity. And there were other medical methods of ascertaining the efficacy of Naturcept to corroborate the human evidence.

A number of expert doctors and scientists have been involved and, well, that's why my organization needs funding. It has been a very expensive proposition; I have been at this for the better part of fifteen years. The majority of the research and development is behind us and I am confident that we now have a substance that works, a product that guarantees that pregnancies will not occur."

Baumgartner, realizing that Nestor was finished, leaned forward in his chair. "So you can prove that Naturcept works?"

"Yes," replied Nestor without hesitation.

"Do you have the exact details and data for producing the product with you?"

"Yes," Nestor answered firmly.

"For how long would the contraceptive results prove one hundred percent effective?"

"Well, that is not precise yet," Nestor answered. "We're working on it. Conservatively speaking, let's say it can work for at least six months, possibly up to a year, but we haven't had time to accurately assess dosage."

"How long does it take to go into effect after consumption?"

"Six or seven days."

"The product would seem to be marketable. You are asking CIDA to back the project and the product financially. Obviously we will have to make some inquiries before any aid is forthcoming."

"I can understand that."

"How exactly would you utilize potential funds?"

"We would have to obtain approval from the governmental drug enforcement agency. Then there is the dissemination, distribution, and marketing. It is a massive undertaking."

"A noble project and a noble sentiment. I detect that you are an idealist by nature, Mr. LaPretre. The product has many practical applications *per se*, which is the biggest point in its favour. However, the community, the public, demands that we act only as a catalyst in stimulating the international flow of money, and although we try to help backward and culturally deprived environments and economically disadvantaged countries, we must always play it safe and consider the economic and religious consequences of our actions, in this or any case. We have to consider our accountability. We are not philanthropists."

Nestor translated this as meaning the maintenance of the illusion of responsibility and effectiveness. He came directly to the point. “I can’t continue with the project unless I get substantial funding from somewhere. Do you think CIDA will back me?” He held his breath as he waited for the response.

Baumgartner took his glasses off and held them up to the light before replacing them on the bridge of his finely-chiseled nose. “Does your paperwork demonstrate your efforts to raise the capital from private investors or organizations? We don’t loan or grant money to those who could raise it elsewhere, or who have personal funds available.”

Nestor was getting impatient. “Look, I’ve paid for all this work with my own private funds, literally sold the family farm. Mainstream scientific agencies will not take me seriously. Even those who believe my claim to be plausible deplore the way I’ve chosen to proceed. Many in the scientific community have their own axes to grind. I’ve come to the end of my rope, and certainly to the end of my financial ability.”

“I can see you feel strongly about that,” Baumgartner soothed, noting the vehemence with which Nestor spoke.

“I’ve disclosed my own capital investment and the sources of whatever else has gone into the project. I’ve prepared further details on that and on some of the technical aspects of my research and its results. I have it all here.” Nestor reached into his briefcase for the paperwork, which he slid with a flourish across the polished desk.

Baumgartner began to read the material. “You are requesting our unconditional backing. Hmm. Our banking principles are severe and uncompromising. All I can state at this time is that we may undertake a feasibility study into the legitimacy—perhaps I should rephrase that—the viability of Naturcept, interfaced with presumptive reactivity of your file, plus a quantification of its cost-effectiveness.”

My God, thought Nestor. “What more could one ask,” he said with a smirk. “When might this become operative?”

“I’ll prioritize it as of now, and try to optimize procurement as soon as possible, if your application is accepted.”

“Thank you, Mr. Baumgartner,” Nestor said, thinking that he had just been fed misinformation, but feeling there was still some chance of success. He stifled the urge to tell him just where to prioritize his government agency.

"One more question," Baumgartner said. "You say you have a precise formula for Naturcept, and that you have it with you. Would you be willing to leave it with me?"

Nestor knew the answer to this question, but pretended to think it over carefully. Then he said, "I'm sure you will understand . . . if my application were to be approved by the Agency, and if they were to actually fund Naturcept with research funds, then by all means I would provide that information. But until such time I have to cover my own ass, an expression with which I am sure government agencies are only too familiar. This is a valuable product to the world and to whoever produces it, of that I am sure."

"I can appreciate your position, Mr. LaPretre. May I ask if anyone else has expressed an interest?"

Nestor paused a moment, again weighing his reply. "Nothing definite, although I do have an inquiry from a foreign organization. But I'd really like to keep this a Canadian enterprise."

"Duly noted, Mr. LaPretre, I assure you. I'll keep that thought in mind." Baumgartner did not rise. They shook hands again and Nestor took his leave.

He began to walk wearily back to his hotel, favouring his injured leg. He had encountered another anaconda, and he was running out of both cash and credit. Someone had to come through, but somehow he had the feeling that it wasn't going to be the Canadian International Development Agency.

In his office, Baumgartner stared out the window at the city of Hull for several minutes. He took his glasses off and carefully cleaned them with his neatly pressed handkerchief. After refolding the hankie and placing it gingerly in his breast pocket, he pressed a button on the intercom and said, "Miss Stevenson, I'll be away from the office for the rest of the day doing field work." By this they both knew he'd be gone for a longer period than usual.

Baumgartner went to a French bistro, le Chat du Noir, to place a call from their pay phone. He dialed a number, and when the Azusipa Dionusos Drug Corporation head office answered, he asked for Finn Mahoney.

CHAPTER TEN

THE SECRETS OF GOD

THEY HAD ALL BEEN VOLUNTEERS in 422 Squadron, screened for above-average motivation, hardiness, and a sense of adventure. Hugo Payne was one of them in 1966 when they received the strike message from the Vietnam headquarters of the USAF.

Armament, fuel, and maintenance crews had been working all night and into early morning, readying the aircraft. The weather reports proved excellent; the twenty-four kites on the mission stood ready on the flight line. Heat shimmered off the concrete runway; the temperature was in the nineties, hotter in the revetments.

Time to climb into the overheated cockpits. God, it was hot. Hugo hooked up his oxygen mask to the aircraft system and tested it. He was flying an F-105F Weasel with an electronic warfare officer, nicknamed a "Bear." Their craft carried radar warning and homing equipment, chaff to confuse enemy radar, radio jamming gear, conventional bombs and cannon, plus air-to-ground missiles that rode down radio beams to destroy the emitter. Not like the early days of flying in World War I, Hugo thought, when all they had were gliders and slingshots. Not even like World War II.

The Wild Weasel's job was to fly in ahead of the strike Thud aircraft—each of which carried two 3,000 pound bombs—and to confuse and jam the Vietcong defenses, particularly their SA-2s, or Sam tracking missiles, which were armed with proximity fuse warheads. Four Wild Weasels were to fly this mission, their job to go in below the Sam's minimum effective altitude of 2,000 feet and knock them out before the bombers arrived on target. The primary danger of this tactic was that they had to fly right into the most lethal part of the enemy anti-aircraft gun envelope to accomplish their task.

Hugo plugged the communications jack into its socket, and hooked up his seat belt and shoulder harness. The crew chief helped make the connections to the ejection seat. He started the engine and let it warm up, as if it wasn't hot enough already. It was button-up-your-overcoat-and-fly time. He advanced the throttle to taxi out of the revetments and closed the plexiglass canopy. With brakes released, it was time for take-off. Six hundred knots at ground speed level. Then way out yonder to where the blue began.

Turning the northeast corner of Thud Ridge, they headed straight into Hanoi. The bombers were overhead and the flak started to roll up as the four-ship suppression flight of Weasels went to work, completely obliterating two clusters of guns along the Red River. Others were still firing. Hugo's Bear couldn't spot any Sam launching sites.

A bomb run, which took seven seconds, was an eternity when diving at the target. MiGs were taking off from an enemy airfield but they weren't fast enough to catch a Weasel. As the second wave of Thud bombers came in, the Sams came into action. So did Hugo and the Weasels. They knocked out eight Sam sites and damaged six others—but not before the enemy got operational. "Something's tracking us," the Bear yelled into the intercom. "Christ almighty! Hit the confetti button!"

He had only enough fuel for one last run. His Bear spotted another Sam site. He and his wingman dove through a wall of 37mm and 57mm flak, blowing up the Sam with their last cluster bomb units. Hugo leveled off, deployed his speed brakes, and had started to pull up when the shit hit the fan. He felt the aircraft lurch. He'd been hit with fifty calibre before, but this was something bigger, maybe a Chinese 37mm cannon. Where in hell had that MiG on his tail come from? The engine sputtered but kept running. Hugo turned hard to the left and hit the afterburners just as another burst hit the front cockpit. That was all he remembered. That and the searing red-hot pain in his right leg and groin.

His Bear managed to get the Weasel back to a forward airstrip, smoke and a flicker of flame partially blocking his vision. Coming in too fast, he jerked up the landing gear to avoid sliding off the strip, skidded several hundred feet, and slid off the right side of the runway. The ambulance got there just in time to pull an unconscious Hugo out of the cockpit before the plane went up in a huge ball of fire.

Hugo could have done without the bilateral orchidectomy. This horticultural expression, referring to pruning, was the surgeon's metaphor for castration. In Hugo's case he lost it all. The surgeon did his best, but the main operation had been performed by a burst of cannon fire aimed at his Wild Weasel.

He got out of Vietnam alive, but not a happy man. The docs had fixed him with plastic and plugs, sewn him up, and provided him with a method by which he could urinate. When he was in his cups he sometimes bemoaned the fact that he had not been screwed for nearly thirty years; at which times he also admitted that this made him feel a little nervous.

"It's not that bad, really," he said, speaking to his secretary as he took another martini from the passing waiter's tray. "I don't want the fruit salad, you can eat the olive," and he passed it to her on the end of the little toothpick.

"I'll tell you something," he continued, staring moodily at her full figure. "From a strictly physical standpoint you also lose the desire to fuck. Therefore, whether such a desire starts in the balls or in the brain is a moot question. The balls are gone, but the brain remembers. Even videos of fornication mean zilch to me, and therein lies the rub, or lack of it."

"You explained all that to me when you hired me, Hugo. You didn't want me to wonder why you never made a pass at me. You swore me to silence and we agreed never to talk about it. Obviously you've had too much to drink, so it's time you went home."

"Hmmmphffff!" he snorted. "Well, at least I've licked two of the world's main problems."

"And what might they be?" she asked, knowing she was being set up.

"Stupidity and lust! Most people are in the fucking dark or in the dark fucking!" He laughed loudly.

She took the half-empty glass from his hand and told him to go home.

Hugo mulled over the suggestion, then quietly exited the hotel, hailed a cab, and gave the driver the address of an apartment in downtown Toronto.

Payne had been nearly twenty-one when it happened. Before his love of aviation led him to become a fighter pilot in the Vietnam war, he had gone to Juliard, and although he had not finished, Hugo had become an excellent musician. He played bass and the valve trombone. After Vietnam, he went back to music and had made a good living at the trade with some better-than-average groups. Not that he needed to, because the Forces paid him a large pension. And his own family were very wealthy. So much so that he was a millionaire, and would be even richer when his mother died. None of it compensated, but it was better than nothing. He coped and he could do more or less what he pleased, because Hugo did not give a damn what happened to him. That philosophy gave him an edge in any situation fraught with danger.

On his way to his condo, Hugo passed the expensive nursing home which housed his grandmother. He realized that he was three-quarters swacked from too many martinis. His mind was playing strange tricks. He told the driver to stop and wait; he just felt like seeing her for a few minutes. He didn't come often enough. Maybe this time, although it was late, she would be lucid.

There was no one at the reception desk so he donned one of the short white coats hanging from a rack. On the second floor he met a nurse, but, concentrating on walking a straight line, he breezed past her in a professional manner. An orderly was scrubbing the floors of the hallway in front of his grandmother's room. Hugo stepped around him and entered. A night light cast a ghostly glow on Theresa, who lay curled in her bed. She wasn't asleep, but she didn't respond when he spoke to her.

Lately, the hospital told him that the best time to visit her was first thing in the morning. Sometimes she would talk then. Usually her dentures were out and it was hard to make out what she was trying to say. She was a tough old lady who had always had low blood pressure, so something else would likely kill her before a heart attack did. Empathy had led him to the conclusion that it was going to have to be him. She was ninety-two years old.

He stood beside the bed and looked down at her. She looked back at him but her gaze went through and past him to something distant. A tear formed slowly and ran down his right cheek as he remembered how well she had treated him as a child, how she always stuck up for him with his parents. "It's not his fault," she'd tell them, "he didn't ask to be brought into this world."

"You didn't ask to come into this world either," Hugo now said to his grandmother, "but I'm sure you'd be asking to get out if I could only get through to you, or you to me, or you to them, or either of us to anybody who can do anything." She lay in her bed, unmoving, likely in pain, possibly without thought. He'd have to get more involved. Would they do anything—the medical profession? Euthanasia was only legal in Holland. There you could have a family meeting with the doctors and the loved one, while he or she could still understand their decision. You could have a farewell party together, and then a lethal drug would be painlessly administered—very civilized. But Holland wouldn't do this for foreigners. Hugo knew his grandmother had to die, and he wanted to spare her the physical distress, the agony.

As he sat watching the wraith who was once so vital, his mind filled with memories of long ago—her singing *Twinkle Twinkle Little Star*, and *Yes, Jesus Loves Me*; the wonderful smell of baking in her kitchen; the coffee, which was mostly warm milk, that she allowed him to have at her house. Hugo swallowed the sob welling up in his throat and turned away from her.

Then he turned back, kissed her on the forehead, and left the room.

His phone was ringing when he entered the apartment, still wearing the white coat. All he wanted was to go to bed, but something told him to pick up the receiver.

The rule was that you never said who you were, and in fact Hugo did not know the exact identity of the caller, who was, in any case, only the bearer of a message:

Rejoice heart and soul, daughter of Zion!
Shout with gladness, daughter of Jerusalem!
See now, your King comes to you,
He is victorious and triumphant,
Humble and riding on a donkey. . . .

It ended with, "Maximum time of possible conception is four days," before the line went dead.

It was a code, of course, the way these messages always were. To Hugo it meant, in the enigmatic jargon of the members, that he should see his immediate superior in the Chivalric Order in which he was a Commandeur—the Priory of Sion—within four days. That superior was Croises, of which there were only three, so this had to be important.

Hugo ran his hand through his sandy-silver hair. They must want him to do a job. Good; it had been a long time since he'd seen some action. He hoped he was as good as perhaps he never was. The Priory hadn't summoned him in ages, maybe because while they could tell him what to do, they couldn't control how he went about doing it.

He felt the familiar pressure in his gut, and it had nothing to do with the Priory of Sion. Although he was used to it, he hated what he had to go through several times a day. It was messy, with the bags and tubes and piss. And that wasn't the worst of it.

Hugo knew something that few people ever have to contend with, and it often plagued him. It was similar to the "phantom leg" syndrome, when one loses a limb and it continues to hurt, even years after the loss. One may go for years without feeling or pain, but then, without warning, even ten or twenty years later, sudden sensation. Hugo was now suffering a bout of the dreaded "phantom penis" syndrome—he thought he had a hard-on, and that was the worst part of all.

Tracking back through the galley-style kitchen of his apartment, he made himself a cup of Ovaltine and sank into an easy chair.

Few people had even heard of the Priory of Sion, and to the extremely small percentage of those who knew anything at all about the shadowy organization, it appeared to be an influential, powerful, and wealthy international secret society, whose members were neither naïve idealists nor religious fanatics.

Hugo went over the creed in his mind: *No solutions for existing world problems will be forthcoming except through new methods and new men. There is a rising tide of resentment and dissatisfaction with the beliefs and dogma of politics and religion as a means of accomplishing worldwide change for the better. The environmental consequences of monetary, trade, agricultural and economic policies, plus national interest, has brought on a universal crisis and no mechanisms exist to promote responsible government behaviour. The hierarchies of the Christians and the Moslems, the liberals and the conservatives, the capitalists and the socialists, are not yet ready to recognize the distinct signs of improvement throughout the laity—a moving current of change abroad in the world. Jesus orchestrated, from behind the scenes, certain critical events in Western history, involving political and religious repercussions with potentially enormous impact, affecting the thinking, the values, the institutions and beliefs of the contemporary world.*

This kind of thinking refreshed Hugo's memory as to why he was involved—the goal of the Priory of Sion was to try to emulate and put into practice the philosophy of Jesus Christ. He knew that beliefs could be dangerous, that people kill in the name of beliefs. And disbelief can be as much an act of faith as belief itself. Some things are just not known. He thought of the Latin logo of the Priory:

Et in Arcadia Ego—Begone! I Conceal the Secrets of God. . . .

CHAPTER ELEVEN

AZUSIPA DIONUSOS

FORMED IN EUROPE IN THE EARLY 1920S, *Azusipa Dionusos first specialized in a variety of popular patent medicines. As the company grew, its directors hired chemists to develop new products, as well as other professionals to expand their research, manufacturing, and advertising and sales facilities.*

Following World War II, the company began to buy out smaller competitors, expanding its operations and markets to the Americas, India, and Southeast Asia. Azusipa survived a hostile take-over bid by an American pharmaceutical corporation in 1983-84, subsequently luring away many of the American company's top personnel. By 1990, Azusipa's research department had identified the areas of fertility and infertility as its largest potential market worldwide.

After announcing record profits for 1994 and being named one among three of the most powerful companies by the American Pharmaceutical Association, Azusipa Dionusos Inc. formulated an aggressive plan of action. In 1995, the company's highly-paid competitor analysts were given a mandate to obtain any and all goods, information, and personnel, by whatever means possible, to attain their goal: to become the *most profitable drug company in the world.*

It wasn't a room so much as a space somewhere in Hotel Limbo, like a bunker used for military operations. The impression arose from the grey cement walls, unrelieved by the similarly coloured filing cabinets which lined three of the walls. There were no windows; ventilation was supplied by an air-conditioning unit somewhere else in the building. In the centre of the room were an oblong table and six chairs on castors; the hard carpeting between the filing cabinets and the table revealed a great deal of wear and tear. Several telephones with long extension cords were on the work table. At each end of the table were computer stations.

Two men sat in the room, one rifling a stack of files, the other hunched over a computer. When Baumgartner's call came in to the unlisted number at Azusipa Dionusos Inc., Finn Mahoney answered.

Azusipa was determined to become number one in the licit international drug business. In operation for years, their strange name came from a combination of ancient Sumerian and Greek words: *ia-u-shush*—Jesus, the seed that saves; *da-ia-una*—meaning Dionysus, the Greek god of healing or fertility, its symbol an erect phallus; *sipa*—stretched horn or penis; *azu*—physician; *nosios*—Greek for healer.

"Yes, it has been a while, Humphrey, that's right," said Finn. "Thought maybe you had retired on us. No. Glad to hear it. How are things at CIDA?" Finn listened, then said, "Well, the Canadian government never did have a good year, never once made a profit. What I say is, 'Put them on commission.' I take it you have something of interest or you wouldn't be calling us at all now, would you?"

Apparently Humphrey agreed; Mahoney listened attentively for several minutes.

"You were right to inform us immediately," he said. "We have a definite interest in that kind of drug, especially if it's the real McCoy. I'm never convinced until our boys independently check it out, though. Reliable information makes correct decisions. But don't worry about that, boyo."

Finn listened further. Mahoney was one of a new breed of competitor intelligence gatherers. He liked to refer to himself and his cohorts as "competitor analysts" instead of thieves, but in reality he was an in-house snoop and hit man for Azusipa Dionusos. After hanging up, he turned to the other man in the room, Mitch Peden, who had been listening to Finn's end of the conversation with Baumgartner.

"There is a man," said Finn, "named Nestor LaPretre. We must have a file on him; he's been working a long time on a new contraceptive drug. Baumgartner seems to think he is legit and has what he claims to have. Said he certainly has every reason to think so from their files. If this is true then LaPretre has one hell of a birth control product on his hands. The bottom line is that it sounds very promising—just what we are looking for. But our pigeon is strapped for cash just like most of these private scientific types, and he's looking for some financing."

The lean, dark-skinned Mitch smiled through thin lips at his younger, baby-faced partner. "That's good. Might make him easier to deal with. I'll run a make on his operation."

"He's between invention and distribution. All we have to do is play both ends against the middle, and make the middle-man part of the deal."

"We *are* the middle-men," replied Peden. "Everyone can have a share, and if the others don't like their end, there are alternate solutions."

"Let's check the files on Mr. LaPretre, and everything we've got on birth control and contraceptives while we're at it."

Technologically, Azusipa was beyond up-to-date. Their automated DNA and sequencer machines, designed to decipher the code of life, helped researchers to identify genes that caused diseases such as breast cancer and asthma. Gene crunchers the world over were trying to map the sum total of genetic information in the human species. They were lagging with regard to plants and other forms of life, but drug companies, including Azusipa, knew that RNA and DNA research was crucial to the quality of life in the future.

The concern of national health institutions was whether it was in the public interest to allow or grant patents and rights to future royalties upon the discovery of a minute gene fragment. Was it truly an invention and did it have utility? A gigantic industry was building up around the lucrative quest to identify genes and cash in on genetic mapping efforts. Opposition came from those who questioned the ethics and mechanics of biotechnical patenting—especially when it was applied to the twenty-three pairs of chromosomes which define a person's characteristics. There was not so much controversy when it came to patenting plant products.

Finn and Mitch were both at the computer now, watching the screen with interest and stopping only occasionally to comment on some new or reformulated data. Azusipa's machines studied pieces of tissue that might contain tens of thousands of genes and eliminated long repetitive strings of genetic material, called "junk DNA," isolating a few hundred base pairs of it. They would then claim sole rights to the discovery if anyone proved this sequence had any use.

Azusipa Dionusos' plan was to become the forerunner in this biological gold rush. They wanted to work in open territory where they stood to make the most money. To do this, they had to obtain the knowledge and services of geneticists and others who were highly skilled in biotechnology.

Men like Finn, fat and cordial on the surface, and Mitch, lean and mean, worked assiduously in their mutual interest. They made a good team, for beneath their opposing exteriors they both did a hard-nosed job for the drug company. The corporate intelligence centre, where they now sat, kept track of the mountains of data which had been culled both legitimately and illegitimately from their drug competitors, food and drug administrations, and government commissions around the world. Azusipa was also part of a Paris-based industrial espionage program that ran against both foreign and domestic pharmaceutical competitors. Finn and Mitch were major-league players in the intelligence service which collected information and manufacturing secrets involving research and marketing. Interception of electronic communications; infiltration of rival companies; breaking into large hotels to copy business documents left in rooms by visiting businessmen, journalists, and diplomats; any "bag" operation or technique that might further their clandestine purpose, they used.

Fully aware of the potential to make millions, Finn and Mitch were polished professionals when it came to obtaining information about new products and how they were made. Possession and control were the name of the game—a drug sought after by hundreds of millions of people could mean billions in profit.

CHAPTER TWELVE

SNATCH AND GRAB

OPUS DEI, DESCRIBED by some as a religious fifth column, recruited its members, after first observing and testing them, from the financial and political elite, and infiltrated all segments of society, from garbage collectors, farmers and fishermen, to university professors and high-ranking professionals. A world-wide diocese, Opus Dei had potential informers everywhere, members under the authority of the movement's leadership. Tendentious and elusive, Opus Dei brought great influence on young and overly religious minds. After being recruited, members were under strong pressure to remain.

Cardinal Bettini had long been a member and an ardent admirer of Opus Dei and its founder, the Very Reverend Josemaria Escriva de Belaguer y Albas of Spain, who was now buried in an underground crypt beneath the luxurious headquarters on the Viale Bruno Buozzi, in the affluent Pariola district in north Rome. The Cardinal was their chief agent inside the Vatican Curia. How much Opus Dei knew about the Cardinal's own little offshoot organization was another matter entirely. Bettini liked to know everybody else's business and wanted no one to know his own. While Opus Dei balked at violence as a strategy, Bettini's small and personally-controlled assemblage were not dissuaded.

When the Cardinal needed an agent in Canada to play a role in this Holy Mafia, he conferred with the top Canadian Opus Lieutenant. As a result, he decided that Charlotte Lockwood might be the ideal person to work on the case of Nestor LaPretre. The information in her file indicated that she had a Master of Divinity degree, was affiliated with McGill University in Montreal, and had, quietly and efficiently, carried out several minor assignments for Opus Dei over the past few years. The Cardinal believed she would follow instructions without question and could easily be kept in the dark as to the true intent of the operation. She would be shipped back to Canada none the wiser.

Bettini read the Vatican's dossier on Nestor LaPretre. He was a backsliding North American Catholic. Raised on a ranch in southern Alberta, of a Francophone father and an English mother, he'd had a good start in life, so there was no excuse for his current attitude and faulty morals. He'd had a rigid Catholic school upbringing and had even applied for admission to a seminary before, apparently, realizing that he didn't have the calling. There'd been one marriage of short duration, which failed for reasons not stated. Brilliant academically, LaPretre had graduated at the top of his class in science from the University of Guelph, noted for its biological expertise. For many years now, Bettini noted, LaPretre had been obsessively involved in contraceptive experimentation through the genetic engineering of plants.

In the days of the Inquisition LaPretre would have been burned at the stake, thought the Cardinal, avenging God for the wrongs inflicted on Him by Nestor's crimes of disbelief and doubt and the sin of flouting conception by his invention of Naturcept. Bettini thought LaPretre needed a Father Confessor, one who would strive to save his wretched soul from the endless torments of hell, someone who would act for an authority far higher than that of earthly judges. LaPretre was a heretic, and Bettini therefore knew that a strict rule of "The Congregation for the Doctrine of the Faith," formerly "The Holy Office," formerly "The Roman Inquisition," must be applied—all his worldly property, especially Naturcept, should be confiscated.

Bettini's view, in simple terms, was that the priest lays down the law, the Bishop disciplines those who disobey, and the Pope excommunicates those whose disobedience persisted. Moral decisions should not be left to the laity. They should passionately obey an active authoritarian clergy. It was a system that worked, thought Cardinal Bettini, eschewing all modern liberal ideas on the subject.

Bettini stared at the replica of the Shroud of Turin on the wall of his study and became agitated at the thought of the heretics who said that the Shroud was not authentic. "Damn all the heretics!" he said, turning to more pertinent matters.

The Cardinal had doubts about the new Pope Cesare Romereo's

doctrinal conservatism within the Church. He was particularly worried about what the new Pope might do because all previous Papal announcements and edicts were no longer infallible unless so stated. Bettini had no idea where the Most Holy Father stood on birth control and anti-conception devices. The opinion of the Church had already been declared by Popes John Paul VI and II. If Romereo was in agreement, then all would be well. But if he wasn't, the Cardinal was prepared. Bettini realized he'd better have a talk with Cesare Romereo to find out which one of them had the biggest problem.

The Cardinal picked up the phone and dialed the Opus Dei number. He instructed the administrator to get another message to Sister Charlotte Lockwood and urge her to obtain the consent of LaPretre to come to Rome immediately to discuss Naturcept. She was to convince him of the urgency in this matter, that in effect, he had no choice. Bettini knew that Charlotte would succeed; she'd been chosen specifically for this mission because of her proven track record for persuading otherwise reticent people that a certain course of action was their own idea, thus a good one.

Charlotte's priestly mentor in Montreal passed on the urgent message from Bettini, but before she could contact Nestor, he contacted her.

Nestor had been thinking that if it came to a choice between CIDA and the Vatican, he might choose that source which had at least demonstrated interest, rather than the one spewing nonsensical bureaucratic rhetoric. The Canadian government continued to drag its feet on co-operation with the United Nations population control program; Canadian cabinets were always divided on this issue. No doubt influenced by the Catholic ministers in cabinet, they regarded the subject as explosive. Nestor had little hope that they would transcend religious considerations and treat the matter as national policy. The same thing applied to the Vatican, but at least he knew they were willing to discuss it. He'd given up on the drug companies because they wanted complete control, not to mention the money and publicity. Nestor refused to subvert his own work to suit their programs.

Nestor arrived at Charlotte's apartment with streaks of dirt on his suit, a bruised and scraped hand, and the sleeve of his jacket ripped from the wrist to the shoulder.

"What happened?" she asked, surprised to see him in this condition. "I was just about to give you a call. Come, come in."

She offered him a comfortable chair and went to the kitchen to make a pot of tea. Back in the living room, she handed him a steaming cup, which he gratefully accepted.

"Ms. Lockwood," said Nestor, "I have to trust someone, and I feel I can trust you." He looked straight into her face. She met his gaze.

"Please, call me Charlotte. And certainly you can trust me. You have no reason not to."

"Someone tried to steal my attaché case not half an hour ago. It's the first time something like this has ever happened; I always guard my data carefully."

"Tell me about it."

"I stopped near the entrance to a park. I was deciding whether or not to take a short cut. Suddenly from behind me I felt a heavy blow across my right hand. A man grabbed my briefcase and jerked it away, trying to run with it at the same time. But I take good care of that case when I'm in public."

"Mr. LaPretre, didn't I warn you that someone might be following you?"

"Well," Nestor's brow furrowed. "I don't remember. Did you?"

"I'm sure I did," she said confidently. "But in any case, you still have it with you."

"Yes. I wear a shoulder harness to protect it. A thin steel chain runs from the harness down my right sleeve, which is clipped to the handle. Snatch-and-grab artists aren't prepared for it. This thug was a big bugger—large, beefy, really husky. He knocked me off my feet as he tried to run, but he couldn't drag me very far. The chain held, and the briefcase was pulled out of his hand. He came back for it, but by then I was scrambling to my feet and there were other people around, so he turned and ran. I started to chase him, but a car pulled up and he jumped in."

"Who could it have been?"

"I have no idea. This guy didn't look at all like the young hoodlums you'd expect to do that kind of thing. I doubt it was a coincidence. Someone wants this attaché case and they were following me to get it."

"Is there anything I can do?" she asked, pouring him more tea.

"I have decided I will go to Rome with you as soon as you can arrange it."

"Fine."

"Someone wants what's in my briefcase very badly. I'm going to have to take further precautions for the trip. But how can I be sure I can trust you?"

"Mr. LaPretre," Charlotte said, "I have a divinity degree and am a tenured professor at McGill. Would you like to see my credentials? Or I can arrange separate flights to Rome if you'd like."

"No, no," Nestor said, flustered, "that isn't necessary."

"Well, that's it then." Charlotte smiled. "Just what further precautions did you have in mind?"

"I'm going to buy an identical case here in Ottawa."

Charlotte looked the case over as he showed her its features. It was about eighteen inches by twelve, four inches thick, good leather.

"I'll split the contents," explained Nestor, "and place some distractions and meaningless paper in each case. The contents of either case would only confuse biologists. They could never figure it out. You'll carry one case inside your luggage, and I'll carry the other."

"I'll arrange our flight right away," Charlotte said, smiling supportively.

CHAPTER THIRTEEN

VATICAN ROULETTE

THE ONLY LIGHT IN THE CHAPEL came from the massive candle in front of the altar before which Cardinal Bettini knelt in prayer. He never asked God for small things, but the thought of a good night's sleep did cross his mind. It was nearly midnight in the Apostolic Palace. The chapel was for the use of the inhabitants of the Vatican's Papal apartment. The candle, nearly two feet in diameter and three in height, had been a gift to Pope John Paul II from the schoolchildren of Poland, who had assiduously saved wax from many small candles and fashioned it into a grandiose gift to the Holy Pontiff.

Suddenly he sensed that he was not alone. Had he heard a rustling, or was it just a feeling of being watched? He turned his head slowly. The flickering candlelight made viewing difficult. Had he seen movement in the shadows near the statue of the Virgin Mary? "Will you join me in prayer?" he asked quietly.

"No," a male voice replied from the gloom.

"I don't recognize your voice."

"You have no reason to. I've never been here before."

"Then what are you doing here now?" Bettini demanded.

"We need to talk."

"Is that so? Then make an appointment with my office."

"No, we'll talk now."

"What about?" Bettini, unsettled, was playing for time.

"Theology, for one thing. Yes, I suppose it would come under that heading."

"This would seem to be the place, but the time is not propitious," Bettini said calmly. He was becoming vexed by this intrusion. "If you are a stranger, how do you come to be here in the Vatican at this time of night? It is long past tourist hours." Who was this man hiding in the privatePapal chapel? Was there reason for apprehension? "How did you get in?"

"Possibly I managed entry by the same means as whoever murdered Pope Luciano Albini," the voice replied firmly.

"Murder!" exclaimed the Cardinal. Chills ran down his spine; there was no way to alert security here in the chapel. "Murder, you say. And through some secret means of entry. Interesting theory—would you care to elucidate?"

"It's easy. Your security is appalling. Six of the Vatican entrances open onto the streets of Rome. Your Swiss Guards are useless, your security cops are mostly interested in talking to pretty girls at sidewalk cafés. The elevator is not guarded and many people have keys. Anyone dressed as a priest can come and go unchallenged. And since the demise of John Paul I, you discovered a hidden stairwell near the Papal apartment. Someone in Pope John Paul I's day likely knew of its existence."

"You seem to know your way around the premises, so if that's your ridiculous murder theory, maybe it was you. I should call the Swiss Guard. They may not be as useless as you think." The Cardinal made a move to get up off his knees, but as he did so he heard a loud cough immediately followed by a "thunk." Wax particles sprayed from the candle and a breast-like swelling sprang from its broad surface, a hole appearing in the centre surrounded by a darker aureole.

"Let's just stay where we are, shall we?" said the voice.

Bettini sank back to his knees. He didn't scare easily, but now he knew that the man was armed. It was best to keep talking. "You mentioned theology . . . by all means let's discuss it. In what aspect are you particularly interested?"

"Birth control."

"Birth control is not theology. It is a form of murder. There are many forms of sin. Is there one to which you would like to confess?"

"None."

The Cardinal had a short fuse. "Then leave!" Gun or no gun, he jumped to his feet. "This is blasphemous. I will not have it. What do you want? You are an intruder by night, a criminal, likely a burglar or worse. So either state your piece or get out. I am not afraid of you."

"I heard you were feisty and wanted to see for myself. Calm down, Your

Eminence. We haven't had our talk, and I'm not leaving until we do. I came here to discuss birth control with you and I think you know why."

"I do? What makes you say that?"

"Naturcept!"

"Naturcept?"

"And I want to talk about Nestor LaPretre."

"Nestor LaPretre?"

"That's a bad habit you have, repeating names. You know what I'm talking about."

"Did you break in here tonight to find someone named Naturcept or La . . . something . . . what?"

"Your Eminence, I haven't broken anything yet. I came only to see you, and perhaps eventually the Pope."

"A strange way to seek a Papal audience. There are other channels, you know."

"True, but I wanted to surprise you. I knew it wouldn't do me any good to see the Pope unless I saw you first. He is new, and you are presently the most influential personage in the Church, a member of both the Curia and Opus Dei."

"You flatter me, Mr? . . ."

"Call me Hugo, if you like."

"Why not? We are old friends by now. But I am tired in the extreme, Mr. Hugo." Although wide awake, the Cardinal attempted to make his voice weak. "Do you bear me any harm?"

"Not unless you do something foolish."

"Then I suggest we repair to my study where we can continue this discussion."

"And where you also have a way of signaling the security forces. I think not. Let's just sit here in the pews like good Christians." Hugo stepped away from the chapel wall and into the light of the giant candle.

When Angostura Bettini saw Hugo Payne for the first time, the impression was not unfavourable. The man was tall and handsome, with steel-grey curly hair, a well-formed nose, and sturdy chin. In clerical garb, his wrinkled forehead made him appear to be a kindly and experienced priest. It was a perfect disguise for night-intruder tactics.

They sat down, warily, at opposite ends of the front pew.

"I have read the infamous rubbish from which you likely derived your theories regarding the alleged murder of John Paul I. It took fantastic speculation to new levels of absurdity," observed the Cardinal, indignation creeping into his voice.

"Seemed logical to me, but I do understand that murder isn't the Vatican's official view of the matter," replied Hugo. "That is not what I came to discuss."

"Then get on with it, please. I get little enough sleep as it is."

"Believe it or not, I am trying to help the Vatican and the Roman Catholic Church. I'm here to try to get you to fight tomorrow's battles, Cardinal, not those of yesterday. The point is . . . your previous *Humanae Vitae* and your Splendour of Truth encyclicals relating to birth control have not been humane in their contribution to world overpopulation. You make up a list of what the Church terms morally unacceptable, intrinsic evils—birth control, premarital sex, homosexuality, masturbation, sterilization, and artificial insemination—you don't enter into any dialogue with lay members. So the Pope must expect Catholics to use their consciences to obey the Church. It's an in-camera monologue on issues of morality that should concern all of us and affects all of us, through overpopulation, hyper-pollution, poverty, hunger, infanticide, to name a few."

"The Lord will provide," Bettini droned. "He is the Shepherd of the Flock."

"Your concern for the poor is touching, but the Lord does not always provide because there are just too many mouths for Him to feed. Abstinence and the rhythm method are bullshit."

"You are well beyond your bounds, my friend," replied Bettini, staring coldly.

"It won't hurt you to listen. The Curia are very good at political expediency. They major in it at theological colleges. We've got six billion people on Earth now; we don't need to try for ten. How bad does overpopulation have to get before you recognize the chaos and misery it produces?"

"You roadless heretic, the only reason Christianity has survived 'til today is due to the organizational and theological structure which the Roman Catholic Church developed. We save individual souls in the name of Jesus through an organized Church. That is our job. We are not into making deals, political or otherwise."

"Don't give me that crap. In the past you made deals with a great number of fascist and repressive dictatorships ... in return for their protection of your institutional rights and privileges, your Church power."

"And you back your opinion with a lethal weapon," Bettini growled in reply.

"So I do. Another example of power politics. Just listen, Bettini—this isn't the Inquisition. You can't enforce your views that way any more. That must irritate you. But why not be reasonable and rethink your position and beliefs once in a while, in the light of modern conditions that didn't exist in the early days of the Church?"

"I believe in one God, who is the Father Almighty, and Christ's incarnation, death, and bodily resurrection on the third day. I believe in the Holy, Catholic, and Apostolic Church."

"Spare me the dogma, Cardinal. You want control over people's minds, and their obedience to your power structure. But you have that already. So, if you espouse a new idea, a new approach to a subject, there is every reason to believe that it will be accepted and therefore stand a much better chance of succeeding. That's why I was sent to talk to you. The Church could do itself a favour. Remember, your faithful aren't all buying your position on this matter any more. They want knowledge and self-discovery, and an awareness of the human condition. You and I sail through history in different boats when it comes to the nature of Christianity, but we want you to seriously rethink your position on birth control. There are compelling reasons why a small change in your doctrine, like condoning Naturcept, would be considered a rational move on your part. Give it a chance; we are trying to help you."

"Damn your eyes. If the Church, as the mystical body of Christ, is the repository of truth, as I believe it to be, then it is my duty to defend her against the progressive faithlessness of liberal dissident Catholics—people like yourself—with their watered-down principles. Your ideas go against all Church doctrine through the ages." Bettini's voice was high-pitched now.

"Edicts made for another time and place," Hugo said calmly. "Stop attributing everything to some nebulous creature with a direct wire to the

Pope. You tell the Pope what to do and you know it. You are not a god. You've got a big enough ecclesiastical army already; why not concentrate on making their lives and those of future generations a little better."

"The Lord looks after his flock very well, you gnostic troublemaker. We have developed rituals to sanction every major event of their lives. We try to provide food for the poor and hope for the hopeless. You are nothing but a shit-disturber! I've had about enough of this business."

"Wait!" Hugo raised his left hand. "*Pax!* We're getting into name-calling here. *Deo Volente*, you and I can do better! As Adlai Stevenson once said, 'He who slings mud, generally loses ground.' I came here to talk specifics only."

Bettini paused, looking down his long nose at Hugo. He smiled. "I hadn't heard that before. That's good. The man was right. I'll admit that you see black and I see white. We can't all have the same vision of Christ. So, I agree, let's eliminate the sermons. We don't have a congregation in any case."

"And nobody is passing the collection plate."

"Right! So just what is it that you want from the Vatican, specifically? Spell it out. As I said before, you've got the gun."

"I hope you'll listen carefully anyway. We want you to change the Church's stand on birth control. Reverse your edicts against it. Persuade the Pope to make this decision officially. We want you to espouse Nestor LaPretre's genetic plant creation and help in its promotion and distribution."

The Cardinal listened with his eyebrows raised while Hugo elaborated upon the proposal. "It's not a natural method of contraception," Bettini demurred. "It's artificial."

"Why do you take that position? It is plant life. It grows on Mother Earth. You've got the perfect out—you won't even lose face by so declaring."

"It is not in accordance with God's law and teaching."

Hugo rose quickly from the pew and began pacing, running his free hand through his hair several times before replying. "We're not asking you to recant the most recent encyclicals, although they are all over like a dog's breakfast. We just want you to declare Naturcept to be natural and therefore an acceptable birth control method. You really don't have to rationalize much to do so." He paused for a moment. "Let me ask you another question."

"Are there no end to your questions?" Bettini sighed.

"Did the Vatican ever own shares in the Instituto Farmacologico Sereno? In fact, perhaps a controlling interest?"

"It may have. You'd have to ask Marcinkus."

"I don't have to. He bought it, and it was held through most of the period covered by your *Humanae Vitae* encyclical."

"So?"

"So one of Sereno's best-selling products was an oral artificial contraceptive called *Luteolos.*"

"We don't dictate the business policy of companies in which we happen to hold shares."

"Come off that crap. And neither do you divulge to your world-wide parishioners where you invest your money. They might just find such investments hypocritical; especially when you are telling your married couples how to conduct their sex life."

"Get to the point. I am extremely tired."

"The Vatican can be very practical, so my point would be well understood by God's ex-banker, Paul Marcinkus, or whoever is controlling your financial affairs at the moment. You needn't mention this argument to the Pope, because it only concerns profit and there are more humanitarian reasons upon which I'm sure he would prefer to base any decision. Consider the world market for Naturcept, especially in Third World countries. They haven't been using any effective contraceptive at all, and that's where most of your Catholics now are. Other forms of birth control have proven inadequate, even dangerous. The profits would be colossal. Think of all the good work you could do with the money. Or, if you prefer, all the cathedrals you could build."

"This question has long been decided. . . ."

"No. The real reason you don't want to change is that some of the influential Curia can't accept a degree of autonomy among the laity, or realize that old rules could and should be changed. You think that would undermine the hierarchy, and therefore your control."

"You certainly do carry on, Mr. Hugo. You seem to think you know how to run the Church better than we do. However, I believe you are serious."

"I certainly am. Birth control is possibly the biggest problem facing the Pope and the Church today. You've got the political climate, the need, and the market—what more do you want? Solve the population problem and make big bucks in the process. You can call Naturcept the Catholic Birth Control Method and get rid of Vatican Roulette. Just think about it."

"Who do you represent?"

Hugo paused. "The Priory of Sion," he said, finally. "You have no doubt heard of their exploits over the centuries. The Priory would like you to decide on the merits of the proposition, as to whether you will promote Naturcept to the Pope and the Vatican."

The bloody Priory of Sion! Of course, thought Bettini.

"Ah . . . Priory of Sion, you say . . . perhaps it will come to me. So . . . they want me to use my influence to become the instrument of the Church that will interpret for mankind the mind of Christ on this issue?"

"Overstated, but yes. You have a chance to correct previous—let's not call them errors—positions. We think you should do it for the mutual good of everyone, including the interests of the Church."

There was a long pause. "How soon do you want an answer?"

"We realize that the actual change would take a little time; but your decision as to policy would be appreciated as soon as possible. How long do you want? Think it over. The ball is in your court, Eminence. Let's say we discuss it again on Saturday."

"Same time, same place?"

"No thanks, I have no desire to meet a welcoming committee."

"You are a prudent man, Mr. Hugo. When and where, then?"

"In Rome. Neutral territory. You know the Ristorante Mastrobologna near the Marcello Theatre? Why don't we have dinner there? Say, eight p.m. on Saturday?"

"Eight on Saturday at Mastrobologna."

"I'll make the arrangements. All you have to do is show up—alone, of course."

"How prudent would that be of me?" Bettini asked, nodding toward Hugo's gun.

"There will be no one but myself. Just a quiet dinner between friends. It's a very public place and I won't be carrying this." Hugo slipped the revolver back into the holster, rose from the pew, and faded into the surrounding darkness.

Cardinal Bettini was one of the few people who knew anything about the identity and history of the Priory of Sion. He had access to the Vatican's secret archives—forty miles of bound registers and boxes of correspondence packed into sixty miles of shelves. They covered subjects from strange scandals to Church records of theology, politics, and commerce. There were documents concerning saints and sinners, popes and antipopes, martyrs and apostates. The Church documented the administration and minutiae of the faith from the time when Rome's earliest Christians recorded the arrival of Saint Peter and his crucifixion by Nero's executioners on Vatican Hill.

The Priory of Sion, in Bettini's view, was a combination of lunatics and Cathar-Merovingian heretics. They were reputed to possess something of fabulous and sacred value, a controversial and historic secret of immense import to the Christian world, knowledge that conferred great power to the possessor—the vanished treasure of the Knights Templar, the Holy Grail.

He sat a few minutes longer in the chapel and then rose from the pew. Why in God's name should the Vatican listen to your blandishments, he thought. My answer to you should be: "*Roma locuta est. Causa finita est.*" He would think about it, but there was nothing he could accomplish this night. But on Saturday, who knows? The Priory's proposition, like any other, would have to be assessed before he would decide what to do.

The Church hierarchy gave no credence to the existence of alleged and hitherto secret writings involving Jesus Christ; but the Cardinal had found it both prudent and expedient to become an expert historical theologian. Never mind the state of present-day teachings; it was prudent also to know how and why it came to be taught. At the same time he was well aware of the need to be cognizant of historical reality, as much as that was possible. In Rome one kept one's own conclusions private, although since the days of Martin Luther, the Protestants could be counted on to shoot off their big mouths.

Back in his own quarters, Angostura remained deep in thought. He certainly didn't want a democratic vote on who should be the Vicar of Christ on Earth, even though the Holy See would be prohibitively favoured to win. But still, he couldn't underestimate the opposition. The Priory was organized, disciplined, and probably sophisticated enough to package resurrected chivalry in an effective manner.

The Priory of Sion, Bettini knew, were alleged to be the keepers of proof of something explosive and invisible to the world at large that could intimidate the Vatican and the Pontiff, and which they thought effectively rendered them immune from the Vatican's punitive wrath. They intended to confront the Church with it, and appeared to be capable of doing so, knowing that it would cause turmoil and dissent—which would threaten Rome's position of power in the world.

And now, the Cardinal pondered, their agent had spoken specifically of birth control, tying it directly to the problems caused by the world's rapid population growth. Could the Priory of Sion prove the Pope did not speak for God in Christ's name in the matter of procreation? By threatening to expose certain documents in their possession relating to new Scriptures and new teachings of Jesus Christ to the glare of publicity, documents which could be scientifically proven to be authentic, could they force the Vatican into a more liberal position? Did they have access to material, Bettini wondered, which placed personal conscience above the dictates of the Vatican?

CHAPTER FOURTEEN

THE DEVIL'S CONGREGATION

THE BRIGHT NOONDAY SUN shone on the strongest building in Rome, the mausoleum of Emperor Hadrian, now called the Castel de Sant Angelo. On its summit, overlooking the six towers and one hundred and sixty-four battlements of the red brick fortress of the Popes, stood a bronze statue of St. Michael Archangel, sword in hand, guarding Rome from her enemies.

Inside the walls of the Apostolic Palace, and connected by an internal staircase to the Pope's apartment below, was a roof terrace. It had been built at great expense by Paul VI so that he could get exercise and fresh air in privacy. Each day after lunch, officially at two in the afternoon, the Pope and his Secretary of State conferred for a short time on current Church matters and world affairs. Sometimes they summoned their respective secretaries to take notes and instructions.

Cardinal Bettini stepped through the door into the sunshine on the terrace. Pope Cesare, dressed in a white sweatsuit, sat relaxed on a bench on the far side, his head back, eyes shut. Bettini started across the courtyard with his head bowed and hands clasped just below the gold cross on his soutane. The Secretary of State did not like doubt; he wanted to find out for certain what he could expect from Cesare. Bettini heard music. He hesitated, glancing up to see that the Pope was playing a portable cassette recorder, likely one of the many gifts that were continually received by the Papal Office from devout followers. The music had a Latin beat; the Pope's right foot tapped to the lively tune.

The Papal office is strictly circumscribed by tradition and changes little from century to century, but each Pope rules or fails to rule with a style of his own. For better or worse, and because he is married to it, the Pope's personality has a profound effect upon the Church. Cardinal Bettini worried about this new Pope's personality as he watched the Papal foot bouncing vigorously to the music. Bettini recalled the personalities of previous Pontiffs.

Jovial and self-confident, John XXIII had loved people, but had been a poor administrator and paid little attention to Church business. By ignoring the bureaucrats, John had permitted them to run the Church as they pleased, which would have been fine with the Cardinal if he had been the bureaucrat in charge. John XXIII had been the one who had introduced the ecumenical council of all the Catholic bishops, saying he wanted to retool the Church for the modern world. Bettini knew that John XXIII had had limited experience—he didn't know a thing about the modern world, what he wanted to accomplish, or how to go about it. But he had certainly succeeded in stirring the pot. The Council had tried to tamper with nearly every area of the Roman Catholic way of life.

After John, there'd been Pope Paul VI. An intellectual who couldn't communicate, Paul was one of the Curia who unfortunately used his skills to organize the whole Vatican II Council. Thankfully, Bettini and his cohorts were able to get to the gloomy Paul before he turned the hierarchy into a democracy. Bettini remembered when they pressured Paul into reaffirming the Church's ban on artificial birth control in spite of all the contrary advice given to him by heretical cardinals and bishops.

No trouble with John Paul I. Thirty-three days and he was gone, thus solving the problem. The less said about that, the better, thought Bettini.

Pope John Paul II—now there was a man with the right stuff. The Cardinal smiled as he pictured John Paul II's face. A good pope, he had hammered home certain truths of the Church "against a tide that believes that anything goes." He had reversed a lot of the harm done by Vatican II. John Paul II knew his role, thought Bettini, when he insisted that the teachings of the Church, the *Punti Firmi*, be obeyed, and that faith had a moral content. The Polish actor had been good, there was no doubt about that, and he never figured that the truth needed to be voted upon. He knew what the truth was, and expected members to listen, write it down, and memorize it. His philosophy had suited Bettini very well.

And now Pope Cesare Romereo I. Something of a wild card, thought Bettini. Cesare might be philosophically close to the liberation theology of Brazil, which had often been called to account by the Vatican for their views. But a majority of cardinals had thought differently. Cesare had remained enigmatic on the subject, becoming the overall choice among the many Church factions vying for power. Bettini, as Secretary of State, had for a short time become the Camerlengo, or Chamberlain, of the Universal Church, in charge until a new pope was elected, and totally in charge of the Conclave which was to elevate a cardinal to popehood. Although supposedly impartial, he certainly hadn't backed Cesare Romereo, whose victory remained galling to him.

Ambling toward Cesare Romereo, Bettini felt bitter toward this *desnortificacao*, this sudden unprecedented southern emphasis in the Church. It was true that there were more Catholics outside of Europe than inside—over half now lived in Latin America, Asia, and Africa. As much as he worried about the future under Cesare Romereo's reign, he lamented the diminishment of local control over the Vatican.

Bettini shuffled his feet heavily and coughed. Cesare's eyes sprang open; he hurriedly snapped off the cassette.

"Ah, Cardinal Bettini, my pleasure. I was just meditating to some music from home. Change takes a little while to get used to, don't you think?"

"Give yourself time, Santissimo Padre. But that is the very subject I wish to discuss," replied the Cardinal.

"You wish to discuss time?"

"No—change. You mentioned change."

"I was referring to change in my personal life and surroundings," Cesare said, glancing around the Roman horizon. "Quite a change. Are you aware that change is what people fear most in life?"

Bettini ignored the question and came right to the point. "I was referring to changes in Vatican policy, in teaching, changes in official Church position. We've had too many of them in the past twenty-five years. It's never good policy to change papal authority and Catholic tradition. The only true Church of Christ should beware." Bettini only half hoped his words didn't sound like a threat.

"If it works, don't fix it?" asked the Pope.

"Yes. My humble opinion is that we should continue on the path taken by John Paul II and stick to traditional values."

"But if it is not working, we have problems. We do have a few, don't we, Your Eminence?"

"Some people think we do, but they exaggerate."

"I think some of the values have become some of the problems," said the Pope, "problems that we can't ignore. Women in the priesthood, for instance. In Canada, Anglicans have elected a female bishop in the Diocese of Toronto."

"We have Henry VIII to blame for that," Bettini said, smiling as he made himself comfortable on the bench a short distance from Cesare.

"There's divorce, too, of course. And priestly celibacy, abortion, contraception, the activities suitable for nuns, our financial structure and investments. I haven't had time, in the few days I've been in office, to think about all those things and to identify all that should or should not be done about them. Never an easy task at best. To change or not to change, one might say, that is the question. Is it not?"

"We can discuss any of those areas in greater detail if you so desire," said Bettini. "Where would you like to begin?"

"I'm not concerned with specifics at the moment. There is something in the atmosphere today that bothers me. The smoke of Satan is in the Church. I can detect faint but lethal wisps swirling around the altar. The trick is to find the source and dampen it before too many are asphyxiated. I have some fear for the faith." The Pope turned to face the Cardinal, who now sat up with his back straight.

Bettini, thinking quickly, was puzzled. Had someone been talking to Cesare behind his back? "Then we must meet the threat. Specifics form the whole. The whole is the status quo, which must be maintained. That is my opinion, Holy Father."

"Ah. You make yourself very clear, Angostura. Now that you've shed some light on our general concerns, perhaps we should discuss more specific matters. Setting aside Church edicts and history for a moment," the Pope said softly, putting the tips of his fingers together, "what is your opinion of contraception?"

"Contraception is intrinsically and gravely evil by reason of natural law." Bettini watched the Pope's face as he spoke. "God entrusted to us the defense and purity of morals in order to preserve the chastity of marriage from defilement by the foul stain of contraceptive devices. This stain is an offense against both the law of God and nature. If we do not confirm and stand by that attitude, God the Supreme Judge will call us to account for the betrayal of his sacred trusts, and we shall fall into the pit."

The Pope was silent for a long moment before he responded. "The Bible says 'increase and multiply.' However, circumstances have changed. The question now becomes: should we change our teaching to suit the circumstances?" The Pope sighed deeply.

Bettini sensed that the Pope truly didn't know the answer. "Holy Father, contraception is only an anticipated homicide, purposeful intervention is a sin; the institution of marriage must remain open to the transmission of life."

"Are you aware that much of the laity no longer espouses reverence and respect for that teaching? And is it not true that a pope may revoke or change the edicts of his predecessors?"

"Holy Father, everything in the universe is subject to the Pontiff." Bettini became aware that his voice had raised in pitch. "Many popes before you have spoken on the subject. To challenge previous papal authority would destroy credibility. I strongly advise against any change of policy in this matter."

Bettini's view was the same as Opus Dei and the Roman Curia. Both were highly complicated hierarchical bodies; the Holy See's civil service in particular, derived their worldwide influence from the Pontiff. They frowned on anything that detracted from the Pope's stature, power, and glory, because it diminished their own.

Romereo's remarks indicated some doubt about the status quo, which reinforced the Cardinal's previous suspicions about him. He decided not to discuss Nestor LaPretre and Naturcept with Pope Cesare—better he not be given any say in the matter. Bettini would deal with that problem in his own way.

The conversation ended a short while later. The Cardinal went back to his office and began to pace back and forth. He had several problems to contend with, the most worrisome being Hugo and the Priory of Sion. He knew he'd have to meet the mysterious Hugo to find out specifically what the Priory had that was of such value to the Vatican that they thought they could barter with the Roman Catholic Church. Bettini shuddered that someone would have the gall to try to blackmail him.

But suppose Hugo did have something of great value to trade. What could be of such importance? Bettini blasted the Priory of Sion to hell and back several times before coming to the realization that he couldn't afford not to find out just what it was they had to deal with.

Resigned, the Cardinal knelt in prayer. "Glory be to God who has judged me worthy to be his servant, who has trusted my ability to fulfill His will and fight the devil's congregation on earth. . . ."

CHAPTER FIFTEEN

THE TEARS OF CHRIST

HUGO PAYNE WAITED in the lounge of the Ristorante Mastrobologna, north of the Teatro Marcello on via Botteghe Oscure near via Caetani. An antique medieval house over five hundred years old, the restaurant consisted of three sumptuously furnished levels. The lounge on the lower floor served a substantially Roman clientele. The restaurant was up one flight, with a *boîte* on the top floor. The furnishings, *objets d'art*, and paintings were all old and worthy, the food of high calibre with prices to match.

Nursing a Campari on the rocks, Hugo glanced at his watch—eight p.m. No Bettini yet, but there was no reason to expect him to be on time. The Cardinal was reputed to be meticulous, and for that reason alone he would likely be a little late if he came at all. A sort of one-upmanship. As Hugo finished his drink, Bettini came up the steps to the lounge. Alone, as requested, he was in mufti, his hands thrust deep in his coat pockets, with nothing to indicate that he was a clergyman. To Hugo he looked less the ascetic and more the conservative businessman.

Smiling a welcome to the Cardinal, Hugo invited him to sit down. "Shall we have a drink before we discuss our problems?"

"I have no problems." Bettini's face remained sombre. "I suggest that we go right in to dinner."

"As you like," Hugo replied, smiling broadly again.

Bettini turned on his heel to approach the maitre d' at the base of the stairs. A waiter sprang forward to take the Cardinal's coat. As he retreated, Hugo said, "From the manner in which you entered, Angostura, I thought you might be packing a gun in one of those pockets."

Turning abruptly, Bettini faced Hugo. "Please refrain from becoming familiar. We agreed that you and I need carry no weapons and I keep my word. We are here strictly on business, and there is no need to be friendly. In any case, who would want to harm you, Mr. Hugo?"

"No one, I'm sure." Hugo was enjoying himself.

The maitre d' seated them at a small table in a private alcove away from the quiet murmur of corporate Rome at the trough. A waiter appeared, leaving menus and a wine list.

"What wine do you recommend, Cardinal?" asked Hugo, glancing through the list of Chiantis, Bordalinos, Frascatis, Orvietes, and Soaves.

Relaxing in his chair, Bettini replied, "As you ask, there is an interesting wine you may not have tried. May I suggest the *Lacrima Christi del Vesuvio*, the Tears of Christ?"

"That seems an appropriate choice, yes."

"It comes in red or white. I'll see if they have some of the red. It's in short supply and I think the better of the two. You will find it quite heavenly." Bettini rose and left the alcove.

Upon his return the Cardinal said, "I've ordered a *mezzo litro* for you, their most aged and best; I'm having a sparkling Verdicchio. Apparently the *spaghetti al vongola* is excellent today. I may as well enjoy the evening, since you are paying for it. Only fair since I have to listen to whatever scurrilous proposal you have in mind." He seated himself again, stretching his long legs before him.

When the wine came, Hugo picked up his glass to taste it. As he did so he saw Bettini staring at the tattoo between the top and middle knuckle of his little finger.

"An interesting mark, Mr. Hugo," the Cardinal said, nodding at the hand. "Does it have any significance?"

"Not really. Like most tattoos, it was done in a fit of youthful enthusiasm. It is the Cross of Lorraine, and to me it means the Priory of Sion—which is not to say that you will find it on other members."

"I see," said Bettini, reaching for his own wine glass. He took a healthy draught and for a moment his face softened. "We may as well get on with it. What exactly is your proposition?"

Hugo cleared his throat and extracted a flat silver cigarette case from an inside pocket. "You think of me as an enemy. Perhaps, but perhaps it's just the opposite." He held the cigarette case out to Bettini, who shook his head.

Hugo's eyes watched the flame as he lit his cigarette. "Let me put it this way: both the Priory of Sion and the Vatican have been in existence since the time of Christ. Despite the power and corruption that creeps into any organization which manages such longevity, we both still perform a function. If we attempted a meeting of the minds rather than remaining adversaries, we could better perform the pastoral function of bringing solace, comfort, protection, and hope to the world. The Priory is a chivalric order whose code of conduct links humanity with the divine. You and I, the Vatican and the Priory, are opposing sides with the same goals." Noting the look of impatience returning to Bettini's eyes, Hugo continued. "Our philosophy forms the basis of our request of the Vatican. That is, we wish to espouse a method of worldwide birth control, so that overpopulation will not destroy the quality of life on this planet."

"Spare me your noble sentiments, sir. They are not in accordance with our *Jus Canonicum*," snapped Bettini.

"Okay, let's get to the point," Hugo continued. "The Priory of Sion is in possession of the Treasure of the Temple of Jerusalem. We can produce it today along with proof of the lineal descendants of Jesus Christ through his children by Mary Magdalene, all of whom fled with Jesus from ancient Israel to France."

Bettini sat bolt upright. "This is blasphemy!" he said, his voice an octave higher as he slammed his wine glass on the table, shattering it. The red wine flowed across the white tablecloth. Hugo noted the Cardinal's trembling body, his cold eyes. "You dare to suggest that Jesus did not die on the cross!"

A waiter appeared at the commotion and gathered up the pieces of glass.

Hugo stared calmly at his guest. "Correct, Cardinal Bettini. And we have reason to believe that there is supporting evidence in the innermost vaults of the Vatican's archives. Perhaps you should check those secret archives more closely, although it may be that even the Pope himself doesn't have security clearance. The Church will never open those files marked 'Closed Forever.' Why? Because it just might reveal the truth, *Et in Arcadia Ego.*"

Bettini glowered, his fists clenched on the table top.

"But you don't want to look in those files, do you?" said Hugo. "And maybe the information is not there. But whether the world at large chooses to believe the documented information we can produce is something else again, and something you can't predict."

"Such profane abuse of God's word wouldn't be believed by the masses in any event," replied Bettini.

"Possibly, but do you want to chance it? These documents would be placed with the most prestigious scientific minds and subjected to the most stringent methodology of the twentieth century, with its linguistic and carbon-dating expertise."

"And people might just as easily turn on you as charlatans. Hundreds of millions of people are just not interested in changing their beliefs, or believing anything that they weren't taught to believe as children by the missionaries of Jesus."

"But I think we can agree," said Hugo, answering Bettini's scowl with a smile, "that the result of such a disclosure would be unpredictable."

Bettini's face was once again impassive. "I will never give credence to your contentions. But out of curiosity, what do these so-called documents of yours reveal?"

"We can produce the lineal descent of Jesus Christ through the Merovingian Dynasty, together with proof of scriptures and teachings of Jesus, which were purposely dropped from the Bible by Roman Catholic censors, but which have been preserved by the family of Mary Magdalene and Jesus. The Priory of Sion possesses the Holy Grail of antiquity that hangs over the Vatican's head like the Sword of Damocles." Hugo took a large mouthful of the Tears of Christ.

"Am I hearing you correctly? How does the Priory of Sion propose to perpetrate this hoax?" Bettini asked.

"We intend to restore the bloodline of Jesus Christ to its rightful place in the world. Whoever that person is has more of a legal and moral claim to his heritage than those who usurped the papacy and continue to hold the position illegally. This can and will be implemented if necessary."

"You are blackmailing us with the Second Coming of Christ?" the Cardinal spat out.

"That's one way to put it, Cardinal. But if you act rationally, I see no problem."

The Cardinal reached for the napkin in his lap and wiped his brow.

"You and your Priory are bluffing, sir. The Holy See does not submit to blackmail."

"No? Well, they have before, as recently as World War II. And you had better hope you're right, because we can produce a messiah equal to Jesus, with proof of authenticity."

The waiter returned with a new glass and their meals.

"And what kind of a man do you say he was?" Bettini asked.

"Certainly he didn't consider himself divine. He was a messiah in the tradition of the Jews, not the Messiah dreamed up by latter-day Christians. The Treasure of Jerusalem consists of incontrovertible proof that the crucifixion was fixed, that Jesus was alive as late as A.D. 45, and that he sired children before and after the event."

"You don't say!" Bettini remarked with raised eyebrow. He took a long draught of Verdicchio.

"I do say. Just what had Jesus done to provoke the Romans to the extent that they would want to crucify him? Nothing. And if the Jews had wanted to kill him, they had the authority to stone him to death. When the Romans crucified somebody, they stayed crucified. Their methods were infallible." Hugo, thoroughly enjoying himself, watched Bettini's face. "First, the culprit was flogged—oh, he'd lose a lot of blood there." He nodded to the wine stain on the tablecloth. "Then he'd be tied by thongs to a wooden beam laid horizontally across his back. He'd be led to the place of execution, strung up, and nailed to a vertical beam. He'd hang from his hands, see. . . ." The Cardinal sat staring at the scraps of food on his plate. "He couldn't breathe unless his feet were nailed to the cross. Then he could press down to take the pressure off his chest. A healthy man with feet fixed could take a week to die, either from exhaustion, dehydration, or blood poisoning. Take your pick."

Bettini's agate eyes sprang open and met Hugo's, never wavering. "You are an evil man, Mr. Hugo," he whispered.

"Touché," replied Hugo, sighing. "However, to continue: if they broke the victim's legs so that he had no support, it was an act of mercy—a *coup de grâce* bringing sudden death by asphyxiation. The Romans were going to break Christ's legs, if you will recall, but were asked not to do so. Why? According to the Fourth Gospel, Jesus' feet were fixed to the cross, thus relieving pressure on his chest, and his legs were not broken. He was in good health, but he only lasted three and a half hours. Again, why? Strange indeed. Pilate was astonished to hear of his death. But was he really surprised? Did Jesus really die? The spear wound in his side is recorded as being inflicted after his death. Jesus died before they could break his legs, thus fulfilling an Old Testament prophecy. Very convenient, worthy of a Machiavelli, a careful plan engineered to fulfill a political prophecy, wouldn't you say?" The Cardinal was about to reply, but Hugo cut him off.

"Christ says he is thirsty, so they give him a sponge soaked in vinegar. Vinegar, like smelling salts, is used to restore someone to consciousness, yet he takes a whiff and passes out. Why? Did the sponge contain not vinegar, say, but opium or belladonna? To have him simulate death, get him down off the cross, that was the strategy. According to Matthew 27:60 and John 19:41, there was a tomb nearby in a garden owned by Joseph of Arimathea, a secret disciple of Jesus. According to Matthew, Mark, and Luke, the crucifixion is only witnessed 'from afar off'; it is mentioned specifically in Luke 23:49." Hugo drank more wine while intently watching the Cardinal's face, waiting for an expression of indignation. But Bettini was slumped in his chair, his plate pushed back and hands folded in prayer-like formation against the edge of the table.

"Who could see from afar what really happened? It was a privately catered affair performed on private property in the Garden of Gethsemane. In short, it was a mock crucifixion, a hoax."

Bettini had suffered through the lengthy recital in silence. He finally spoke. "You amaze me with this charade. What you are stating could only have been accomplished with the collusion of the Romans."

Hugo wished he'd brought some small piece of evidence with which to antagonize the Cardinal even further. "Exactly! Now you are grasping the facts. Was Pontius Pilate corrupt, susceptible to bribes? Would he exchange Jesus' life for big money and a guarantee of no further political agitation? You can bet your holy ass he would! So he grants the body of Christ to Joseph. A crucified man was not entitled to burial by Roman law; the body was left on the cross to be picked clean by the vultures. Joseph asked for a 'living body,' by the correct translation of his very words, and Pilate, pretending to think Jesus is dead, gives him the body.

"Why did Joseph have such influence? He was a wealthy member of the Jewish Sanhedrin, of royal blood, and reasonably friendly with Pontius Pilate. He was also the brother-in-law of Jesus. He would therefore have no trouble staging an execution on his own grounds, in which a substitute took Jesus' place on the cross. Which explains why Jesus' wounds healed quickly—he never had any. Or Christ might have been on the cross but did not actually die. Toward evening they hustled him into an adjacent tomb, where a couple of Essenes were waiting to treat him, probably with vinegar this time. Then he disappeared. He's gone. Where? Historians have proposed that he went to the Kashmir in India; that he died in Masada when that Fortress fell to the Romans in A.D. 74; that he was in Alexandria, Egypt, where he founded the Rose-Croix."

Hugo paused for another drink, then took a deep, cleansing breath. "Is it true that your Pope John XXIII was an adherent of the Rosicrucians?" he asked.

"*De mortuis nil nisi bonum!* You tend to mythomania, Mr. Hugo," said Bettini caustically. "*Cui bono?*"

"All right, I won't speak of the dead. Let's speak of your own Opus Dei, Cardinal. How many members do you have worldwide? One hundred thousand? Was Pope John Paul II one of yours? Your own records state Opus has members in over six hundred newspapers, reviews, and scientific publications around the world. Opus Dei could indeed be very influential in selling population control to the masses."

"Give me strength, *pro Deo et ecclesia!*" Bettini intoned and crossed himself before pouring another glass of wine for them both.

With deliberate movements, Hugo again reached for his cigarette case and slowly went through the ritual of lighting up. "Ah, the flames of hell, eh, Cardinal? We know you know about the Priory of Sion, but we don't know just how *much* you know." Hugo deliberately exhaled smoke toward Bettini, who did not react. When it became obvious that the Cardinal was not going to speak, Hugo went on.

"The holy family—wife, children, brother-in-law Joseph of Arimathea, and Jesus—were smuggled out of the Holy Land to Marseilles. There was plenty of traffic between those two points in ancient times. Mary Magdalene did indeed bring the Holy Grail, the royal blood of the House of David, into France; we have the records to prove it."

"Your story does not concur with our long-established religious teachings," said Bettini, now very calm.

"What I have told you in no way detracts from the idealistic message of Jesus, in offering hope to the poor, afflicted, and oppressed of his day or the present. When Jesus failed to ascend the Jewish throne and remove the Roman yoke from their necks, his family placed priority on the preservation of the bloodline and went into exile. We maintain that bloodline today."

"And we still have the Church!" replied Bettini emphatically.

"Indeed. It's a big power base you don't want to lose. In his day Jesus was the spiritual leader, the high priest, the religious oracle, as well as the king of a body politic whose principles and culture were primarily of a religious nature. Every Jewish King of Israel and the Old Testament House of David was anointed as such, the Priest Messiah or Christ. There was nothing divine about messiahs in those days. To assert that you were literally the son of God was an extreme blasphemy, and utterly unthinkable for Jesus. He was much like your Pope of today, or the Ayatollah to the Muslims in Iran, where religion and the state are one."

The conversation ceased for several moments, while Hugo smoked and the Cardinal seemed lost in thought. Finally Bettini said coldly, "Mr. Hugo, I did not come here to discuss your dubious theology. I am not at all impressed."

"Fine. Just ask yourself this—what would the implications be for the Vatican, if the records from the Temple of Jerusalem were released, proving that Jesus was only a messiah, a man thought of by Palestinians to be their rightful king, and whose throne had been usurped by you Romans. This messiah was married, had children, and did not die on the cross at all. We can establish without a doubt that the Merovingian dynasty of France, where Jesus and Mary and their family migrated after the staged crucifixion, still exists today. We can produce someone who, by strict scriptural definition, is a biblical Messiah, who has a more legitimate claim to the papacy than your present Pope from South America, or any of the previous incumbents now passed on to the Old Popes' Home."

"I tell you again, it's preposterous!" The Cardinal's eyes had come back to life.

Hugo butted his cigarette and sat back, resting his elbows on the curved arms of the ornate chair. "The Church wouldn't welcome a new challenge. And," Hugo paused, "there are precedents. You've made deals before in order to stay in control, many throughout history, so why pretend otherwise? In fact you are famous for making deals, especially if they are to your advantage."

Bettini appeared to have found his smile again. He leaned forward in his chair. "Could you enlighten me with a recent illustration?"

"All right. Erich Priebke, a former German Nazi SS captain who was wanted in connection with the worst war crime committed in Italy in World War II—the killing of three hundred thirty-five Italians at the Ardeatine Caves outside Rome in March of 1944—revealed that he took part in the massacre, but was helped out of Italy to the Argentine by the Vatican. That came to light fifty years later. How much did the Vatican get for that?"

"Are you going to take the word of a Nazi war criminal instead of ours? Surely you can come up with something better."

"The history of the Merovingian ruler Clovis I, the most powerful potentate in Western Europe back in 496 A.D., was recorded—all particulars and details—in an account entitled *The Life of St. Remy*. Then, strangely enough, this record was deliberately destroyed by the Roman Catholic Church two and a half centuries later, and only a few scattered manuscript pages are known to remain . . . of which we have copies. Your Church made a deal with Clovis to impose Roman Catholic doctrine on all of Europe by means of his secular and military might. In the Church's greatest hour of need he converted to your creed. He kicked ass on all other forms of Christianity, including the fearsome Visigoths who adhered to Aryan Christianity. One of your priests, who of course is now a saint, got to Clovis' wife. She nagged Clovis into converting to Roman Catholicism. Does this sound familiar? Clovis became the first Catholic King of the Franks.

"Part of the trade was that he got to be secular King of the Holy Roman Empire, the successor to the Caesars, ruling all peoples and other kings. The Church and the State pledged allegiance to one another in perpetuity. A great triumph for the Roman Church, and the one thing that established your Church as the supreme spiritual authority in the west. The Church made the deal with the bloodline of Christ, just as God is said to have made one with King David."

The Cardinal sat back in his chair with one arm outstretched, tapping his long fingers on the table.

"One hundred and seventy-five years later, Dagobert II was King of the Franks, a direct descendant of Clovis. Your Church participated in the assassination of Dagobert II. It is well-documented, Cardinal; I am sure you are familiar with it. Don't tell me you never make deals."

"You only relate one side of that Dagobert story."

"So you do recall the ancient saga, then."

"Well enough to know that King Dagobert and the Franks became considerably less fervent than they might have been as adherents of the one true Christian faith. Dagobert was a blackmailer in our books, only nominally loyal to the Roman Church and the Papal States. If your theory is correct then he would have leaned toward Aryan Christianity, a potential abrogation of the ecclesiastical end of the deal we made with his ancestor Clovis I."

"In any event, it is a matter of historical fact that you had an agent in Dagobert's palace—the mayor, Pepin 'the Fat' d' Heristal, who ran the place. He was apparently not one to shrink from treachery when the situation and his paymaster called for it. According to records King Dagobert went hunting on December twenty-third, in A.D. 679, and when he took a noonday nap under a tree, a servant, on Fat Pepin's orders, ran a lance through his eye and out the back of his head."

"Why are we talking about sixth-century assassinations?" asked Bettini.

"Because we are talking about the bloodline of Christ. Your Church was so interested in it back then that they tried to eliminate Christ's descendants entirely. They returned to Dagobert's castle and tried to exterminate the rest of his family. Luckily they didn't entirely succeed."

"The Vatican wasn't responsible."

"Come off it. They were the paymasters, the co-conspirators. The Roman Catholic Church aided and abetted regicide, helped murder the descendants of Christ!"

"Another ridiculous contention and reconstruction of fact, Mr. Hugo. The Church later canonized Dagobert II as Saint Dagobert."

"But why did they wait two centuries after his death to do it? It was a belated attempt to make amends and to clear your ecclesiastic conscience, to make the record look good. And don't forget that the Pope of the time, by Apostolic Authority, endorsed a Pepin to be named King of the Frankish Empire."

"Again, Mr. Hugo, what is your interest in these matters? Why have you asked me here?"

"Because, as I've said, the Priory of Sion is in possession of records of the bloodline of Jesus Christ. The Vatican must take us seriously. We have incontestable evidence of the many deals beneficial to your Church that have been made in the past. We would like you to promote and market worldwide the natural birth control referred to as Naturcept. Without the endorsement of the Vatican, our mission would be very difficult indeed. And without your endorsement our public relations department would be quite zealous in their campaign to discredit the Church. Now do I make myself clear?"

Cardinal Bettini leaned across the table, piercing Hugo Payne with his stare. "Yes, Mr. Hugo. Now you certainly do. Let me see if I understand correctly," said the Cardinal, his mind carefully sorting out the pieces. "You want the Vatican to revise all edicts and encyclicals as they pertain to the use of contraceptive birth control or you will blackmail us into so doing, with certain potentially damaging and incontrovertible information which you allege to hold in regard to Jesus Christ Our Saviour, and the Pope's present position? Is that about it?" He assayed what he considered a friendly smile.

Smiling or not, Hugo knew Bettini could not be trusted. However, he believed that the Vatican would at least consider the proposal, because there was a big faction in the North American and European Church who had already agreed with what the Priory was trying to do. And he knew from Bettini's reputation that he'd had no choice but to play hardball with the Cardinal.

Hugo nodded and said, "So, then, Cardinal, how long is it going to take you to decide? And how soon can a change of policy be implemented?" It was Hugo's turn to be pleasant.

The Cardinal bowed his head and rubbed the bridge of his nose. "As you can appreciate, this is a delicate matter and will have to be handled carefully. If we agree, and it is not likely, it would take several months, perhaps even a year or two to prepare for such a policy change."

"Will you want to review the evidence on Naturcept before a decision is made?"

"We will get back to you about that sooner than you think, Mr. Hugo. Have no fear." Bettini stood.

"I shall be in the San Giorgio Hotel for one week," said Hugo, still seated. "I request some sort of a reply during that time. If none is forthcoming I shall have to assume, and report to the Priory, that the Vatican does not wish to co-operate in any way."

Bettini reached across the table to shake Hugo's hand. "Thank you for the enlightening conversation. As you well know, we might respond to a request, but not to blackmail."

"Of course not, Your Eminence. Heaven forbid. I appreciate the time you have taken and certainly hope that any future relations between us will be of a friendly nature."

As the Cardinal walked away, he turned back to say, "I can recommend the *torta deliziosa* if you like bitter chocolate. And you might like to try their espresso Galiano; it is excellent."

CHAPTER SIXTEEN

DOWN BY THE RIVERSIDE

A BLACK LIMOUSINE WITH TINTED windows waited for the Cardinal at the curb. Upon his entry, the car drove slowly down the street, stopping where it met the Via Arenula. A few moments later the rear door opened and two men stepped out. The limo then drove toward Vittorio Emmanuele, heading for the Opus Dei headquarters on Viale Bruno Buozzi.

One of the men turned right and walked down Arenula toward the river, the other remained lounging on a bench at the corner of the Via Botteghe Oscure.

Meanwhile Hugo decided that there was little he could do but wait, and therefore enjoy what the Italians called *dolce far niente*, the sweetness of doing nothing. For starters he finished the carafe of red wine from Naples. The waiter asked if there were anything else the American gentleman might care to order, and on a whim Hugo said, "Yes, I'll have a dessert, but I don't want chocolate. A small sorbet, *per favore.* And also an espresso Galiano."

The waiter soon returned with the sorbet and espresso, remarking, "Tomorrow is Sunday, so try to live with gusto tonight." Hugo nodded his agreement and asked for the bill.

"*Subito!*" the waiter replied and hurried away.

But in Rome that could be slower than the second coming, and was. Hugo paid, descended the stairs, and walked out into the ink-black night. Somehow the fresh air didn't seem as invigorating as he had thought it would be. He strolled slowly down Botteghe and turned into Arenula. He was headed across the Tiber on the Garibaldi bridge, just above the Isola Tiberina, toward the crowded, chaotic, but mellow Transvestere quarter—an area of twisting gnarled streets which were very narrow, having been made for chariots. In some parts living accommodations were a hopeless jumble, but this suited his purpose, for if anyone was following him he could suddenly duck into a narrow alley or a certain doorway and resurface two blocks away.

His life was far from gratifying, but it was good enough for Hugo to want to take more than basic precautions. He saw no evidence of a tail as he walked through an area of the Arenula with cafés, fruit stands, flower and book stalls. All of a sudden he experienced a sort of vertigo. Doltish and giddy, he was aware that his pace had slowed; he had trouble placing one foot in front of the other. As he approached the Ponte Garibaldi, the bridge across the Tiber into Transvestere wavered under the dim lights. Perhaps the Tears of Christ had been too sweet for his stomach, or had the Caffe Galiano been off? The realization that Cardinal Bettini had suggested them both dawned on him.

He was part way across the bridge when he decided he'd better go to the balustrade and try to vomit.

Two men suddenly appeared at his side.

"Can we help you, señor?"

"Are you having difficulty?" asked the other.

"No. I'll be all right, thank you," Hugo replied, leaning against the railing. He turned to look at one of the men. He believed that people's eyes mirrored their intentions—but the light on the bridge was as bad as Hugo felt. The man behind him suddenly, quietly and quickly, pistol-whipped him across the back of the head.

They were already waiting, he thought, as the blow spun him around, slammed him against a cement pillar, and left him slumping half on the sidewalk and half against the bridge railing.

The men stood over him, talking as if he were a drunken companion. A switch knife sprang into the hand of one of his assailants, who bent over Hugo's prostrate form as the blade flickered open.

"Hold his hand," he whispered tersely to his companion, then calmly proceeded to insert the blade into a knuckle joint, severing Hugo's little finger. A spurt of blood hit the pavement.

The excruciating pain snapped Hugo's brain back into consciousness. It screamed, Do something now, or you'll sleep forever on this bloody bridge. He heard one of the men say, "Better take a look and see if we got the right finger."

"You mean the left. Turn it to the light and let's see the tattoo. I can always cut off the other one before I stick him."

While they took a look at his severed finger, Hugo sprang to his feet with every bit of energy adrenaline could pump into his body, salvaging the couple of seconds he needed before they did him in. He was vaguely aware of running along the bridge, the river flowing somewhere below. He knew he'd never outrun his assailants. The sons of bitches drugged me, his befuddled senses told him, and I tipped them extra to do it.

With time running out, Hugo moved to dive over the railing when the man with the pistol shot him in the back. He went over the balustrade on the upstream side of the Ponte Garibaldi like a rag doll. Full of raw pain, in slow motion a thought formulated in his brain. He had no idea where he had been on the bridge when he went over the edge. He didn't know whether he would strike water, land, cement, or a building.

Hugo hit the water at a bad angle, nearly feet first. He momentarily felt immense relief. He sank a long way, but fought furiously back to the surface, where he had no trouble spewing the contents of his guts. His body struck a piling under the bridge, to which he clung with his good hand. Knowing he had to move before he bled to death or drowned, Hugo struggled to keep his head above water, to suck in as much oxygen as he could.

There was no moon, but the lights of the street running alongside the Tiber shone on the water. Downstream was the only island in the Tiber, which Hugo had observed many times. All he could see was a silhouette of the skyline, but he thought he could make out the single arch of the Ponte Rotto, now called the broken bridge, all that remained of the original Tiber bridge. He knew the killers would be watching for him along the banks, probably from the Garibaldi Bridge.

Taking note of his injuries, he grasped his left wrist with his right hand and squeezed hard, hoping to stop the flow of blood from his missing finger. He didn't know how bad the gunshot wound was, nor how much blood he was losing. His back and chest hurt like hell. His head ached and one leg had been wrenched when he hit the water. Hugo heard shouting from above, took several deep breaths, pushed outward treading water as best he could, then let himself sink underwater into the current. Trusting himself to the Tiber, thoughts of Romulus wafted through his brain.

When he could hold his breath no longer he exhaled as slowly as possible while kicking his way toward the surface. He gulped air quickly then submerged again.

After several breaths Hugo struck a small out-cropping of jagged rocks at the prow of the island. Shoving off from the projections, he floated down the river's right-hand channel. He was tiring fast; he could no longer find the strength to continue. He felt his conscious mind turning grey, fading into black.

The current carried Hugo's body up against a quay which projected from the side of Isola Tiberina, perhaps the same spot where the snake had landed two thousand years before. He had just enough moxy left to crawl half-way out of the water onto the first of what looked like steps in a high masonry wall, before succumbing to unconsciousness.

Isola Tiberina, a man-made island, was built at the river ford by the Tarquins in the early days of Rome. Over time, it built up and metamorphosed into the genuine article, which, with the aid of high cement revetments, now had the appearance of a large ocean liner. Whether it had a beach depended on the height at which the Tiber happened to be flowing. When the river was low a person could walk around the island, with occasional steps leading down to the river's edge. Due to the recent rains, the river had more depth and a faster flow than its usual sluggish pace.

Aesculapius, the Greek god of medicine, had a mascot, a pet snake, which, in pictures, can be observed curling around his staff. As Aesculapius came up the River Tiber from Ostia, his pet snake rushed ahead, crawled onto the island, and nestled on a rock near the island's top end. As a consequence, the snake's master decided to erect a hospital on the island, which has maintained an unbroken record of service to Rome ever since.

Friar Ambrose closed and locked the doors of the small Church of St. John the Calybite. He had been working late and decided to take some evening air before returning to his quarters at St. Bartolomeo on the south-eastern end of Isola Tiberina. The island is sometimes called Isola Tiberina di San Bartolomeo because of the hospital complex which occupies that part of the island along with the imposing church of the Apostle Bartholomew. The friar belonged to the Brothers of St. John of God, which the Roman population referred to in friendly terms as *fatebene fratelli*, or do-good brothers. They treated the sick, the poor, and the aged from the Roman ghettos, and conducted a medical school for aspiring physicians.

Friar Ambrose contemplated visiting the fruit peddler at her stand on the Ponte Fabrico leading to the east side of the Tiber. He decided against it, being needful only of a walk before a good night's sleep. He moved along the promenade on the west bank near the Ponte Rotto, a good spot to watch the rapids below. He was about to continue when he saw something move at the water's edge at the bottom of the steps leading down to the water. Brother Ambrose went to investigate, and the dice of fate rolled seven for Hugo Payne.

CHAPTER SEVENTEEN

ST. AMBROSE GOES MARCHING IN

HUGO'S EYES WERE STILL CLOSED but he was conscious. Every bone ached, and his head felt like a fur-bearing doorknob. Images of recent events began to float in front of him. He opened his eyes, not knowing what to expect. To his surprise, he was alive and alone in a bed in a clean white room, the sun streaming through a large window. Looking and feeling himself over as best he could, he found that there were bandages around his head and chest, the latter heavily padded on the left side. His left hand looked like a white catcher's mitt with three fingers protruding at the far end. The little finger throbbed terribly, but then he remembered that he no longer had one.

Bettini! The son of a bitch was not going to get away with this, thought Hugo. He now realized that the Cardinal was more dangerous than he had given him credit for—on his way to polarizing the Church with his tactics. The Catholic Church had enough problems without creating a split in its ranks. Something had to be done about him.

He heard noises. Somebody was approaching from down the hall. The door opened and a white-clad figure, a young doctor, Hugo presumed, entered with a nurse in tow. Hugo cocked an eye toward them and tried to smile.

"You've had a close call, señor," was the medic's first remark. "You were lucky that the Friar found you when he did."

He was going to have to rely on his weak Italian. "I'm glad someone did," Hugo replied in a low voice. Speaking any language hurt his chest. "I don't remember what happened. I don't remember being found."

"Nothing?"

"Not much."

"Obviously you were attacked by someone—you can't shoot yourself in the back like that. And what happened to your finger and head?"

Hugo quickly pondered what to tell the man. As little as possible was best; until he had time to assess the situation, nothing was to be gained by telling anyone anything at all.

"Where was I found?"

"At the bottom of the stone steps near the Ponte Rotto."

"And where am I now?"

"In the Hospital of the Brothers of St. John of God on the Isola Tiberna."

"And you are? . . ."

"An intern here at the hospital. My name is Guiseppe."

"Could I have a report on my condition?"

"Certainly. You are missing the little finger of your left hand, but it has been operated on and stitched; you have a wound through the musculature of your left side, which was deep but missed anything vital, very fortunately for you. It seems to have been a small bore bullet which passed right through, nicking a couple of ribs. That's been patched up nicely and should heal reasonably quickly. You lost a lot of blood but you were given a transfusion. Oh yes, you have a concussion from a blow on the head. Other than that I'd say you were in good health."

Unsure if he understood the last comment, Hugo smiled anyway. "Thank you for fixing me up."

"That's what we're here for. So what happened?"

Hugo didn't know himself exactly what had happened. He wished they would leave him alone to think. "I must have been robbed," was the first and most obvious thing that came to mind.

"You still had a wallet with a good deal of cash in it, but we could find no identification. I won't question you further, though I must report this." This time the intern spoke slowly enough for Hugo to understand clearly.

"Since I can't remember, what is there to report?"

"Just who you are, where you were found, your precise injuries. But maybe you will remember later; concussion often causes short-term memory loss. Too bad these things happen in Rome. They must have thrown you into the Tiber somewhere, thinking you dead. You would have been if Friar Ambrose hadn't found you."

Hugo was exhausted; he only wanted to sleep. "Who?"

"Friar Ambrose, a priest at the local church . . . out for a walk."

"I'd like to thank him," said Hugo weakly. "Is there a way for me to talk to him?"

"He will be in to see you before very long. His Order ministers to the sick here. You can thank God you were mugged near a hospital."

"Yeah, what a break!" Hugo moaned, then whispered, "Do you mind?" turning his head slightly towards the door.

"Certainly, but just one more question. You seem to have been hurt quite a while ago, señor. I noticed old surgery scars."

Hugo thought that was an interesting way to put it—old surgery scars.

"I thought, well. . . ." The intern paused. "I wouldn't have mentioned it at all, except for something I read about recently." Hugo had shut his eyes.

"Really don't like to talk about it."

"I keep up on recent medical discoveries, read a lot of international periodicals."

"So?" Hugo whispered.

"So I'll bring around the article I read. You may find it helpful. Now you just rest. The attendants here will see to your needs."

"Thank you, Doctor. And when I wake up again I'd like to see this friar, the man who saved my life. Can this be arranged?"

"Certainly."

The intern and nurse left. Hugo fell asleep trying to make sense of what had happened and what his next step should be.

The next morning Hugo had already been served breakfast and was sitting up in bed, although not without some discomfort, when there was a knock on the door. It opened slowly, revealing the quintessential monk—fringe of hair, bald pate, roly-poly physique, and a broad smile with a tooth missing. If monks had a charity he'd be the poster boy, Hugo thought, pleased that at least he'd retained his sense of humour.

Friar Ambrose approached and extended his hand, which Hugo shook as vigorously as his injuries would permit.

"I've been wanting to talk to you and thank you, Friar," Hugo said to the monk, who continued to hold his hand.

"Don't mention it, my son. It was God's will that I took that route on my evening stroll." His pink face wrinkled in pleasure. "Call me Ambrose. You have been very fortunate. Everything, I am told, will heal satisfactorily. You will be well soon."

"But not if they discover I'm still alive." Hugo whispered.

Friar Ambrose furrowed his brow momentarily, but then smiled again. "I am here to garner information so that I may make a report through the proper channels and to the proper authorities. It is one of my duties for this hospital."

"But you should be aware of one thing, Friar."

"And what is that?"

"You saved my life, and you are now, according to my philosophy, responsible for me."

"There are many philosophies in this world of ours. I have heard of that belief. It is probably another myth, but I have learned not to differentiate in my ministrations to the sick and needy. Doing so today causes a great deal of trouble."

His demeanor, his soft voice, indicated to Hugo that this was a man who could be trusted. In any case, Hugo had few options.

"Time is extremely important, Friar Ambrose. Having saved me from certain death once, I will only release you from your moral responsibility for my continued welfare if you agree to do it again." Hugo watched the Friar's face intently.

"Do it again? I don't understand. I don't know who you are. You were thrown in my path by whatever fates run with the Tiber. But, by the grace of God, I do not understand." He appeared genuinely perplexed.

"My life is still in danger," Hugo revealed. "Certain people, if they knew I was still alive, would come here to the hospital and kill me without compunction. I'm asking you—pleading with you—to keep my presence here to yourself, strictly between you and me, at least for a few days." He felt sweat soaking into the bedsheets.

"That would be difficult."

"But it could be done? If they know I am in this hospital they will come here to finish the job, I can assure you."

"We wouldn't want that."

"Nor would I! Our paths will likely only cross this once. But I am asking for a favour. See to it that there is no report of this incident, no story in the newspapers. You don't have any names or details yet, so you never saw nor heard of me. Give me a day or two to recuperate and let me disappear into the night. Forget I was ever here. . . ."

Friar Ambrose interrupted. "You ask a lot. . . . There are others involved, and this is a very ethical institution."

"I will make you an offer in all sincerity, Ambrose, and with gratitude. I very much need you to believe me. I am in a position to see to it that a substantial donation is made to this hospital or to whichever church you name. Would you accept such an offer?"

"As I was saying, we are an ethical institution and have to consider whether that would sully our religious scruples. Whether my conscience would allow. . . ."

It was Hugo's turn to interrupt. "This gift would come from an organization that is attempting to do some good in this troubled world, just as you do here. I am a member of a wealthy and high-minded group, and I can assure you that an anonymous donation will arrive in due course, whatever your decision is."

"Well . . . you talked of a philosophy of life, but you never mentioned religion. . . ." The Friar paused, seeming to consider the proposition.

"I am of Christian persuasion, Friar Ambrose," Hugo continued. "I am on your side and so is my organization. I'm on a mission and I can't complete it if I am dead." Hugo was trying to be honest without giving away too much. He felt he could trust Ambrose, but from past experience he knew it was better to err on the side of caution.

"Why didn't you say you were Catholic, my son?" This fact seemed to determine the friar's decision. "I'm sure something can be arranged. I'll have to ask the intern when it might be medically safe for you to leave."

"Thank the Lord, Friar," said Hugo, "that I don't often have the chance to thank one man for saving my life twice. Now would you like to accompany me on a little walk?"

"But you are seriously injured. I don't recommend it."

"I have to see how I make out. Come on, Friar. You can catch me if I fall," Hugo chuckled.

The Friar laughed before saying, "All right. I can show you a little of the facility." He helped Hugo out of bed. Once he was mobile, heavily favouring his left side and in some pain, they went for a slow stroll through the halls of the hospital.

St. Bartholomew's cared primarily for patients long past the prime of their lives. About twenty elders sat around various tables and settees or in wheelchairs; some stared into space half comatose, others were a little more alert. These latter followed Hugo and Ambrose with their eyes, but said nothing. Hugo noticed a woman who alternately tapped the table with her fingernails then clapped her hands with closed eyes, as if to some inner music, her open mouth uttering unintelligible sounds. The other women at her table occasionally looked in her direction but generally ignored her, showing no reaction to what would ordinarily be very irritating.

One old man looked as though his nose and jaw had fallen into his mouth, forming a round black hole that threatened to suck in the whole room, the hospital, the whole world. A birdlike woman looked Hugo over and said with some belligerence, "Might as well have stayed in bed. We get up and here we sit. Let's go home, I'm sick of sitting." At least it was a sign of life. A young priest moved quietly around the room throwing a sponge rubber ball at anyone capable of catching it and throwing it back.

Another old man sat stiffly upright as if he were in the military, his eyes shut, saying and doing nothing. The woman next to him said, "Why don't you mind your own business, you empty-minded old fool. You haven't got the guts to make a pass at me, have you?" No pleasing her, thought Hugo, glad her attention wasn't aimed at him.

Ambrose suggested a rest, so they sat at a table with several old women. Hugo observed one in the act of secreting paper napkins up her sleeves. She saw him watching her and said, "In case you get to go for a picnic in the woods or go for a drive and get caught short . . . you should have something to wipe your ass!" Hugo could tell from her appearance that she would never have said or done something like that in her younger, saner days.

Suddenly, for a moment, Hugo saw his grandmother Theresa sitting in a chair, staring at him with soft eyes. He shook his head and she was gone.

What bothered him most was the distressed voice he could hear down the hall—an old woman, alternately crying and repeating a phrase again and again. Her Italian dialect was hard to decipher, perhaps because of her age and distraught condition. He asked Ambrose what she was saying; it was, "Please, please come back. Come back, I want you to come back. For God's sake, come back to me."

"I can't stand this," said Hugo. "Let's get out of here." Walking down the hall, they came to the door of the room from which came the plaintive cries. Hugo fought the urge, but was compelled by something stronger than himself to enter the room. An old lady sat propped in bed. Hugo could discern great charm and beauty in the face now ravaged by age and grief as she uttered her continual plea. He turned away quickly, and as he did so, he noticed the name on her door: Camille Navona.

As they continued down the hall he asked the Friar, "Do you know why she says that? It's very unnerving."

The Friar placed his arm gently around Hugo's shoulders. "People at this age often return to a part of their childhood or youth, to a time and place, or to something which has strongly affected their lives."

"And this woman? What happened to her?"

"She had a lover long ago. He was killed at the front in World War I. She was married later, but it was not a happy union. Her children predeceased her. She has been grieving all her life, but only recently does she feel free to express herself. At her age she is like wine—*in vino veritas*—in old age there remains only the truth of what she feels ruined her life. Everything else fades; that is all she can think of. Very sad."

"Too damned sad. How do you stand it? All of this . . ." he waved his right arm in an arc ". . . this sadness is a good argument for euthanasia."

Friar Ambrose removed his arm from Hugo's shoulders. "No, no, my friend, you mustn't think that way. All life is sacred. Euthanasia is a very serious offense to the divine commandments."

Hugo deferred to the Friar. After all, Ambrose was his host and the man had saved his life.

When Ambrose had gone, Hugo noticed an envelope on his table. On the flap, penciled in Italian, was written: "The article I mentioned you might find interesting, Guiseppe." Hugo opened the flap and began to read the contents as he lay in bed. The heading immediately caught his attention.

NEW SEX ORGAN MADE WITH ARM SKIN

> In a new surgical procedure, doctors at the University of Chicago Medical Centre are using skin from the forearm to fashion a new penis to replace an organ lost to accident or disease. They say the

> new organs are more sensitive and function better than previously reconstructed penises.
>
> One of the doctors, Laurence Levine, a urologist, said at least one thousand people in North America might require such reconstruction annually, because their organs are destroyed by cancer, injury or birth defects.
>
> The technique, employed by Dr. Levine and his colleagues, Drs. Lawrence Gottlieb and Lawrence Zachary, plastic surgeons, involves a flap of skin and fascia, the fibrous tissue under the skin's surface that encloses muscles, taken from the underside of the arm.
>
> This flap is used to create a new organ with two tubes, one a urethra and the other for later insertion of a prosthetic device to aid sexual function. Blood vessels and nerve endings are connected using surgical techniques.
>
> Dr. Levine said the team has performed six of these operations in the past eighteen months with "a high degree of success."

"*Merde!*" said Hugo out loud. "Now they tell me." Why couldn't this threesome have come up with that ten or fifteen years ago? Science was increasing its discoveries exponentially. Maybe there was still a chance for him.

CHAPTER EIGHTEEN

THE SMOKE OF SATAN

FINN BENT OVER THE large-scale map of Rome. "I swear to God and three other Irishmen," he said, "there are just too many blasted main roads, Mitch. Where do we do it? Not on the Via Ostiense going up to this Pyramid, or the Via di St. Greggorio past the Coliseum. Certainly not on the main drag, the Via del Corso." He stared intently at the map.

"Slow down, Finn," Mitch replied. "Their regular vehicles have been tailed from the airport and the route is always the same. Follow me on the map. The driver, before he gets to the Coliseum, turns off Viale Aventino, past the Circus Maximus, and along the Via del Cerchi. Then he cuts up San Teadro, turns left into this small street called de Fienili, goes a few hundred yards and cuts right onto Via Foraggi, which runs slightly downhill right to the wall of the Roman Forum. Then they go left on to Consolazione to get back onto the Via del Fiord Imperiali and through the Piazza Venezia."

"So?" asked Finn.

"So, the Via Foraggi, which is very narrow, has a bend at the wide spot in the middle, so you can't see the length of the street from either end. It's quiet, and they sometimes stop at a little wine shop near the bottom end."

"Traffic?"

"Very little until they get back on to Via Consolazione."

"Unusual for Rome. Yeah, we need a street like Foraggi. Let's check it out personally, boyo."

"They won't use more than one car, and they won't be expecting anything, so we don't have to be fancy. Come on, let's take a look."

The cab took Nestor and Charlotte through the city in the early morning hours to catch a connecting flight from Toronto to Amsterdam. From there they would go on to Rome. Nestor tried to be pleasant, but his mind was still half-asleep as he watched the street lights, the stone walls, and the still trees of Ottawa slide past the cab windows.

Charlotte was wide awake; the trip promised the excitement of an adventure hitherto unexperienced. The Opus Dei agent in Montreal had provided cash and instructions; all she had to do was accompany Mr. LaPretre until they arrived in Rome, where they were to be met by official Vatican representatives. She would get to see Rome and maybe some other parts of Italy as well; something she had always wanted to do. She particularly looked forward to seeing the Vatican, until now just a phantasm in her mind. Perhaps, if all went well, she'd have an opportunity to speak with the Pope again. He had once attended a symposium she'd chaired in Sao Paulo, and had been one of the few who'd posed difficult questions.

They had talked about why she was doing this, Nestor wanting to know her role. She told him she belonged to a Catholic Order which performed administrative services for the Church; that she had enrolled in the Order through a Monsignor in Montreal who had taken a fatherly interest in her. Her more recent focus, she told Nestor, was genealogy; she was hoping to take a side trip to Paris to look up records of her mother's family lineage.

Charlotte asked Nestor to explain what it was that warranted the Vatican's interest in him. Nestor replied in layman's terms, telling her about his plant and DNA tissue crossbreeding experiments, and Naturcept.

Charlotte had her own opinion on the subject, but she listened carefully and made no comment. One of Nestor's cases was inside her own luggage, locked, while Nestor carried the other. She didn't know what the contents were, nor would she try to find out. He said he trusted her and he could.

It was a pleasant first-class journey across the Atlantic. Nestor taught her how to play gin rummy.

The flight bearing Nestor and Charlotte landed at the Leonardo da Vinci International Airport at Fiumicino, near Ostia, twenty-two miles from Rome. They were met at Customs by a representative of Cardinal Bettini, sent to escort them into the Imperial City. A customs official, accompanied by a priest in black soutane, came right into the baggage area, and to the chagrin of the other passengers, their luggage was scooped up and they were shown immediately through a side door marked for employees only.

The V.I.P. treatment—no inspection or stupid questions—settled Nestor's nerves. He had never liked dealing with Customs minions. The problems getting plant material from one country to another for scientific purposes, even with permits, was sometimes ludicrous. Too often the agent was a power-mad civil servant who knew nothing about transporting plant specimens and was too arrogant to admit it.

A large Mercedes awaited their arrival at a passenger loading zone. In addition to the priest, who introduced himself as Monsignor Brian Kelleher, there was a driver and a large florid balding man with a crooked nose and thick eyebrows who appeared to be a bodyguard.

Father Brian, as he asked them to call him, was friendly, helpful, and well-organized. Observing his charges, he noticed that LaPretre was certainly unprepossessing in appearance. He didn't weigh much more than the woman, and the glasses and beard gave him a scholarly touch, though to Kelleher Nestor appeared more a buffoon than a serious scientist. The Monsignor upbraided himself for judging by appearances; he was well aware of the respect Mr. LaPretre commanded in the scientific community.

The Lockwood woman was a different matter, a pleasant contrast. She appeared to have Christian humility, along with lovely eyes and a comely shape. Again he chided himself for thinking of her as a woman rather than an agent of God, as she was.

They headed down the north-south Highway of the Sun, which melded into the Ostiense. It was approaching one o'clock; the traffic was somewhat lighter during the afternoon closing of shops for lunch and siesta. Kelleher explained that at the height of the rush hour his rosary beads usually got a rigorous workout during the course of the low-flying trip into town. Arnold, the bodyguard, sat in front with the driver, while Father Brian conversed with the guests in back, asking about their trans-Atlantic trip. Nestor and Charlotte thanked him for their swift passage through customs. The Monsignor acknowledged that the cloth did, at times, have some influence in the Italian sector.

Kelleher acted as their unofficial tour guide as they progressed along the streets and avenues of Rome. He claimed that Rome was the world's most beautiful, charming, and enigmatic city, with an incredible diversity of ancient buildings and magnificent churches. Most interesting of all, he said, were the Roman people themselves—clear-skinned, beautiful, and full of life.

The vehicle was brought to a stop by a traffic officer near a cluster of men on a corner, who were loudly praising a passing group of women. "That is one of the national pastimes in Italy," said Kelleher, nodding toward the little pageant.

"Don't the women object to the remarks the men are making?" asked Charlotte.

"My view of human nature leads me to believe that they take no offense whatsoever," replied Kelleher. "They probably quietly thank the watchers for their good taste."

"How long have you been in Rome?" asked Charlotte.

"Since I was a young priest," answered Kelleher. "I was a missionary in Colombia, when, if you'll pardon the expression, a talent-spotter of Cardinal Bettini's heard about me. The Cardinal is very conservative, so perhaps his interest was piqued because I refused to aid, abet, or engage in acts of civil disobedience. I do not espouse Church-bound social action, nor the theology of liberation based on Marxism. There is a great deal of empathy for that among the priesthood of South America. I was there to minister to the bodies and souls of the Christian community, not to fight alongside the guerrillas against what some considered a repressive regime."

Charlotte remembered her own short stay in Rio years ago, and found herself wondering if the conditions in the barrios had gotten much worse. There had been far too many street children even then. She tried to put the thought out of her head, for although she agreed with Kelleher about the Church not meddling in liberation politics, she knew that Nestor had a good point when it came to overpopulation and poverty.

"I've been there, although only for a short visit," she said. "I realize there is no need to become radical if there is nothing to reform, but when I think about the tragic human conditions I saw, I sometimes wonder if the Church shouldn't try to bring more influence to bear at the top. I had the pleasure of meeting the new Pope there when he was Bishop Romereo. He regarded the poor as the people of God, and felt that something should be done to alleviate their terrible economic plight. I agree with him." Charlotte was surprised at her own words; after all, she had decided to remain uninvolved with politics during her mission.

The fact that she had met the Pope was not lost on Monsignor Kelleher. Her opinion, coming from one he knew to be an oblate in Opus Dei, surprised him, and sparked a flicker of guilt within him.

"Some of those priests are right," said Nestor. "I've been in Latin America many times with my work, and I've noticed that the more regressive the juntas and dictatorships, the more radical the priests become. Many are tortured and killed; some kind of action against social injustice may be the only solution."

Kelleher backtracked a little. "I realize the situation is getting worse," he observed, "but when I was there I believed that the Church should retain its traditions, and preserve a neutral integrity. Otherwise the Church would be persecuted throughout all of South America, and wouldn't survive to accomplish any good works at all—the type of things which cannot be accomplished where conflict between government and the priesthood exist. But it is not my place to decide these things. It is in the hands of the College of Cardinals, the Secretary of State, and the Pope." Kelleher suspected that he might be talking too freely, and lapsed again into a polite distanced manner. He did his job with patience and attention to detail, with the ability and strength to work hard for extremely long periods. But lately these traits had begun to pall, to seem trivial compared to the larger issues confronting the Church, and, indeed, the world.

Charlotte slyly observed the priest, whose curly silver hair and soft Irish lilt presented quite a contrast to the severe soutane with the stiff white Roman collar. She thought she detected an aura of sadness about him. "What part of Ireland was your home?" she asked.

"Dublin," he sighed. "I go back there occasionally, but I do have a genuine affection for this city," he said, gesturing out the window.

The Mercedes turned off the Viale Aventino, heading west along the edge of the Circus Maximus, then proceeded along Via San Teadoro, cut left and moved slowly along Via de Fienili, then right down the narrow incline of Foraggi.

There was no traffic on the Via Foraggi. Near the middle, the street widened into a piazza featuring a small statue on a pedestal to one side of the street. Someone had parked a Volkswagen van facing Fienili; it was half on the narrow sidewalk and jammed against the building.

A paunchy Benedictine monk in a brown robe and cowl hobbled up the cobbled road. He signaled frantically to the Mercedes with the small Vatican flag on its hood, with license plates marked S.C.V. for the State della Citta de Vaticano. Rome was presently the host of a Benedictine Abbot's Congress, which the Order held at regular intervals.

Kelleher suggested to the driver that they stop to ask what the old man wanted. They pulled to a stop and the monk came haltingly across the cobblestones as the driver rolled down the window. The Monsignor heard the hiss and saw the smoke. He tried to close the window back up as the canister of tear gas was first shoved into his face and then thrown into the car. The monk ducked with surprising speed behind the vehicle just as a street cleaner trundled a rubbish cart off the sidewalk directly in front of the limo, effectively blocking forward passage. The bodyguard jumped out of the car, clawing a gun out of a shoulder holster as he did so. The monk, coming from behind the car, blind-sided Arnold, executing a perfect block just below the knees. The bodyguard flew through the air, managed one complete turn, then landed hard on his back on the stone pavement. Without hesitation, the street cleaner whacked him over the head with a broom handle.

The rest of the occupants emerged from the car spluttering, tears flowing from the sudden onslaught of gas to their eyes and olfactory nerves.

The Volkswagen van had backed up behind the Mercedes and two men jumped out, leaving only a driver at the wheel. The workman jerked the driver from the Mercedes and flung him across the hood. Disarming him, the workman spun the driver around and delivered an uppercut to the jaw that sent the man sprawling into a doorway, where he slid slowly to the ground.

As Charlotte exited the Mercedes, she bumped into the man from the Volkswagen. Barely able to see, she sensed that this man was an enemy and swung her shoulder bag wildly in his direction. The man responded by slamming her into a stone wall. Kelleher, dimly able to make out what was happening, headed straight for the attackers. One had a gun pointed directly at him; he shouted and motioned both Kelleher and Charlotte back against the wall. The other man, grabbing the blinded Nestor LaPretre in a full-nelson, ran him and the attaché case through the open back doors of the van, jumping in behind him.

The remaining assailants, including the monk, also dove into the back of the van, which then drove back down Foraggi at high speed, honking its horn. The Volkswagen van roared out of the bottom of the street and tore off in the opposite direction, onto Via San Teadoro.

At the scene of the abduction there was an abandoned Mercedes, two unconscious members of the Cardinal's mafia, and Monsignor Kelleher and Charlotte Lockwood, still in shock and crying from the tear gas. Kelleher wrapped his arms around Charlotte to comfort her.

During the confrontation, a green Fiat had turned into the Via Foraggi and halted half way up and in the middle of the street, blocking it. The lone occupant had sat watching as the action unfolded before him.

In the Fiat, Hugo Payne shifted gears and began to follow this new quarry, again at a discreet distance.

The Opus Dei vehicles had radio communication with their office and each other. The need for this was not extensive, but came in handy at times. The driver of the limousine had the radio switched on when the assault occurred, and although the receptionist-dispatcher didn't know what had happened, she certainly understood that something had gone very wrong. She had heard unusual sounds and could get no answer to her repeated inquiries. When the effects of the tear gas had abated, Kelleher returned to the car, where several onlookers had gathered. He turned off the motor and asked for help on the radio, giving the location and describing the situation as best he could. Charlotte did what she could for the driver and Arnold, but the latter, particularly, wasn't going to regain consciousness for a long time. He had suffered a bad concussion.

After the emergency crews had arrived, Monsignor Kelleher and Charlotte Lockwood made their way to Opus Dei headquarters.

Cardinal Bettini flew into a black rage when he was told that LaPretre and his briefcase were gone. His first thought was that Hugo of the Priory of Sion was responsible, but he was dead—of that he was certain. His own agents had delivered Hugo's tattooed finger, as ordered, and had reported his demise. They could be trusted and relied upon in such matters.

Bettini visualized Opus Dei as the first legion of the true believers in Christ under his personal prelacy, and had devoutly hoped that they might have become sufficiently entrenched by the end of the reign of Pope John Paul II that one of their own men might have been elected as the next Pontiff. But it didn't work that way, and they were saddled with this South American Cesare. And now his problems were becoming even more complicated.

Lockwood and Kelleher sat patiently as Bettini paced his office. They were genuinely puzzled by the Cardinal's extreme agitation.

Who, Bettini wondered, had kidnapped LaPretre? Perhaps Hugo had accomplices in Rome, or the Priory of Sion had sent more of their lunatic gangsters who believed in the Holy Grail. Maybe that was it. They hadn't received the message: do not mess with the faithful in their own habitat, for the faithful are sustained in righteousness by higher powers. He had almost had LaPretre and Naturcept in his hands. But now he realized there was only one thing to do. He must find the scientist and silence him once and for all, and he must destroy the contraceptive formula.

Finally, the Cardinal sat down to face Lockwood and Kelleher. He fought to remain calm and keep his hands still. His mood improved somewhat when Charlotte told him that she had in her luggage an attaché case which she believed might contain some of Nestor's records. The case was retrieved immediately from the trunk of the Mercedes and delivered into Bettini's hands. Charlotte did not know the combination; an old security guard was called in to pick the lock.

A consultant who was conversant in scientific matters was invited to join them; the contents were inspected and read. The expert concluded that the contents constituted only part of the formula.

The Cardinal turned to Charlotte and asked if she could explain. She told him about the two attaché cases which Nestor had used as a precautionary measure against theft. "Henceforth, Ms. Lockwood," Bettini hissed, "you must report all such details in advance. No matter that you may consider them minor."

The events of the day had put Charlotte on her guard. First Nestor's kidnapping, and now the Cardinal's reaction, seemed to her to be worlds away from what she had perceived to be an important issue concerning religious doctrine.

Softening a little, Bettini took Charlotte's hand. "This must have been very traumatic for you, señora. A terrible thing to have happened on your first day in Rome. You could have been badly hurt. I am very concerned about what harm may have come to our mutual friend, Mr. LaPretre, but rest assured that the Vatican will stop at nothing in order to find him and redress this wrongful action. It is obvious that these bandits did not obtain all of the valuable records of his product. We will find them and negotiate his release."

"Your Grace, I certainly hope so," said Charlotte, a little suspicious of his sudden calm. "What shall I do for now?"

"We have adequate accommodation here, where you can sufficiently recover from your experience. Hold yourself in readiness, my dear. There may yet be use for you in this situation."

Monsignor Kelleher assumed that the session was over. He rose, shook Charlotte's hand, said goodbye to the Cardinal and departed.

CHAPTER NINETEEN

BIG PENIS IN THE SKY

JUST PAST THE VILLA DORIA PAMPHILI, the Volkswagen van bearing Nestor and his abductors suddenly turned off the Via Aurelis Antica onto a side road. Coming around a bend in the highway, Hugo was just in time to see the vehicle disappear into the trees. Braking, he attempted to follow, having to cross oncoming traffic to do so. This held him up, but he finally eased his way slowly down the winding road into what appeared to be abandoned farmland. An Italian sign read, "Private Property—Dead End." The dirt track passed through lines of large gnarled and twisted fruit trees with low bushes, creating a tangle of underbrush. In time the track through the abandoned orchard came to a small ancient cemetery. Hugo stopped the Fiat near the edge of the trees, not wishing to cross open ground in the car until he was certain what lay ahead. The trail did not appear to go far; he could see rock-strewn hills in most directions and no sign of any other road.

Hugo didn't want to lose contact with those he pursued; he decided to trust the dead-end sign. He backed the Fiat into the trees and picked up his knapsack containing a camera and a pair of binoculars and slung it over his shoulder. He walked into the cemetery. On the far side of the graveyard, Hugo saw that the track disappeared into another distorted fruit forest. There was no one in sight. Reaching cover once again, he proceeded cautiously along the tree line, soon discovering that the road switch-backed down into what appeared to be an abandoned rock quarry. Working his way to the quarry, he found an upper vantage point from which he peered down into the pit. He saw a number of men clustered around the Volkswagen van and another car. He reached for the binoculars for a closer look. Two mobile trailers stood among sun-faded outbuildings of what had once been a farmyard, which now resembled a junkyard.

The crater itself was extensive, likely quarried out hundreds of years previously, as various piles of stone and tufa rubble lay heaped about, overgrown with weeds and grass. At some time since the days of Constantine, someone must have transformed the site into a mixed farming operation. There were remnants of dilapidated fencing which had once formed animal corrals, an antiquated stone-walled barn with a sagging wooden roof built against the cliff on the far side of the quarry, and a shepherd's shack thirty yards in front of the barn. Smoke rose from the chimney of the hut; an old Italian in rough clothing sat in a chair outside the front door, a shotgun across his knees. The ruggedness of the scene seemed to Hugo to cover the secrets of the past with layers of debris from the present.

Squirming more comfortably into a prone position amid the scraggly bushes, Hugo trained the binoculars on the men who were taking LaPretre from the back of the Volkswagen van. Quickly removing a Nikon F3 camera from his knapsack, he focused the zoom lens on every man he could see, trying to get a clear shot of their faces as they carried an apparently unconscious Nestor from the van into the southernmost trailer. Nothing about their clothing seemed clerical. He took a good look and a few shots of the shack, the outbuildings, the barn, and the terrain of the quarry floor.

The sound of voices drifted up from below, and although he couldn't make out what was being said, the actions of some seemed to indicate they might be considering departure. Hugo turned and ran down the road as fast as he could, considering his recent injuries, and across the cemetery to his Fiat. He reversed the car onto the track, proceeded back to the Via Aurelia Antica, and headed into Rome.

He would return, but first he had to figure out a plan—one which would require sound management and timing, but whose succcss would depend on the identity of these people. He had to know his audience before he could determine what kind of show they'd likely get.

Back in Rome, Hugo took the film to a fast-photo processing plant, and when they were finished, he faxed the pictures of the men to a Priory office in Paris, with a request for identification. Then he returned to his minuscule quarters in the Transevere and crawled into bed, his wounds aching.

Seated on chairs on either side of a wooden table in a small, sparsely furnished room, they silently and patiently waited for Nestor LaPretre to awaken from the drug which had been administered in the back of the Volkswagen. Finn Mahoney was the more relaxed of the two, his chair tilted back against the wall, his hands folded loosely across his pot-belly.

At last Nestor began to move. He blinked his eyes at the strange surroundings, the lone light bulb dangling from the ceiling, the badly painted picture of a sad circus clown on one wall, and two strangers seated across the room. Having lost his glasses, he squinted first at one, then the other. One was rosy-cheeked, rotund, and pleasant, the other astonishingly angular and ugly.

"My name is Finn," said the larger one. "May I call you Nestor?"

Nestor stared at him silently. Still confused, he didn't know what was expected of him, or who these men were. Finally he said, "If you like; it is my name."

Finn smiled at him again. There was a further silence.

Suddenly Nestor demanded in as loud a voice as he could muster, "Why am I here? I want an explanation!" There was another lengthy silence.

"We'll be giving you one," Finn said finally, waving a pudgy hand, "but it's a question of where to start, you see. The subject matter is so difficult that we could probably start a long way back in history, if that would be to your liking."

Nestor furrowed his brow. "Who are you? What am I doing here?"

Finn ignored the questions. "Our present Christian civilization has been living with and seeking moral truth and religious comfort from a lie for two thousand years. At the moment you are caught up in this situation because you are trying to alleviate some aspects of the lie. How does that grab you for an explanation, boyo? Esoteric enough for you?"

"Listen Finn, let's not get into that crap," said the other man. "I don't want to hear your theories again. Stick to the point, for once in your goddamn life!"

"Whoever you are, I don't care about two thousand years ago," Nestor said. "I want to know what's going on right now. What the hell is this all about?"

"All in the fullness of time, my friend," said Finn.

Nestor shifted his weight on the cot against the wall to look around the small room. There was one door, one little window closed by a shutter of some kind.

"You have something you'd like to tell us, haven't you, Mr. LaPretre?" The other man spoke tersely, his arms folded across his chest.

"I don't know what you are talking about," Nestor said, turning to look at him.

"You know what I mean, all right," he said loudly.

"Don't get him mad, Nestor. He can get very mean when he's mad," said Finn slowly. "Now I'm a peaceable man by nature. I hate to witness violence in any form, although sometimes I have to when he loses his temper. By the way, meet Mitch."

For a few brief seconds Nestor wondered if he should try to fight his way out of the room like in the movies, but quickly dismissed the idea. He didn't like violence either, especially if it was done to him. "Look, you are holding me against my will. It seems to me . . ."

"Not interested, LaPretre," interrupted Mitch. "Now there was something in that briefcase of yours about a birth control formula, but only half of it is there. That's a little bit unfair, don't you think, after all the trouble we went to?"

"After all you . . ." The picture was becoming clearer to Nestor now. "What about me?" he demanded.

Finn sighed and said, "Would you believe we are only trying to help you?"

"No."

"I'm not surprised," said Finn. "And while we are not exactly philanthropists, we *would* like to help you." Finn turned to his partner. "We don't wish to harm him, do we?"

"Not if he is willing to be reasonable," Mitch replied.

"Reasonable about what?" Nestor realized it was a stupid question even as he uttered it.

Mitch leaned toward Nestor. "Read my lips," he said, his face darkening. "You have the formulas and the seed stock somewhere, and you have information on Naturcept in your head. We want it. All of it."

Nestor, who had worked his way to a sitting position, stared at Mitch in silence.

"Who has the rest of it, Nestor?" Finn asked softly. "Your girlfriend?"

"She's not my girlfriend. She works for the Vatican."

Finn laughed loudly.

"What's wrong with that? She was merely obeying instructions, acting as an emissary to bring me to Rome to talk to the Pope. What have you done to her? She doesn't know anything about Naturcept."

"Never mind her. Did you really think that the Vatican was going to help you?" asked Finn.

"I hoped they would. They spoke as if they might."

"I think you should study your history a little more before you get into the religious end of this birth control business, friend. You're a heretic—they used to send people like you to the gallows or the stake with true Christian piety and the wish that God have mercy on their souls. Your work destroys the seed of life, which emanates from the Big Penis in the Sky. Why would the Vatican regard you as anything but a modern day Onan?" asked Finn, now serious. "We, on the other hand, are prepared to make you an offer you can't refuse, on condition you don't deal with anyone else."

Nestor's head was no longer muddled. "Oh, I see. You say you want to deal with me, but . . . you want to rip me off!"

"Well, now, boyo, you may be right. And we couldn't just let you talk to the opposition first, could we? Especially since they had more than talking in mind. Why not just get out of the drug business entirely and let us handle it for you; we are better equipped than you."

"And if I don't co-operate?"

"I told you not to make my friend here mad. You see, if we don't get Naturcept, then maybe nobody gets it."

"Without me," Nestor said brazenly, "no one gets Naturcept!"

"Without you. . . . Exactly! Look, we want you to help us produce it. We're not entirely greedy. We want you to reap some benefits from your own invention. That wouldn't be too bad now, would it?" Finn asked.

"I don't know you people; I don't trust you. You're bullshitting me." Nestor's leg had begun to throb.

"Your mind doesn't seem to be assimilating the facts here, LaPretre," Mitch said. "But no matter, you can stay here until it does. There are a lot of bad people out there. You'll be safer here," he said, his grin becoming sardonic.

"We'll be back to see you when you may be in a more receptive frame of mind," Finn smiled at Nestor. "Maybe it was too soon to talk to you anyway. We all make mistakes. Let's hope you will be guided by reason in the long run."

The pair rose and walked out of the room. The sturdy green door slammed behind them, shaking the room. Realizing that he must be in a trailer, Nestor heard the door being bolted from the other side as he got up to check it. He could see nothing but black when he tried to peer out the window. Lying down again on the bed, his head aching, he stared straight ahead at the toilet in the open bathroom.

CHAPTER TWENTY

THE SACRED MUSHROOM

"YOU'RE IN A BIT OF A BIND here, Nestor, I'll be the first to admit that," said Finn Mahoney. "But let me give you a word of advice: when you're in a dark room standing naked next to a bureau, never slam the drawers! And don't think of me as an enemy. I'm just here to talk to you."

"What should I think of you as, then," asked Nestor. "A friend?"

"Don't get feisty. I'm just a minion of a certain drug interest that wants your plant substance produced and marketed. By them."

"They have a strange way of going about it," Nestor said curtly.

"So it must certainly seem to you, laddie, but then you are not in possession of all the facts. When our Canadian agents discovered that you were about to bring Naturcept to Rome, we had reason to believe it might get lost forever, and you with it. We can't have that, can we now? Admittedly, my principals are selfish. They want Naturcept all for themselves. They are, you might say, in some ways misguided: if they can't have a product, they don't want anyone else to have it. Bye the bye, would you like a libation?"

"No thanks," answered Nestor, even though a stiff belt would ease the throbbing in his left calf.

"Too bad. I hate to drink alone. You have to realize, Nestor, that my people play hardball, but they don't get serious until the final innings. If you hadn't been offering your Naturcept business to others when we first heard about it, we might have been instructed to start some negotiations."

"So why didn't they do so?" Nestor asked. "I was looking for a backer."

"My people are not into 'backing.' They want control. However, let's assume that you and I can now cut a deal. It's not going to be easy because we're into a much bigger game at the moment."

"I have no idea what you are talking about," said Nestor, hoping that Finn might spill some useful information.

"I admit to several addictions," replied Finn in a confidential tone. "History, particularly religious history, the drug business, and philosophy."

Nestor nodded, encouraging his captor to continue.

"You are presently caught in a stand-off between an orthodox religion and your own scientific discipline. Some day those two may make their peace, but I doubt it. If you were dealing with some of the more enlightened elements of religion in the Catholic Church, you might resolve that conflict and effect the results you strive for, but it wouldn't be easy."

"Apparently I'm not going anywhere soon. If you want to explain, go ahead." After many hours alone and in silence, Nestor welcomed any conversation, however ill-intentioned.

"May every hair on your head turn into a candle to light your way to heaven. Where to begin? The Apostle Paul warned Timothy, I think it is First Timothy in the Bible; he said, 'Oh Timothy, keep that which is committed to thy trust, avoiding profane and vain babblings, and oppositions of science falsely so called: which some professing have erred concerning the faith.' So even back then the Church and science didn't trust each other and they never have since. The Church believes in the power of faith, and science in the power of reason."

"That isn't news to me," replied Nestor. "I'll have that drink now."

"Another addiction," said Finn as he raised his eyebrows and grinned in self-parody. He rose from his chair, unlocked the door, and went down a narrow hallway. Nestor heard him talking to someone in Italian. He returned and sat down again. "Now, where was I?"

"You were saying something about faith and reason."

"Ah, yes. You see, Christians, like all other religious manifestations of the Near East, were originally and ultimately derived from an ancient Sumerian fertility cult. In those times everything centred around a God they didn't understand. Uncertainty about God's will has always kept man in perpetual subjugation and subjection to religious masters, of which the Muslims and Catholics are prime examples. Natural disasters inevitably struck, sending men scurrying to some priest or other to understand the nature of the sin he must have committed, and to find out how he could atone."

Nestor sensed this was going to be a long session. He wished the drinks would arrive soon as he tried to find a comfortable position. A burning desire to be at home in his greenhouse on Vancouver Island flooded him.

"Now that's where drugs first came into it," said Finn, "because those priests were the first druggists. Pharmacists vie with hookers for the title of the oldest profession. The two may even be in cahoots. Worship of fertility led to the mysterious drug cults of antiquity and then later to similar manifestations in Christianity."

"I hate to say this, Finn," said Nestor, stretching out on the bed, "but would you get to the point?"

"You sure know how to hurt a guy, Nestor," Finn said, flashing a grin. "The point is that Christ was a mushroom—the mushroom called Fly Agraric, the mandrake or *amanita muscaria*, the one with the red-and-white-spotted cap. In it is a very powerful hallucinatory drug."

Nestor digested this statement, but decided to remain non-committal. "Right up my alley. I know the mushroom well, of course."

"Good. This mushroom and the drug it produced was worshipped for millennia by what are now called Christians. The juice or distillation of the fly-agraric was in Greek spelled *khristos*, meaning good, honest, health-bestowing; even non-believers referred to it as 'christos.' This 'Christ-food' was a portion of the deadly mushroom which produced a disturbing hallucinatory effect when it was ingested, causing superstitious notions and inspiring so-called prophets, who raved in madness. They were tasting the nectar of the gods, the undiluted Word, and for a short period of time these prophets understood all things with certainty, and felt their souls were free from earthly doubts and fears. The drug offered spiritual release from sin and gave the soul a chance for complete absorption into the godhead. The word 'crucified' comes from 'Christ-food.' Even today the Vatican assures the Catholic worshipper that through the miracle of transubstantiation he or she is actually eating Christ's flesh and drinking his blood, through which they will receive salvation."

Finn shifted in the chair, his hands clasped behind his head. "The point is that they are no longer getting the real thing. The Judeo-Christian drug cult has removed the fly-agraric drug, which takes all the flight to heaven out of the ceremony. Not nearly so much fun today. Except for the priest—if he buys really good wine he can drink the rest of the bottle later. I don't remember to what church I no longer belong, but these days churches are trying to get by on a variety of wines, cheap or otherwise. The Baptists likely even use Welch's grape juice—diluted, of course. Cheap is cheap; you can't get high on that stuff."

There was a knock on the door and Finn rose to open it. A muscular young Italian man entered, and, nodding to Finn, placed a bottle of Schnapps on the table along with two tumblers.

"Could you not get Bushmills like I asked?" said Finn, his tone registering disappointment.

The youth shrugged. "It's not easy in Italy," he said. "This is all the foreign liquor I could get on such short notice. They never heard of Bushmills."

"More's the pity. But this is all right. Do you know this stuff?" Finn asked Nestor as the man left the room.

"I'll try anything once." He watched Finn pour three fingers of the liquor into each glass. "Your theory seems highly iconoclastic to me," Nestor said.

"S'truth, boyo," said Finn, raising his glass. "A toast. 'Niver piss into the wind when wearing light brown trousers.'" He tossed back his drink in one gulp.

"Cheers," answered Nestor, taking a sip and choking as the liquor burned his throat. Finn continued.

"I'm not trying to knock the faith for anyone who can hack it. If some Christian ethics seem worthwhile to you today, what does it matter if the cult was originally derived from a drug culture or from a real live prophet, in each case named 'Christ'? By the way, that's not the way to drink Schnapps. Down the hatch!"

Not to be outdone, Nestor tried it. It scorched his tonsils and seared his esophagus, but he got it down. He sputtered, "But what about the Bible? That's not what it says."

Finn shook his head. "The Bible is merely a cover-up story. You have to remember that these Christian Jews were expelled from Rome because they were making assholes of themselves as far as the Romans were concerned, causing civil disturbances 'at the instigation of christus,' or Christ mushrooms, whose consumption led to commotion and discord, and thus the subsequent vilification and contempt of the Romans. It's all chronicled by the Roman historians. They regarded users of the drug, whom they called Christians, as despicable dope addicts, whose arrest, arraignment, and conviction on anti-social charges and consignment to the gladiatorial arena of the Coliseum, was eminently justifiable."

"Let me get this straight, Mahoney. You're telling me that the Bible is all fiction?"

"Basically a crock, yes. The Old Testament, the patriarchal legends, the sojourn in Egypt—that is rooted in the religion of the holy fungus, which came from the underlying fertility philosophy of the ancient Near East. When the Romans took over that world, the old religion became unfashionable. The mushroom cult was driven underground, its members persecuted and hideously tortured if they pursued their religious ideas. That's the history of religion—torture everyone who does not hold your views, until they confess to their sins. Then kill them for being guilty.

"By the time of the New Testament," Finn continued, "the Christian practitioners had to invent a story, a tale which bore no relation to fact. Like the CIA or the FBI today. So they wrote an allegory in such a way that it would not bring the wrath of their enemies, the Romans, upon them. At the same time, by using ingenious literary devices, the story was passed on to the initiates and those who came after, the precious names of the herbs and the manner of their use and accompanying incantations carefully hidden."

"I don't remember reading anything about mushrooms or drugs, or even oblique references to them, in the Bible," said Nestor. "So how do you know all this?"

"It is common knowledge among theologians. In the drug business we identify any and all references to drugs throughout the ages. We have no religious water to sprinkle. We have no reason to suppress the information contained in the Dead Sea Scrolls or the later literary discoveries in the ruins of the ascetic Essene community and the old library at Qumran. Information in those documents has been verified by noted linguistic authorities, particularly of the Sumerian language, and bears out what I'm saying. You're not likely to hear this from religious organizations. Quite the reverse, for they have a vested interest in suppressing such information."

"We've been lied to about Christianity, is that what you are telling me?" asked Nestor.

"Think about it. When was the last time you were told the real truth about anything? Society is based on misinformation dreamed up by advertising executives and perpetuated by simpleton politicians. If someone tries to uncover the real truth, it means pain and sacrifice for us all. People don't go for that, so most don't look too hard for the truth. They don't want to read about it or hear about it, and if they do, they'll likely suppress it, because they don't like it. But the truth is still there waiting to be exposed."

"You have a point, I'll grant you that." Nestor sat up on the cot and leaned against the wall, pulling his knees to his chest with his arms.

"Take your Naturcept, for instance. The truth is that not enough people out there realize that overpopulation is a problem."

"I won't argue that, Finn. I recently read an article which stated that an expected doubling of the world's population by 2050 threatens to thwart any attempts to clean up the environment. The use of the verb 'threatens' is what bothered me. It isn't a threat, it is a fact, an absolute certainty, yet the politicians treat this as only a possibility. They don't want to face the truth—that human proliferation now makes us a species of weed."

Finn nodded. "I believe the evidence of the expert scientific chappies when it comes to analyzing and translating those ancient writings. They support the approach of the old-time gnostic sects of the Christian religion. But any reference to their views was turfed out of the Bible by the R.C.s some fifteen hundred years ago."

"This could be very interesting," Nestor sighed. "I think I'll have another shot, if you don't mind." He leaned over carefully and held out his glass. The throbbing had crawled up his leg to become a niggling pain in his hip.

Finn poured for them both. They snapped back their shots, and Finn continued. "So the New Testament writers wove a story about a hero named Jesus Christ, who, after a short ministry in Palestine, fell foul of the machinations of other Jewish leaders, who in turn coerced a Roman governor into putting him to death. From the Old Testament they dug out a story that foretold of the coming of a messiah. If you are a linguistic expert you can find innumerable references to the sacred mushroom in the bible and related documentation, a lot of which, however, has since been expunged."

The second shot had begun to take effect. Nestor felt much better, his plight not so precarious. "A lot of Christians today would call that blasphemous bullshit."

"Sure they would, but then most of them never even read the Bible, let alone the Dead Sea Scrolls. They've never studied language or history. In fact, many of them are illiterate, so they only see the surface.

"The story of the old dope artists, their attempt to pass on cult information, gradually failed, faded away, backfired on them. An organization which accepted the authenticity of their myth at face value emerged, an organization which founded a world-wide faith upon their hero, as if he had really existed in the scenarios they had invented. This was the story of his life, death, and resurrection. That became the most important act of a still unprovable god."

"In other words, we've all been duped?" Nestor was feeling warm, conspiratorial, the pain all but forgotten.

"Precisely. And now you have Naturcept, which is contrary to their vision of the holy teachings as related in the book they created. You have discovered another drug, like the French RU-486, anathema to the religious establishment of today. You are in big trouble, boyo. Because not only are the Christians now socially acceptable, they form a large part of secular authority. But luckily, they are not as strong today as they once were. At one time the Vatican ruled a large portion of the known world. My advice to you is don't mess with them—deal with us."

"I'll deal with whoever can do the job. But," and Nestor raised his glass in salute, "your tactics leave a lot to be desired."

"Too true. Let's have another kick at the cat, Nestor, m'boy." Finn got to his feet, stretched, then poured out two more liberal shots.

"Quite the happy hour we're having," Nestor murmured.

"Yes, and now that our minds are drugged and tongues loosened, there is something more to the point I have to tell you. We are working on a deal that may take a few days to resolve. When you know the details, you'll see that it is to our mutual benefit. But for the moment . . . I like to talk, especially when I'm drinking. Did I tell you that? Wouldn't be Irish if I didn't." Finn raised his eyebrows before swallowing the fiery liquid and wiping his mouth with the back of his hand. "We are all bound by the thin threads of taboos, fetishes, and secret fears," he continued. "Fear is the most powerful narcotic of all." He paused. "You know, I believe fear is the basis upon which the Jewish, Christian, and Islamic religions all operate; and although the Christians gave up magic mushrooms, they are still able to operate on the drug of fear. But I do digress. . . ."

Nestor stretched his arms high into the air. "Just get on with it, Mahoney. I haven't got all day, you know." They both broke up with laughter.

"Ah, the elixir of alcohol," Finn said, shaking the laugh off. "Another drug. Say, Nestor, why did you call it Naturcept, anyway?"

"Well," said Nestor, composing himself, "some of the DNA, and the names of the plants I crossbred, led me in that general direction, terola . . . termano . . . terminologically speaking." His thoughts were flying in all directions. He looked deep into his tumbler and another thought intruded. "Dammit, man, you've locked me in this room, and I want out. Let me out!" Nestor yelled.

"Nestor! Try to extend your thirst for knowledge, divine knowledge. You've searched for it in your field and found it. You should now search in other fields, as men have searched for truth for thousands of years. Did you know that in ancient times a farmer likely copulated with his wife in the fields in order to encourage the crops to grow?"

"No, I didn't," said Nestor, shaking his head in disbelief, "but I do have the feeling that I'm going to get screwed." He sank back on the bed, realizing that Finn, like the evangelists he abhorred, was determined to go on.

"That's all right. I'll recap the story so far. Now the mushroom was copiously endowed with the sperm of God, and the Christians, over centuries of experiments, cultivated mushrooms which sent their users into religious ecstasies—which were as mysterious to them as the power of a woman to fascinate her partner's penis into erection. The few who knew the secrets of these plants were the chosen of God, bound by fearsome oaths to keep the secrets of the cult. These favoured few did not shout their gospel from the pulpit like evangelists nowadays. They rarely dared to commit their knowledge to writing; it was passed on by word of mouth from priest to priest, who depended on trained memories dedicated to the recitation of their scriptures. But there came a time when the cult was seriously disrupted by persecution and war, their prophets decimated, and they had to be sure of passing on the information. I told you that, didn't I?"

"You did," Nestor said wearily, "and I can see you are going to tell it all over again. Do I have a choice?"

"No, you don't, you are the definitive captive audience . . . anyway, this is my party. So . . . at some point in history there was the Jewish Zealot Revolt against the Romans. About A.D. 66. The drug-influenced Zealots wanted to take on the Roman Empire. They had terrific defense and good goaltending at Masada, but their scoring ability was zero. They held the Roman Legionnaires scoreless for the first half, but then the Romans swarmed and blew the Zealots out of the arena. The Zealots became despised, fans turned into a mob, and many of the Zealots were heavily penalized. The penalty for drawing blood in those days was to be slain. The Zealot team was dumped from the league and those who were left had to play in the streets of Jerusalem, using petrified donkey droppings. Their remaining followers made up stories of a former time of glory, a time when their team, the Bethlehem Nazarenes, had been led by a superstar named Jesus Christ. By writing this story down they spread their knowledge of the magic drug, which was secreted in the text, the magic drug that had once made them a feared force in the big leagues." Finn paused to snap back another glass.

Nestor was again getting into the spirit of things. "I always wondered what prompted the Zealots to make such a stand at Masada, and then, to the last man, woman, and child, kill themselves afterwards. They took it a little hard, don't you think?"

"Righto, m'boy. It's only hearsay, but do you think for one minute that they could have done that unless they were on something? No way." Finn smiled broadly.

"The Christians that remained told and wrote stories about the superstar who had scored more goals than John the Baptist, and had always won the most valuable player award. He had played before the time of their expulsion from the league, and he was such a great and gentlemanly exponent of the religious game, that even the hated teams from Babylon respected, if not loved, him. The memory of Christ became the peg, the great hope, around which they built a new dynasty, a new religious cult. They traded for some players from the Legionnaires, and a new team emerged. They hired a new coach called Paul, who'd been an All-Italy forward before he stayed out in the desert sun too long without protection.

He preached that Jesus Christ had existed, had been betrayed by his own fans, and had been purposely slain by a rival team from Jerusalem, captained by Pontius Pilate. The Romans maintained that Jesus and the Nazarenes had been enhancing their performances using the phallic form of a mushroom, a replica of the ancient fertility god, which was known to them as the 'son of god.' The juice of the christus mushroom was the purest form of their god's own spermatozoa, which was regarded as God himself, manifest on earth. The Romans, aided by the non-Christian population, claimed that this had been unfair competition and unsportsmanlike conduct, and who can say that they were wrong."

Finn reached for the bottle again, poured, and in one co-ordinated movement, they clinked their glasses together, downed the liquid, and banged their tumblers onto the table in unison. Nestor lay back on the bed.

"So divine was the Holy Plant that only God himself could supply the price of redemption for robbing Mother Earth of her only begotten offspring. The new Christian team thought that God so loved them that he had done this for them only, in order to forgive them their sins and acts of deceit and corruption—which acts incidentally, they engaged in at every available opportunity. The Christians believed that they were destined to win the Holy Grail and enter into the player's Kingdom of Heaven."

"You do go on, Finn," Nestor cut in, a little too loudly. "What about this deal you mentioned?"

"Faith and bejasus, boyo, don't be interruptin' me when I'm tellin' a story," Finn boomed. "Ah, the sins of the fathers. . . . Now, where was I? Oh, yes . . . what began as an attempt to boost the confidence of their remaining fans and to fool their opponents with tales of their former glory just didn't work. Their old nemesis, the Roman Legionnaires, came down and whipped their asses again, and the playoffs were over at Masada."

Finn closed his eyes, smiling, and balanced his chair on its back legs against the wall. "Still, you had to hand it to those Christians, Nestor," he said, "because they never gave up their dreams of victory. They were so bloody sure that their brand of virtuous play would triumph. You could smell the odour of sanctity when you went into their dressing room. So right did they think they were, that their virtue became a vice. What had started out as a hoax, a cover story for the mushroom cult, became a trap even unto themselves. What they had forgotten was the sacred mushroom which had given them their original name, the holy plant which caused them to see more clearly and accurately, and to convey a physical and mental power beyond the range of normal human experience."

Finn had run out of steam. With his voice silent, they both sat engulfed in their own thoughts until they fell asleep.

Nestor awoke to find himself staring into an empty tumbler still clutched in his right hand. His left buttock ached. He looked across at his captor, whose eyes were closed. Nestor got up as quietly as he could, the bed-springs squeaking only slightly. Silently, limping, he made his way to the door. The knob turned, but it was locked from the outside.

"Not nice, Nestor," said Finn, opening one eye. "We were taking the afternoon off, remember? Having a friendly chat. Look, this isn't the worst thing that ever happened to you. If humans knew what would befall them in their lives they would run screaming into the woods. . . . So, why don't we just kill the rest of this jug, old pal?" Finn proceeded to split what was left in the bottle into two portions, and handed one to Nestor.

"Okay," Nestor said. "But then I'd really like two things. First, a drink of water—I'm dying of thirst—and then, I'd like to get the hell out of here."

"Patience, boyo. It will be resolved. Where were we?"

"You had taken a quantum leap into the antiquity of soccer as it relates to religion, or vice-versa. From which I have to assume that you are intoxicated. The last I remember was you running off at the mouth, repeating yourself."

"Oh, yeah, now I remember."

"Finn, tell me exactly what you want from me. I know it's Naturcept, but you know I don't have the entire formula with me. What are you going to do now? Are you going to level with me?"

"Maybe," said Finn, uncharacteristically brief.

"I don't get this. You've gone out of your way to be friendly toward me. I have a feeling that you are basically a good guy."

This remark stung Finn to the quick. "No, I'm not, boyo! Get that thought out of your head. I wouldn't want you making a big mistake." He leaned forward aggressively, his eyes on Nestor. "Would it bother me much if you got knocked off? Naw, I'd sell you down the Tiber for the price of a shot of Bushmills. I'd steal your glass eye and say you could see better without it."

"I don't believe you."

"And why not?"

"Because you wouldn't sit there and tell me that if it were true."

"Nestor, just so you don't misunderstand me later—if push comes to shove, I can be a right bastard."

Nestor shrugged. "I can't say that I haven't been warned."

"You don't get into this business because you are an upright citizen. But that doesn't mean I won't help you for the right price."

Nestor thought this over for some minutes. "Again, I'm asking you, what exactly do you want from me?"

"My company wants exclusive rights to produce and distribute Naturcept. We will get it one way or another. We kidnapped you because you were about to deal with parties who are less scrupulous than ourselves. That's the truth." Finn was doing his best to soften Nestor up.

"I was only going to talk to them."

"Look, you don't know much about the inner workings of the Vatican, not by a long shot, my friend. They have drug companies of their own or, at best, very large investments in them. Once you fell into their hands, it's game over for us all. Another company would get the product, and you and my organization would be history as far as Naturcept was concerned. You asked me to level with you. I have. It won't be long now. The pharmaceutical facts of life will be explained to you. You will be made an offer that you can't refuse."

Finn picked up the empty glasses and bottle and, reeling to the door, banged on it. The guard opened up and let him out.

Nestor heard the bolts shoot home once more.

CHAPTER TWENTY-ONE

QUERY IN THE QUARRY

THE PRIORY HAD MANY CONTACTS throughout the world, and soon Hugo got a reply to his fax inquiry. Sion had identified one of the men as a Finn Mahoney, who worked for a drug corporation called Azusipa Dionusos. The company had a reputation for industrial espionage, for cajoling governments or their representatives into compliance with favourable legislation through bribery, and for penetrating and coercing ethnic communities. Their methods were often economic, occasionally strong-arm. Mahoney was reputed to be as hard as a situation required, but had no personal record involving violence.

Obviously they wanted Naturcept. As usual with drug companies, they probably wanted it as cheaply as possible. Killing LaPretre would make no sense in this instance. They wouldn't want the formula to fall into rival hands, but did they know about the double-dealing Bettini's fanaticism regarding Vatican policy? Hugo Payne realized he'd have to enter the Lion's Den to find out Azusipa's intentions.

The sky was dirty grey, the scudding clouds intermittently drizzling rain as Hugo pulled off the Via Aurelia Antica into the trees. Water dripped through the leaves as he tied a white handkerchief to the aerial of the car. He then drove through the woods and cemetery, down the track and into the quarry, where he braked to a halt.

Suddenly a man came out of the shack at a run, his shotgun levelled. Hugo gingerly emerged from the car. He pointed at the flag and began to walk slowly forward, hands held out in front of him. The guard pulled the shotgun muzzle up and Hugo halted.

"This is private property," the man growled. "Can't you read?"

"Certainly."

"What do you want?"

"I want to talk to Finn Mahoney," Hugo replied, ignoring the man's pugnacity.

"No one here by that name. And if there was he wouldn't want to see you."

"Why not ask him?" asked Hugo firmly. "He is going to be mightily pissed off with you if we don't get to talk."

The man hesitated, shifting both his gun and his stance. "All right, but stay right where you are. Don't move."

Hugo stood still, hands at his sides.

The man proceeded to the most southerly trailer. He was about to knock when the door opened and Mahoney stepped out.

"I'll take care of this," he said. He looked at Hugo. "And what can I do for you, friend?"

"You can let me talk to Nestor LaPretre," said Hugo slowly, watching a scowl ripple across Finn's features.

"Listen carefully. I don't know who it is you're looking for, but he isn't here. Why don't you just be on your way."

"I also came to talk to you."

"This is an excellent place to get hurt. You are rapidly becoming a candidate."

"That's not a winning attitude, Mr. Mahoney. You will be interested in what I have to say, I can assure you."

Finn cocked his head suspiciously. "Will I now? Perhaps you would care to elaborate? You seem to know my name."

"And your business," Hugo shot back.

"You don't say! Well perhaps you'd better not leave at all." Finn signaled to the guard, who aimed his shotgun at Hugo.

"Let's stay calm now," Hugo said evenly. "I want to talk about Naturcept."

Mahoney's shoulders straightened, his eyes narrowed.

"Couldn't we get out of this drizzle? We might have mutual interests. Talking can't hurt, and it might help." Hugo continued in his placating tone.

Finn stared in silence, then said, "I'll have to check you for weapons."

"By all means." Hugo raised his arms in acquiescence. Finn came forward and patted him down while the Italian covered him with the shotgun.

Finn motioned Hugo to accompany him to the trailer. It was a mobile unit with a side entrance, a large window at the front end providing light for the small living room. There was a chesterfield along one wall, an easy chair in a corner, a coffee table, and a TV against another wall. A corridor led further back past a small open kitchen to the bathroom and bedroom. Pointing Hugo to the chair in the corner, Finn sat on the armrest of the divan, near the door.

"So," Finn said coldly, "you know my name, and you mentioned LaPretre and Naturcept. But you haven't introduced yourself, which isn't very polite. Now's your chance. After that I'd advise you to keep on talking. It better be good!"

"I'll come right to the point and tell you why I'm here."

"That is the idea," said Finn. "I'm all ears."

"I'm with an organization which is also interested in the contraceptive. Not in the way you are, though."

Mahoney scowled but remained silent.

"I know what business you are in. My organization has nothing to do with pharmaceuticals, but we have a strong desire to see that Naturcept comes into production and is distributed worldwide."

"And what would you get out of it?"

"Naturally you are skeptical."

"And why do you say that?"

"Everyone in industrial espionage distrusts everyone else," said Hugo.

"And you are a horse's ass if you came here to tell me you are after the same thing."

"As I said, we are not competitors. If anything, we see the Vatican, or certain elements within it, as our adversaries."

"A cockamamie tale. You are more likely to be associated with those elements. Why would I believe otherwise?"

Hugo knew this was his chance to set the hook. "Because like you, I followed the limo with LaPretre and the woman from the airport. I witnessed the abduction, and I followed your vehicle. It wasn't hard."

Finn bit his lip. "Bad luck on our part," he said. "Or good tailing on yours. But that doesn't convince me of anything."

Hugo tried without success to suppress a smile. “Then I watched you at the quarry. Some pretty good moves on your part, I have to admit. Maybe we can help each other.”

“Now why would we do that?” asked Finn.

“Because we could then pool our knowledge and our resources, to mutual benefit.”

Crossing to the window, Finn looked out at the slanting rain. He pulled out a pack of French filter-tip cigarettes and lit one. Taking a drag, he let smoke drift slowly from his nostrils.

“I am aware of things you don’t know,” Hugo continued. “You have the ace in the hole, Nestor LaPretre. But you kidnapped him in a foreign country. The Italian authorities won’t be thrilled about that if they find out. You snatched him from the arms of the most influential religious state in the world. Why haven’t they told the Italian police?”

Finn thought on this for a moment. “Did your organization? . . .”

“No,” said Hugo, “but I can explain it.”

“I’m going to call in a colleague before we go any further. You just sit tight.” Finn went to the door, signaling the guard to come into the trailer. “If he tries to leave, shoot him.” That done, he left, and through the window Hugo watched him move towards the other trailer.

Hugo heard a car motor start up. The sound faded into the distance as the vehicle drove away. Hugo and the guard sat in silence for fifteen minutes, until the car returned. When Finn came into the trailer, he was followed by Mitch Peden.

Dismissing the guard, Finn said to Hugo, “How do we know you haven’t got someone waiting in the weeds up there?

“I am alone, I can assure you. No one else knows my whereabouts. I came in good faith.”

“That’s an interesting way to put it. I have persuaded my doubting friend that we should listen to what you have to say before deciding on a course of action.” Mitch stood ramrod straight with his arms folded in front of him, his flinty eyes staring at Hugo. “So start talking.”

“First, I’d like to establish why both of us wanted LaPretre out of the hands of the Vatican. I’ll tell you my reasons, and I’d like to know yours.”

“To hell with him,” interjected Mitch. “He wants to pick our brains. I don’t like this.”

"If we are going to talk, we have to start somewhere," said Mahoney. "Let's give it a try, Mitch. It can't hurt." He looked at Hugo. "All right. We know that the Vatican has a large investment and influence in huge drug corporations. But this is not common knowledge. Their interests are well hidden behind shell companies in obscure parts of the world. These companies are not constrained by religious doctrine."

"Interesting," said Hugo, although he knew this already. Best to draw out Azusipa Dionusos, elicit more information if he could.

"There's a new Pope, and LaPretre is a Catholic," Finn continued. "He might be able to convince the Vatican to adopt Naturcept as a natural method of contraception. If he did, the Vatican's interests would control it. Think of what that would do to the rest of us in the business. Naturcept could be bigger and better than the Pill. It could be the most lucrative product in history to date. We wanted to prevent LaPretre from making a deal with what amounts to a rival company, and persuade him to make one with us. That's why we put the snatch on him. Now, what's your story?" With Mitch in the room standing guard, Finn leaned back on the chesterfield, stretching his legs.

"Obviously you think you are dealing with the Vatican," said Hugo.

"Correct."

"Wrong. It's not the Vatican who wants LaPretre so badly. It's one man and his vigilante clique. Cardinal Angostura Bettini, a fanatic, who is very influential in both the Curia and a cult called Opus Dei."

Finn's expression changed. "Ah, the Opus Dei—this is news to us. How do you know this? Did LaPretre know who he was dealing with?"

"No. Neither do I for sure. Bettini has his own agenda, his own small organization. He's into all the right-wing corners of the Church, and he is a dangerous man."

"Just how do you figure that?" Mitch cut in.

Hugo removed his left hand from his pocket and held it up. The stump of his little finger still hadn't healed. "And if you would help me off with my coat I will show you a bullet hole in my back."

Finn gave Hugo a hand with the jacket and shirt. Mitch stepped closer to get a better look. Hugo turned slowly, playing for sympathy.

"And," asked Finn, "you think Bettini is the guy who did it?"

"*Why* would he do it?" asked Mitch.

"You still haven't told us who you are and what you want from us," Finn said.

"Why don't you get LaPretre and bring him in on the discussion?" Hugo asked. It was time to start reeling Finn in.

"No, that's not a good idea," Mitch barked.

At least Hugo now knew LaPretre was still alive. "He's going to need an explanation and a damn good one."

"That's my department," said Finn, "and I'm already working on it. Now start talking."

Hugo held nothing back: only the truth would get the job done now. Had he known that Mahoney was an atheist with his own theories of religion, and that he would scoff at both the Vatican and the Priory of Sion versions of the origin and meaning of Christianity, it would have made no difference. Hugo was pragmatic; his proposed alliance seemed the best approach. He explained everything he knew about Cardinal Bettini and his private organization. The Cardinal had gone too far, as evidenced by his intention to destroy both LaPretre and Naturcept. Such action would reflect badly on both the Church and Opus Dei, but more importantly, it would prevent either the Priory of Sion or Azusipa Dionusos from getting what they wanted. Hugo concluded that together they should convince LaPretre that his life was in danger, not from them, but from the man whom he thought of as his potential benefactor.

"Your story sounds plausible, but convincing LaPretre won't be easy," said Finn. "But before we get to that, you still have to convince *me*. Why should my organization join forces with yours? What's in it for us? The way it is now, we throw LaPretre a bone, get the product for ourselves, and make the biggest profits in the history of the corporate drug world. Can you make us a better offer?"

It was time for some fancy footwork, thought Hugo, "Getting the product will be no easy task," he said softly. "And you're forgetting two things—Bettini's power and ruthlessness, and the fact that without Church backing, you're not likely to make those huge profits. Better to have the Church's endorsement and support, wouldn't you say?" He could see Mahoney's mind at work. Hugo continued.

"We have to get past Bettini. Get to the real Church. I don't think Opus Dei is cognizant of his agenda. I spent some time in Spain and they are no boy scouts when it comes to right-wing beliefs, but they don't go as far as Bettini. The new Pope has his own views. So far no one knows for sure what they are. If he can be convinced that Naturcept is natural, and therefore compatible with Church doctrine, he may endorse it. Your company wants exclusive rights to production and distribution, but there will have to be some conditions. You'd have to give something in exchange. . . ."

"Like how much?" demanded Mitch.

"To get something like this through the Vatican you'd have to be willing to put something substantial on the collection plate." Hugo felt in control again.

"You mean a kickback to the Church?" asked Finn.

"And why not—it's the usual practice. If you offer to provide Naturcept at cost—or free—to underdeveloped, overpopulated areas of the world, to the people who need it most but can't afford it, you would still make magnificent profits. Think about what it would mean in the rich areas of the world if the Church openly supported Naturcept. For that matter, even if they didn't openly condemn it. It would still be extremely lucrative."

"What if the Vatican won't endorse the product?" asked Mitch.

"My organization, the Priory of Sion, believes they will, for good reason. If they don't, they aren't going to deal with LaPretre or Naturcept at all, so Azusipa would be free to make their own arrangements with him. That is, if they can after what they've put him through." Hugo was careful to use the more distanced pronoun; he couldn't afford to alienate Finn and Mitch personally. "This is a win-win situation for you."

"From what you say, it looks like we prevented LaPretre's demise. He should be grateful," said Finn, "and he badly needs financing."

"Don't forget Bettini in this scenario," said Hugo. "If he and his influence are not dealt with, you could very well end up with nothing. In Italy violent elimination is not uncommon. And you can be damn sure they're looking for you right now. What happens when they find you?"

"Well now, boyo, we're well equipped to handle that situation when the time comes," Finn replied. "For now, we have to convince LaPretre that we had his best interests at heart when we nabbed him."

"You'll have to convince him of more than that. Azusipa would be well-advised to try a little sincerity as to their *modus operandi.*" Hugo couldn't resist getting a dig in, but received no reaction. "Do you have the formula?"

"That does pose a problem," said Finn. "LaPretre may be an amateur, but he's a cautious one. We have half the formula and this Bettini has the other half. Only LaPretre can combine them. The woman must have had the other half with her. We didn't figure on that. We should have grabbed her too."

Hugo thought it was time to net the fish. "Do I take it, then, that we can work together on this?"

"Not so fast, Payne," Finn answered. "One step at a time."

"All right then. Does Bettini have any idea who kidnapped LaPretre or why?"

"Well, now, I doubt that," replied Finn. "They must be sitting there wondering who we might be."

Mitch spoke up. "Finn, you crazy black Irishman, why are you listening to this? I still don't trust this guy."

"Just hold on, Mitch, I'll handle this. As you are well aware, I'm hard to convince. And we're not committed to anything yet. But our boy Hugo's story rings true—only a nut could concoct such a tale, and he appears sane to me. If the Church brought LaPretre to Rome for legitimate reasons, then when we snatched him, they would have raised bloody hell. There is no official report because LaPretre was brought here on the sly. It makes sense, doesn't it? And I doubt Bettini has given up. He likely has more agents in this town than we do. Who knows if even our loyal peasants out there," he nodded toward the door, "can be trusted."

Hugo had correctly sensed that Finn might be like chocolate-covered toffee—you had to chew on him a long time, and he might stick to your teeth, but eventually truth and persistence would make him malleable. "We have to figure that Bettini's thugs are going to find you sometime, particularly if you stay in Italy. He plays rough. The best defense is a good offense. Perhaps we should set a trap and let Bettini find us. We can organize a definitive deal in which all our differences are settled. . . ."

Mitch and Finn looked at him quizzically.

"You let Bettini know that you are holding LaPretre and his formula for ransom for a few million dollars, some amount Bettini can get his hands on easily. The Cardinal wants LaPretre and Naturcept, so he will come."

"It might work," said Finn, "but we still have to persuade LaPretre to trust us and to play his part. That's the only way any plan could be effective."

"Of course," Hugo said. "But what if LaPretre won't play ball?"

"Then I'll shove the bat up his arse," Mitch said tersely.

"I think he'll go along," Finn said calmly. "I'd venture that right about now, he'd go along with just about anything."

"Let's assume," said Hugo, appearing to think out loud, "that we can convince LaPretre that he is in grave danger—which he is, but not from us—and that we are legitimately on his side and have his welfare at heart. We would still have to design a trap for Bettini."

Mitch's frown turned into a smile. "I like it!" he exclaimed.

"So, are we in agreement?" Hugo looked at Mitch and Finn, but neither spoke. "All right, then. It's time we put our heads together to come up with a plan."

They sat in silence, each mulling over the problem from his own point of view. Hugo hoped his fishing expedition would pay off.

The rain, now a downpour striking the picture windowpane, obscured the dismal scene outside. In the next trailer, Nestor lay locked in the small room, dozing, waiting for something to happen, anything. . . .

Mitch jumped to his feet. "Come on," he said with a note of excitement in his voice, "follow me." He began to root around in the kitchen cupboard, coming up with three large flashlights. He hustled Finn and Hugo out of the trailer into the rain and the gathering dusk, and ran them across the farmyard to the old barn against the quarry wall.

Mitch raised the bar that kept the weathered door closed and ushered them inside. With all three brandishing flashlights, they entered the gloom. Rotting hay on a stone floor, sagging rafters—the roof would cave in any year now. Rats scampered into a corner where the stone masonry of the barn met the quarry wall. The barn was bigger than it appeared, the rear portion a wide tunnel dug into the cliffside, and lined on each side with the remains of animal stalls. Mitch entered one of these and pushed aside an old trough, revealing a rough area of rock wall. On close inspection

Hugo could see the outline of long-eroded stone pillars, which surrounded the tunneled opening in the cliff. Mitch shone his flashlight high above the pillars. Faintly discernible in the rock were the chiseled letters, CHI-RHO, and the sign of a fish.

"What is this?" Hugo asked.

"Let me introduce you to a catacomb," said Mitch eloquently, belying his former gruffness, "but watch out for those who have yielded up the ghost, and here have been gathered unto their people."

CHAPTER TWENTY-TWO

CAVERN OF THE CROSS

THE ROMAN CATACOMBS are evidence of a faith much simpler and direct than of later times. The largest passage is near the cemetery of Callistus on the Appian Way, believed to be six miles long. Called the Crypt of the Popes, not all relics have been removed from it, because fourteen popes and 170,000 martyrs are buried there. Many other vaults have been subject to rampant destruction. But new catacombs are found from time to time, or regions of existing ones are opened up, and more light is cast on the thought, worship, and practices of early Christians.

Historians claim that catacomb burials ceased after the fifth century, but pictures and religious objects of worship continued to be placed there. The faithful resorted to the subterranean basilicas as spots of particular sanctity. They were not often used for that purpose, however, since, as underground cemeteries, they were places of darkness and mouldy air.

A catacomb began with a tunnel or a set of steps dug into the hillside or ground leading down to the first passageway. Here narrow burial tombs were dug into the sides of the tunnel. When the original passage had been used up, others were dug at right angles, which led to other tunnels parallel to the first passage. Then another stairway would be constructed to carry the tomb up into the hill. Deviations from straight lines became necessary where and when diggers met with tufa or other unsuitable ground.

The geological features around Rome were conducive to easy construction of these beehives of the dead. The standard graves were small, but larger floor-to-ceiling walk-in vaults were built for more important individuals. In these vaults, as well as at entrances and corridor intersections, the walls might be carved or painted with garlands of leaves or foliage, vines, bunches of grapes, peacocks, doves and other birds, sea creatures, or cubicula with pillars at the entrance. Pictures were generally of martyrs or saints, apostles, the Virgin, or of the Lord himself.

Few rooms of any size date from the centuries of Christian persecution. Larger rooms for worship came later. These were spacious and very well decorated, and contained rudimentary ventilation systems. Some had been recently wired with electricity for tourists, but in centuries past, when the catacombs were for worship alone, light would have been supplied by wall torches. This also explained why larger caverns were few in number.

Nestor felt a chill when Finn, Mitch, and Hugo took him into the catacombs to further explain their plan. If they were telling him the truth, Nestor thought he'd better go along with them; he had nothing to lose. He had few options. He was not about to become the opposing voice which must be silenced. No one would ever find his body here. The innumerable back passages of the catacombs, and those he had traversed to get to the high-ceilinged, circular chamber in which he now stood, were ideal for concealing murder.

High-powered battery flashlights had been placed around the room; their bodies threw large shadows against the walls of this place of ancient Christian worship. At the centre of the cavern several steps encircled a wooden cross of considerable size—an early Roman Christian crucifix upon which many had likely died. The sporadic lighting had a frightening and beautiful effect.

For some time, they peered around the gloom in silence. Pictures in panel form surrounded the cavern, which was divided in half by two entrance porticoes. Old Testament scenes on one side connected symbolically with those of the New Testament on the other. The once-brilliant colours were now faded and subdued; like life itself, not as strong and vibrant as they once had been, but still distinguishable, as were the tabloid actions the panels depicted. Several showed the life of the Psalmist David, to whose Royal house Jesus Christ had belonged. Panels on the Old Testament side showed God saving his loyal followers from certain death, like the Three Hebrew Children in the Fiery Furnace, Daniel in the Lion's Den, Jonah in the Belly of the Whale. One was of Cain slaying Abel, another the Sacrifice of Isaac. The scene at the entrance depicted Adam and Eve in the Garden of Eden, whose original sin made it necessary for

Christ to give his life for the salvation of humankind. The last scene, and the largest, was on the ceiling, depicting the Last Judgment.

In an alcove was a representation of an arena where gladiators fought and Christians died. From this sphere of struggle, Nestor thought, there emanated a malignant impression of calamity. Perhaps the painter-sculptor had intended to show that good may come from evil, for the horrors of gladiatorial shows produced one of the finest and magnificent achievements of all time—the Roman Amphitheatre. Most of man's heroes have trod some arena or other, thought Nestor, staring in amazement at the magnificent artwork. As he walked across the dirt floor, trying to ignore the pain that shot up his leg each time he put weight on his left side, part of a poem from English class flickered through his mind: "Then in this magic circle raise the dead; heroes have trod this spot—´tis on their dust ye tread."

As impressed with the cavern as Nestor was, he preferred the often monotonous repetition of lab work; even the creatures of the jungles and deserts he frequented acted according to type. But this situation threw him off balance. The laws of predictability were no good to him now. He felt useless, small.

On the New Testament side the panels depicted the public life of Christ—the Manger, and Joseph holding the reins of a donkey on which the Virgin sat, with Christ's small head peeking over her shoulder. There was also the Annunciation to the Shepherds, Adoration of the Magi, the Baptism scene and the Marriage Feast at Canaan, the Miracle of the Loaves and Fishes, the Entry into Jerusalem, the Denial of Peter and the Resurrection on Easter Sunday, and the Women coming to the Tomb. Christ appeared with Peter and Paul, between them the Lamb, as in the Book of Revelations, standing on the Holy Mountain of Zion, out of which flowed the Four Rivers of Paradise.

They sat down on the steps leading to the cross. Mitch had been their guide, having visited several times with the peasant from the farmstead. Nestor was the first one to break the silence, addressing Finn in a hushed voice. "I don't see any mushrooms!"

"More's the pity," replied Finn, "but that doesn't disprove my premise. These pictures were probably painted many centuries after Christ was supposed to have lived and died, and likely by brainwashed artists."

Nestor didn't bother to reply. Teachings long since forgotten surged into his brain as he gazed upon the religious panoply. He tried to remember some of what he had been taught. St. Thomas Aquinas, who had committed his mind and heart completely to divine revelation, was reputed to have established the distinction between reason and faith, and Pope John Paul II said the rest of Christianity should do likewise. Aquinas felt that reason soared to lofty heights but could go no higher, whereas faith had the higher and more reliable assistance of God as enunciated by the Pope. That may be so, thought Nestor as he peered at this magnificent display, but in the realm between faith and reason all people wander in confusion, the real human problem forever hidden.

Both Mitch and Hugo's thoughts were less philosophically focused. "Let's have another look at the gladiators," Mitch said to Hugo. "Come over here." They followed Mitch to the gladiator tabloid in the large alcove just off the main cavern, where two figures were engaged in mortal combat against a backdrop of wounded, dead, and dying. One was a myrmello, a name derived from the ensign of a fish on his high-visored helmet. He carried a large rectangular shield and a short dagger-like sword, and had a greave plate on his left leg, which, with the shield, gave him a protective barrier along his entire left side from neck to knee. A leather belt covered his thighs and genitals, and leather bands protected his exposed right arm which held the short sword.

The myrmello fought against a retiarius or net-fighter, who was an agile, quick-footed daredevil. The retiarius fought bare-headed, wore a cloth tunic, and was armed only with a sharp trident and a large net in which he hoped to snare his opponent. He wore the same belt and leg bands as the myrmello, his left shoulder guarded by a metal shoulder-piece. His strategy relied on quickness, speed of foot, and the ability to provoke, irritate, and exhaust his heavily armoured opponent, baiting him into lumbering across the arena. Once he was cornered, he was as good as dead.

Scattered around the floor of the alcove were a number of gladiator artifacts and weapons. Hugo took note. This particular catacomb had to be a very recent discovery or it would long since have been ransacked by thieves, vandals and antiquarians—undoubtedly one reason for the close guard of the Italian gypsy-peasants. They were likely in someone's employ, well-paid while the owners decided how to best exploit their religious find.

Hugo looked up and saw, carved in the rock, the Latin motto of the gladiators: *I undertake to be burnt by fire, to be bound in chains, to be beaten, to die by the sword.* Speaking the quote aloud, his mind coursed with images of the gladiators in the arena.

CHAPTER TWENTY-THREE

SHEPHERDS OF THE FLOCK

PRIESTLY SINS, BOTH OF THE FLESH and of the mind, are not uncommon in a Church that is governed by celibate men out of touch with reality. Now in his forties, Father Brian Kelleher had never married, had never raised children, had never discussed contraception with a woman. He had never considered how women around the world, many living in poverty and subjected to back-breaking drudgery, could become fearful of the consequences of love. Except for a short stint in Colombia, he had grown up in the sheltered life of Church bureaucracy, where he had been taught to adhere to the rules laid down by his infallible superiors, particularly the Cardinal whom he had served faithfully.

When Kelleher had been recruited into Opus Dei, Bettini had told him that the organization was the watchdog of the true Church, and at first had maintained that all dissent and heresy should not be tolerated. Bettini wanted to withdraw all support from those organizations which were undermining the teachings of the Church, were ambiguous about them, or neglected the teachings entirely. In reality, the Cardinal had said, any such patronage is contradictory to the purpose for which the Church institutions were founded. Dissidents were to be regarded as misleading and scandalous apostates.

Brian noticed, however, as time went on, that the Cardinal's tolerance level had declined even further, until he readily used the verb "destroy" in reference to perceived enemies of the Church, not only those without, but those within the Church itself. This was of increasing concern to Brian.

Brian's thoughts turned to Charlotte Lockwood. They had been talking a lot of late, as the Cardinal had placed him in charge of her stay in Rome. Bettini needed time to work out a strategy for the LaPretre conundrum—he was determined to find LaPretre. Kelleher realized Bettini would have to call in a few debts in order to get more agents on the job.

There was something about Ms. Lockwood that bothered Brian. Certainly she was intelligent and attractive, and they got along well. But he knew there was more to it than that. He found himself eagerly asking her to accompany him on an afternoon walking tour.

Brian decided they should take in the Pincio, the Borhese Gardens, and the great Roman Park, Villa Borhese. They strolled toward the Pincio Gardens in the early afternoon sun, St. Peters and Vatican Hill on the horizon. They passed the Villa Medici on a viaduct that crossed over the main road, and onward into the landscaped acres of the public park lying northeast of the Villa Borhese.

Small fissures were forming in Brian's thinking, conflicting with the stringent demands of the Catholic Church, as though he were about to embark upon a traitorous journey. Charlotte evoked in him a peculiar exhilaration he felt bound to suppress.

They roamed through the park on the way to the beautiful formal Giardino Del Largo, with its Temple of Aesculapius jutting out into the lake. As they approached the large fountain, Father Brian felt the call of nature. There was a small building with public washrooms on the far side of the fountain. Brian asked Charlotte to wait under a tree near the cool, falling water. Charlotte sat on a bench. Suddenly, a well-dressed Italian man sat down next to her. Charlotte glanced at him, then turned to gaze at the fountain.

"Take this message from Nestor LaPretre to Cardinal Bettini," the man whispered clearly in English, "and to none other than Bettini." He dropped an envelope into her lap and quickly walked away.

Charlotte was so surprised that by the time she realized what had happened, it was too late to run after the man. She glanced around, but he had already disappeared into the crowd. When Brian returned, he saw the look on her face and asked her what was wrong. She related the strange incident and showed him the envelope in her hand. "I should have gone after him," she said, angry at herself.

"You couldn't have done much," said Brian. "Whoever it was must have been following us. At least we have established contact. Best we get the message to the Cardinal."

✧ ✧ ✧

They sat in Cardinal Bettini's office at Opus Dei headquarters, watching him open the note. Straightening the piece of paper out, Bettini read aloud:

> They are holding me for a ransom of two million dollars U.S. If you agree to pay, send Ms. Lockwood, dressed in a nun's habit and accompanied by Monsignor Kelleher, to St. Maria Cathedral in Transvestere, Sunday between one and three p.m. Monsignor Kelleher is to wait in the sacristy at the east entrance while she circulates among the crowd, stopping to observe and pray at all of the relics and chapels on the premises. During this time she will be contacted with further instructions. The money must be in large denominations and held by Cardinal Bettini, who is to wait in a car outside the Cathedral. The Cardinal is allowed a driver and two bodyguards. He must deliver the money personally to my abductors in exchange for myself and my papers.
>
> Signed,
> Nestor LaPretre.

Bettini thought he could live with the demands. He was determined to get LaPretre, even if he had to pay two million dollars. Whether that would become necessary, only time would reveal.

The Cardinal turned to Charlotte. "You will accommodate us, Ms. Lockwood, with our problem?"

"Yes, I'll do all I can to help Mr. LaPretre."

Bettini's face remained impassive as he said, "You realize, don't you, that what he is doing is against the teachings of the Catholic faith?"

Charlotte sensed his displeasure. "Yes, I know that, Your Eminence," she stated firmly. "But I believe that the authorities have decided that Naturcept deserves closer scrutiny. And Mr. LaPretre's arguments are both sensible and logical."

Bettini turned away from her. This was not what he had expected. Maybe his information was wrong. Was she really Opus Dei material? In any case, she had helped get LaPretre to Rome on short notice. The Cardinal understood now that if LaPretre was fortuitously killed in a rescue attempt, it would have to look like an accident. Otherwise Lockwood might have to meet a similar fate. He hoped that would not be necessary.

"Your Eminence," continued Charlotte, "as I've said, I am willing to help rescue Nestor." She had grown quite fond of the odd little scientist.

Brian sat silently, somewhat perplexed. He knew Bettini's views on contraception and concurred with them. Why, then, had Bettini even been willing to discuss Naturcept with Nestor? And why did he seem so anxious to get his hands on LaPretre and Naturcept now?

"There appears to be a fair degree of danger here, Cardinal," Brian interjected, finally.

The Cardinal looked at him, bemused. "Indeed."

"I really don't mind," said Charlotte.

"You show good spirit," the Cardinal told her. "We will give you the best protection possible. However, I doubt they intend to harm the intermediary." Charlotte smiled benignly as Bettini continued. "I'll arrange for the ransom money from God's banker—it will be money well-spent. And Brian, would you be so kind as to take Charlotte to the good Mother Superior at the Vatican hostel to have her outfitted with a habit?"

Brian nodded and looked toward Charlotte, who faced him with a glint in her eye. Confused, he stared at the floor as his face reddened.

Bettini's mind had already begun to work on the LaPretre rescue problem. He couldn't be sure that they would kill him if he didn't present the ransom money. But for a mere two million dollars, he could be sure that LaPretre and his formula would disappear, and it would look as if the kidnappers did it. It was a perfect cover. It is difficult, Oh Lord, being the Shepherd of your Flock, he mused.

CHAPTER TWENTY-FOUR

CHI-RHO

ON SUNDAY AT NOON, Charlotte donned the nun's habit. It was one worn by the Order of the Precious Blood, slightly different from what she was familiar with. Pulling on the headpiece, she went to Monsignor Kelleher's office for his inspection. She was excited by the thought of a new adventure.

"I wish you could walk around the Cathedral with me," she told Brian.

"I'll be as close as possible," he replied. "But the ransom note instructions were explicit, and it is you they will contact. When they do, you know what to do—just come to me in the sacristy. You'll only be alone for a while, and Cardinal Bettini and the bodyguards will be just outside. It should be fine; we don't think anyone intends to hurt you."

Father Brian felt more confident because of the decision to outfit them both with two-way radios. It would be easy for Charlotte to conceal the mechanism in her habit. As soon as they were given their instructions, he would send a message to a group of Cardinal Bettini's men, who would then proceed to the location where the exchange was to take place. Bettini could also convey instructions from the radio in his vehicle; they knew that the kidnappers would take every precaution against being followed to the rendezvous.

When they were ready, Brian and Charlotte descended from the Apostolic Palace to the street, where a Vatican car and chauffeur awaited them. It was five minutes to one when they were dropped at the main entrance to St. Maria Cathedral and entered its front portal. Father Brian proceeded to the sacristy, while Charlotte began her rounds as instructed, stopping at the relics to observe, and at the little chapels to pray.

Her first prayer, of thanksgiving for having the opportunity to do God's work in such an intriguing manner, was sincere. But then Charlotte's mind wandered to thoughts of her research. She had traced her father's roots as far back as she cared to; her mother's were what interested her now. She needed to gain access to the European records she was sure existed.

It was nearing two o'clock and she still had not been contacted. She repeated her prayers before the effigy of St. Paul, trying to remain alert while a choir sang the Hallelujah Chorus.

Next Charlotte knelt before another of the Holy Relics upon which much of religious faith is built. In a ruby- and emerald-studded casket, watched over by two solid silver angels, was part of the foreskin of Christ, which the Church maintained was the only known sliver of Jesus himself. She wondered who would have saved such an item—could it have been the Virgin Mother, or the rabbi who performed the circumcision? She knew that other churches and shrines claim an imposing array of relics: the skull of John the Baptist, the bones of the Magi, the robe of Jesus, the hand of St. Gregory, the foot of Mary Magdalene. Could any of these things be truly authentic, she wondered, and realized that the leap of faith needed to be a true believer was being undermined by reason and logic. The thought surprised her.

Charlotte entered a little chapel, a candle shop devoted to various minor saints and their numerous shrines, statues, and calvaries. Here she could pay homage to many with one prayer. She paid for a candle, placed it on the altar, and had just knelt down on the steps before the Brethren of the Lord—James, Joseph, Simon, and Judas—when one of the statues spoke to her. Closer inspection of the dim recess revealed someone behind a bronze screen.

"Ms. Lockwood, don't react." The voice was flat, cold.

"All right," she replied.

"You can hear me clearly?"

"Yes."

"Go directly to the sacristy and remove your costume, including the headpiece and your undergarments. You will find a brown paper parcel on one of the shelves. In it is a simple dress. Put it on. If you appear to be wearing anything other than the dress when you come back, the deal is off. Move fast."

Charlotte hurried to the sacristy. Brian had heard the message and found the package by the time she arrived.

"You can tell me what they say when you come back," Brian said. "It's likely still okay."

"You'll have to help me out of this," Charlotte said as she fumbled with the nun's habit, reaching for the brown bag at the same time.

Brian helped her with both the nun's regalia and the microphone hidden beneath. The absurdity of the situation struck him, but there was no time for introspection. The crisp black material fell to the floor, followed by her panties and bra. As Charlotte slipped the dress over her head, shoulders, and hips, an involuntary gasp escaped Brian's lips. He hoped she hadn't noticed.

She turned to face him. "Here we go again. Wish me luck," she said and slipped out the door and into the cathedral.

Back in front of the little chapel of the Brethren of the Lord, she took the same position as before and waited, self-conscious in the unfamiliar tight dress in this place of worship.

"Go outside onto the Via Venezia," the voice intoned. "About twenty yards in front of Bettini's car sits a white one, empty. The keys are in the ignition. Get in and start the motor, then go back to Bettini and tell him that he and his men must leave their own vehicle and use the white car. Don't wait for an answer. Go immediately to the white car and get in the back seat. Got that?"

"Yes."

"Then repeat it as if you are praying."

Charlotte could feel sweat beading between her breasts as she repeated the instructions.

"After Bettini and his men join you in the white car, tell him that a blue jeep with a lone driver will swing out of traffic, slow down for a few moments as it passes, then continue on its way. Bettini is to follow that jeep. Do you have all that straight?"

"I have."

"If my instructions aren't followed exactly," the voice said tersely, "the deal is off. Now go."

Charlotte did as she was told. Walking out into the Via Venezia from the west door she worried that Brian would not know what had happened, but there was nothing she could do about that. She spotted Bettini and his men in a black vehicle, and then saw the white car. She walked to it, got in, and started the motor. Leaving it running, she walked back and delivered the short message to Bettini.

"Wait, what do you think you are doing?" he called after her as she walked back to the white car. Bettini cursed loudly. However much it rankled, the Cardinal knew he had to follow someone else's scenario, at least for now. He, his chauffeur, and the bodyguards left the black sedan and climbed into the white car, where Ms. Lockwood sat expressionless in the back seat. She explained quickly what was to happen next.

A minute or two later Mitch Peden drove a blue jeep slowly past them. As he saw them pull out to follow, he sped up and took a long, torturous route to the Via Aurelia Antica. Mitch watched the white car in his rearview mirror. So far, the plan was working.

CHAPTER TWENTY-FIVE

'TIS ON THEIR DUST YE TREAD

THE WHITE CAR BEARING the Cardinal's entourage followed Mitch off the Aurelia Antica near the Villa Doria Pamphili and onto the dirt track which wound through the maze of tombstones. Among the men with the Cardinal were the same ones he had used to eliminate Hugo—lean, hungry, and armed, conscious of their present danger.

Mitch braked to a halt in the middle of the narrow roadway. As he jumped out, he pulled a black silk scarf up under his eyes and snapped down the brim of his hat. At the same time four masked men rose from behind headstones near the road. With no place to veer off, the white car was forced to stop. Bettini and his men cautiously stepped onto the dusty road.

Mitch signaled Bettini to approach. When he was few feet away, Mitch held his hand up. "Did you bring the cash?" he asked abruptly.

"It's in the briefcase," Bettini replied, "but I don't see Mr. LaPretre."

"Nor will you unless we come to some agreement regarding your religious goon squad."

"You told me to bring them. What about your own?" asked Bettini, nodding toward the men behind the tombstones. "They don't exactly appear to be angels of mercy."

"There is no need for either group, I assure you. Why don't we just leave them all here to have fun together, while you, the girl, and the money come with me to the exchange. All these men," Mitch waved to both sides, "are undoubtedly armed, so let's try to be careful, shall we?"

"I don't see LaPretre and I don't trust you."

"We send the lady to find out if LaPretre is okay. She can report back to you. It's on the up and up; we don't want trouble. You'll get LaPretre; all we want is the money."

The two men stared coolly at one another under the Italian sun. Bettini didn't like the situation, but these criminals would gain nothing by harming the woman. She may have baited LaPretre, but the Cardinal now suspected her of being infirm of faith. Ultimately, Bettini thought, she's expendable.

"All right, if she will go. I'll go back and ask her."

Bettini returned with Charlotte. "Señora, I want you to search both myself and this *gentleman*." The sarcasm did not go unnoticed by Mitch.

Charlotte complied. Neither man was carrying a weapon. Mitch assigned one of his men to guide Charlotte, and the two disappeared down the trail, vanishing into the trees surrounding the rock quarry.

The two groups of men waited, the silent heat of the cemetery oppressive around them as they stood sweating. Bettini went back to the car, and Peden sat down on the jeep's fender. The Cardinal took small notice of a flock of crows which circled in the dry, hot wind—an omen which would certainly have given pause to any ancient Roman augurer.

When Charlotte and her companion returned a half-hour later, she went directly to Bettini. Seating herself on a tombstone, she noted that it bore the inscription, "The Hand of the Lord was upon me . . . and set me down in the midst of the valley which was full of bones."

Yes, she had seen Nestor. He was in good health and spirits. Anxious to meet with the Pope, he wanted the ransom money turned over as soon as possible. He also told Charlotte that he had a friend in the kidnappers' camp who would help if necessary.

"Who is he?" the Cardinal asked.

"I don't know," she said.

"Where is Mr. LaPretre?"

"Inside an old barn in a rock quarry surrounded by cliffs."

"Is there more than one way out of this quarry?"

"Only the road we are now on."

"Who was with LaPretre?"

"Another man. And a guard."

"Is this man armed?"

"I didn't see any weapons. Nestor's arms were tied behind his back at the elbows, so he had very little use of his hands." Charlotte could feel a chill emanating from the Cardinal. She wondered why.

"What did the guard look like?"

"He had a black scarf over his face."

Bettini picked up the case containing the two million dollars. He motioned Charlotte to follow him and walked over to Mitch.

"Are we in agreement?" asked Mitch.

"Yes. All guards, yours and mine, are to stay here. Let's get this over with."

Mitch led the way to a meeting with destiny.

The barn door opened in squeaky protest, unaccustomed to the traffic, and the small group stepped into the sudden gloom and coolness of the old structure. Picking up a flashlight and handing others to Charlotte and Bettini, Mitch continued back into the stall. He put his shoulder to one side of the back wall under the "CHI-RHO" sign. When the passage opened up, Bettini stopped and looked quizzically at Charlotte.

"They are down this passage," said Mitch. "Much farther down."

Bettini recognized a catacomb when he saw one and he didn't like them. He found it hard to believe that in the middle ages, nearly all the catacombs in Rome had been lost, their entrances clogged with debris or covered with vegetation. Many of them had remained hidden until the nineteenth century, and this vault proved that some were still undiscovered. Bettini didn't like the atmosphere, the dim light from the flashlights, the tunnels that branched off into the dark, and above all, the silence. He didn't like catacombs even though he knew they were the sepulchres from which the Church had literally risen from the dead into the light of day. He hoped he wouldn't have to remain here long.

They travelled down a long passage, the tombs of the martyrs rising all around, tier upon tier, their occupants long since dead. Ornamental carvings in the rock appeared fitfully as the flashlights lit their way.

Charlotte was increasingly nervous; she had only been as far as the barn and this strange, cold and musty place was unexpected. As the passage turned into steps leading upward, she was determined not to show fear.

"Look," said Bettini, his voice echoing loudly off the walls, "what's going on here? We should have met LaPretre and your man long before this."

"We are coming to them," Mitch reassured him. "Watch these stairs, they twist and are steep. Our friends are just up here."

As they wound upward the corridor brightened, until suddenly they emerged into a cavern, the like of which Bettini, and certainly Charlotte, had never before seen. The Christians had transformed a large natural cave into a place of worship, and even Bettini, who had seen smaller versions, stood transfixed by its beauty. The focal point was the cross, and although a masked man and Nestor LaPretre stood in front of it, Bettini could not resist gazing around the chamber. His brain immediately registered the value of this find to the Church. Two million was a mere bagatelle in comparison.

Finally the Cardinal returned to the business at hand. "Are you all right, Mr. LaPretre?"

"Yes, I am," Nestor said firmly.

"Do you have all your documents with you?"

"I have them here." Nestor pointed to his shoulder bag.

Bettini placed the satchel of money on the ground in front of Mitch. "And here is the money. Count it if you like, but you will find it all there, unmarked as requested. Now if you will please release Mr. LaPretre and guide us out of here, we will be on our way." His voice carried throughout the cavern. Another voice joined in, an echo travelling back around the curved wall, something out of a nightmare.

"Not quite yet, Cardinal," said the voice. From a large alcove on the far side a man walked across the dusty floor and up the steps to the cross, where he stopped, his face glowing under one of the lights.

"Hugo!" Bettini uttered the name like an expletive. "But . . . you're dead!"

"You *thought* I was. You'd best make sure next time, Angostura."

Bettini remained silent, his brain racing for an explanation, a solution.

"What, no cries of happiness? Well I can't blame you for that. After all, the last time we met I was very impolite. I actually had the temerity to give you the finger," and Hugo held up his left hand. "Now, will you," and Hugo pointed to Mitch, "guard the entrance, and you," indicating the masked guard, "escort the lady and Mr. LaPretre to the other side of this church. Cardinal Bettini and I have a personal matter to settle."

CHAPTER TWENTY-SIX

JETTATORI: THE EVIL EYE

FINN MAHONEY WAITED in another farm house on the table land atop the cliffs surrounding the rock quarry. One of the Italian custodians of the catacomb waited with him. He would have liked to be in the cavern below watching the action, but he had a different role to play. Having originally kidnapped Nestor, Finn was now going to come to his rescue. The plan required him to appear to be above reproach later, so now he must play the part of the good Samaritan. From all reports, the plan was working so far. Finn was glad that his old friend Brian Kelleher had been left out of the equation.

Finn didn't ordinarily care who won any contest, unless he had money riding on the outcome. But this time he hoped Hugo Payne would kick the living shit out of Bettini—so that a partnership between Azusipa Dionusos and the Vatican could be realized. If that didn't happen, then Nestor would be free to deal Naturcept as he saw fit. And since LaPretre had exhausted all other sources of funding, Finn knew he'd have to deal with Azusipa.

The drug companies were going to have to position themselves for a difficult future, given the global changes to medical practices. It was no longer a matter of providing pills, powders, and potions for profit, but one of managing health-care. The control of a contraceptive panacea would provide massive profits for many years; Finn was sure that Naturcept would soon be at the forefront of the population control movement.

Mahoney got up to pour himself another coffee. If Bettini were to win, he couldn't be allowed to go without paying his debts and clearing his accounts with his Maker. The very capable Mitch Peden, Finn knew, might have to extend *quietus* to the Cardinal, and discharge him from his earthly obligations of office.

Finn decided he wouldn't dwell on that scenario for long—it posed far too many problems. Bettini's agents were still in the cemetery, and if the Cardinal failed to return. . . . And while the custodians who guarded the catacombs had been well-paid for accommodating Azusipa, they believed they were getting the ransom money, a fortune to them, in exchange for their participation. The Gypsy band had not yet realized that careful exploitation of the religious treasure trove in the cavern of the cross could bring in more money than they could ever fathom. Finn shook his head slowly as he thought of the great fortune awaiting the right entrepreneurial spirit.

Sometime soon Bettini's troopers, and later the Roman police, would swarm the whole area. Finn suspected that the Gypsy guards would prefer to disappear with their two million as quickly as possible and head for the hills, rather than risk a gunfight. And by that time, he and Mitch, he hoped, would have the opportunity to emulate the caretakers of the Cavern.

Kelleher sat in his office and anxiously awaited the return of Cardinal Bettini and Charlotte, now long overdue from their mission to free Nestor LaPretre. Something had gone exceedingly wrong. His radio contact with Bettini had suddenly failed and he had no idea where to send reinforcements. He'd hung around the sacristy for a time, but soon realized the futility of waiting there.

Too nervous to sit, Brian began to pace the office, his mind reeling with recent events. After several minutes, he stopped walking long enough to call Opus Dei headquarters. They hadn't heard from the Cardinal, nor had the limousine returned to the car pool.

The Monsignor continued his nervous perambulation, staring at the floor, his hands behind his back. He had always been devout, taking his faith for granted. But now his thoughts were disconcerting, alternating between fear and excitement. Could this be the beginning of what was euphemistically referred to as a "crisis of faith"?

And what of Charlotte Lockwood? Surely the seeds of doubt had been within him long before he met her. But as a man of the cloth, he must be beyond, above, carnal thoughts.

At one time she would have been considered a jettatori, a person endowed with the evil eye. He knew it was crazy, but somehow he'd have to come to terms with what frightened him.

He remembered the case of Cardinal Danielou and Mimi Santoni. In Paris in 1979, Cardinal Jean Danielou, the author of forty religious books, was found dead in the home of a nightclub stripper. He was sixty-nine and she was twenty-four. The police found a great deal of cash in his clothes, and believed he had died of a ruptured blood vessel. Neither the police nor Church authorities would disclose any other details. His friends came forward to state that he had been trying to guide Mimi to salvation, and was assisting her financially. The Vatican file contained opinions on the case which Brian had read, but only God would really know what happened. And Mimi, of course—which in that case would mean that Mimi knew as much as God.

Brian realized that his situation paled in comparison. He also knew that very few women in the Church's history had ever had any decision-making power or influence in the papal administration. The only exceptions he could think of were Queen Christina of Sweden in the 1650s; Lucrezia Borgia, daughter of Pope Alexander VI; and Catherine of Sienna. Not a long list. He wondered if perhaps Charlotte wielded more influence than he knew, had somehow been sent to test his faith. The Monsignor took a little white book, the *Cameno*, from his desk drawer. He felt a need to review some of the nine hundred ninety-nine spiritual maxims designed to help one achieve perfection. It encouraged austerity, physical and emotional health, and humility, while urging the reader to strive for leadership. It was the handbook of Opus Dei.

Tiring of the platitudes with which he was overly familiar, and finding no answers or comfort, Kelleher again called Opus Dei headquarters and talked to his administrative counterpart, only to find that, no, Bettini had still not returned. Nor had he sent any messages. The limousine was also still missing.

Kelleher glanced at his watch—nine-thirty p.m. They had been gone since early afternoon and had not expected to be more than a few hours.

Brian reached for the Naturcept/LaPretre file and placed it in the centre of his desk. What information would next be entered?

✧ ✧ ✧

In the cavern, the guard did as he had been instructed by Hugo. He nudged Charlotte towards Nestor, then ushered the two of them across the underground cathedral to the portal between the panels of the Old Testament and the gladiator alcove. Nestor grimaced each time he stepped on his left foot.

Once in the dark passage, they travelled for what seemed a great distance. Charlotte was not pleased with her fading flashlight, nor the coolness for which she was not dressed. The nun's habit would have been both warmer and more appropriate. Talons of fear clutched her.

Charlotte, Nestor, and the guard finally stopped before a vacant cubicula with pillars at the entrance and stone seats along each side. A large vault beside them indicated that the deceased must have been a martyr of some rank, someone in the ancient history of the early Christians.

Charlotte shivered, but whether from fear, the cold, or something else, she wasn't sure. Nestor clumsily put an arm around her as they sat on one of the benches, their contact both comforting and warming.

The guard lit several candles mounted on the walls. "This might provide some heat," he said. "If not, you can always pray. I'm going back to the cavern."

"Wait, I'm coming back with you," said Nestor. He didn't want to miss whatever spectacle he knew would be forthcoming. After all, a lot was riding on it.

"And leave me here alone?" asked Charlotte, her voice as cold as the tomb.

Nestor held her firmly by the shoulders. "Yes. Something of great importance is about to happen. We need you to stay here." His authoritative tone surprised her.

She tried again. "You'd leave me here alone? In spite of. . . ." The steely determination she saw in Nestor's eyes stopped her cold.

"I have to," he said, quickly pulling off his jacket and throwing it around her shoulders. "A friend will be here for you soon."

Nestor, Finn, and Mitch had decided that Charlotte must be made to believe that Finn was a friendly rescuer who could not be linked with the kidnappers. Otherwise she might prove to be more of a hindrance than a help. Better to have her think the Gypsies were the culprits—they had always made good scapegoats.

"If not, I'll be back myself. Hang on just a little longer."

Nestor and the guard walked away. Charlotte was left on the stone bench, shivering in the tomb of the unknown Christian, with only the smoky light of the sputtering candles for company. She thought about lighting more candles against the cold and the infernal dread that was all around her. But the candle supply was almost gone.

Her mind began to play tricks on her; the flickering shadows incited her imagination. She recalled tales of novitiates at night in the dormitories of the convent; visions of Dracula, demons inhabiting the bodies of men and women. There could be plenty revenants here, she thought, where all was night. Apparitions are not always seen, but can be felt and heard. She was tired and afraid.

As Charlotte sat waiting, listening, her fear gradually began to take a different form. Why, she wondered, had she been left in this damp to sit passively while the world went on without her? Was she not one of God's children too, worthy of taking part? Her anger grew. She felt she had been relegated to the role of handmaiden and vowed never to let herself be put in this position again.

Looking around, Charlotte considered finding her way out of the catacombs. She mentally tried to retrace her steps, to remember the route they had come, but the twists and turns, ascents and descents of the many passageways they had traversed confused her. Even if there were enough candles to light her way, the chances of her getting out were slim. She was more likely to become forever lost in the labyrinthine underworld of the dead.

Resigned, Charlotte wrapped her arms around her knees and began to rock back and forth. As her thoughts wandered, a scene popped into her mind. She recalled the inception of the new Catholic catechism, inaugurated by the Vatican under Pope John Paul II in 1990. The point of discussion was birth control. A woman—pale, sickly, emaciated—asked a question of the presiding priest. "I am thirty years old, Father, married, and have five children already. The rhythm method doesn't work. My doctor says having more children may kill me. If I must use more efficient methods of contraception, what attitude does the Church take?" And the priest answered, "To do so would be no less than prostitution." The woman had stood motionless for a moment, looking as if he had struck her a physical blow. Then, before she turned and walked from the room, she said, "In that case, Father, how much should I charge my husband?" Charlotte smiled at the memory.

Why had this come to mind? Charlotte wondered. Was her faith failing her, just as the priest's reply to the unfortunate woman had been a slap in the face, a diminishment of her soul? She knew such thoughts were contrary to her avowed acceptance of Church beliefs and utter anathema to Opus Dei. But surely in this sacred place, all thoughts were induced by God.

On the cliffs above, Finn let himself through a small trap door in the pantry floor of the ancient farmhouse. He aimed a small light as he made his way down the winding stairwell and along the passage. At the first left turn he could see a faint glow in the distance. That vault could be the last resting place of Matthew, Mark, Luke, John, or James—no one would ever know. Charlotte was there now.

How was he going to approach her from out of the sepulchral Stygian murk? Any sound would alarm her. The light from the dimly gleaming tapers threw flickering shadows along the passage.

"Charlotte Lockwood," he said in a low voice.

She heard her name and her heart stopped. She looked toward the entrance.

"Don't be frightened," said Finn quickly, stepping out of the dark into the small chamber.

Charlotte could not see Finn clearly, but she faced the unknown and asked, "For God's sake, who are you?"

"A friend. Nestor sent me."

Charlotte forced a smile, hugging herself again to contain her tremors.

"You know, I think I know whose tomb this must have been," said Finn. "St. Anthony's. You probably don't know about him, do you? But if this is his grave, he'll certainly think you are a ghost."

Charlotte's shoulders dropped. "Why would he think that?" she asked.

"Because he suffered temptation in his search for godliness. He was pursued by and was susceptible to women; in particular a beautiful redhead who, he maintained, always tried to seduce him. He'll think you are that ghost."

"You're joking . . . but thank you," Charlotte said, smiling easily now, "for relieving the tension."

"No, I'm not joking. That's the knock they put on Anthony. Nestor tells me that you are something of a theologian, but perhaps you never went for saint psychology. Personally I think Anthony suffered from suppressed sexual desires which he had banished to his unconscious. After all, he was the founder of Christian Monasticism and he likely never had sex. But that is irrelevant. I'm here to lead you out of this dank dungeon of the dead. Leave the lights on for St. Anthony."

Finn offered Charlotte his hand, which she ignored, following him with a firm step and head held high. Her senses were more alert than ever.

CHAPTER TWENTY-SEVEN

MORITORI SALUTANT

BETTINI REGAINED HIS SPEECH. "Just how do you propose we settle this matter, Mr. Hugo?"

"Simple—a primitive but time-honoured method—Trial by Combat."

"Surely you jest."

"No. There is no judge, no jury, here. Only the dead, some of whom likely perished under similar circumstances. Trial by combat is more than you offered me. So I am throwing down the gauntlet."

Fighting in a gladiatorial amphitheatre had been imposed upon the early Christians because of alleged sacrilege, imposed because of their apparently anarchistic, anti-social, treasonable refusal to pay homage to the Emperor of Rome. They would not pledge earthly allegiance to the Emperor, preferring defiance and a steadfast belief in their own God and Jesus Christ. Bettini was now in such an arena and a duel was being imposed upon him, a modern Christian, in much the same manner.

"Why should I consent?" Bettini asked.

"I'll tell you why, Cardinal. We dined together, which is the gladiatorial custom before a fight. But the most compelling reason for you to consent is this: by the laws of the Roman Gladiators, if you choose not to fight, then you are declared the loser. And when the thumbs go down, the loser is executed."

Bettini thought for a long moment. "I'm older; you have the advantage."

"Not so, Cardinal. I'm weaker, thanks to you. I'd advise you to say, 'I am ready to defend myself with my body,' the time-honoured reply of the gladiators."

Realizing that Hugo was serious, Angostura again took a long time to reply. "What of the winner?"

"He walks out of here with Nestor LaPretre and anything that came with him."

"And the two million dollars?"

"My deal with the kidnappers precludes that as a prize. It goes to them when the fight is finished. They'd likely kill you for it anyway, so you can consider it a life insurance premium."

Bettini wasn't ready to commit himself. He tried desperately to think of a way out.

"You have no choice, Cardinal, except that of weapons. The Priory of Sion offered you a deal, but you wouldn't accept it. You refuse to espouse a Christian attitude to our proposition. Be a man. Honour the five wounds of God, who will give the victory to him who is in the right. A harsh way to settle anything—but effective as hell. Otherwise, remember, it's thumbs down!"

Realizing that he was indeed trapped, Bettini shouted, "May you roast in Hell forever, Hugo, you dog of the devil. Name the weapons. You have harassed me for the last time."

"Follow me. And don't try anything; the guards won't let you out. They won't interfere because they don't give a damn who wins."

The men walked over to the gladiator alcove. Hugo, Finn, and Mitch had managed to salvage the materials required to outfit one myrmello and one retiarius gladiator. These lay on opposite sides of the alcove.

"Heads or tails, call it in the air," Hugo said, flipping the coin at the ceiling, "for first choice."

As it started to fall, Bettini said, "Heads." The coin hit the sand. Bettini had won.

He looked from one outfit to the other for several moments, finally choosing the heavier, defense-oriented armour and weaponry of the myrmello. They dressed in silence. Bettini took longer to don the heavy paraphernalia. He was thankful for the regular workouts which had left him in good physical condition.

After indicating their readiness, the men squared off on opposite sides of the gladiatorial alcove.

"Do you recall the gladiator's salute to the Emperor?" asked Hugo.

"I believe I do," answered Bettini. "We'll make it to the cross." They raised their right hands and cried, "*Ave, imperator, moritori te salutant!*" Their weapons held high, the words echoed around the chamber: "Hail, Emperor, greetings from men about to die!"

The Cardinal then added quietly, "Or not."

Hugo smiled at Bettini's confidence. They began to circle one another, waiting for an opening.

Bettini chose to move in so that Hugo would have no room to throw his net. Hugo was poorly equipped for a slugging match, so he shied away from Bettini's charges. The Cardinal managed to get close enough for several swings of the broad sword, which Hugo fended off with his trident before stepping back.

The best thing to do, Bettini figured, would be to work Hugo into a corner, but there were no corners here. Hugo twirled his net like a lariat, preparing to throw and entangle Bettini.

Bettini, conserving his strength and breath as best he could, worked his way to the alcove in which the statues of the gladiators stood.

He stood in front of the alcove catching his breath. Neither man was used to the extreme exertion. Hugo threw his net, imagining the entangled Bettini with a dagger at his throat. At the last second the Cardinal leaped back into the recess, and the net struck the overhead arch. Jumping quickly out of the alcove, Bettini moved to attack with his swinging sword. Hugo parried the heavy blow with an upraised forearm. The force of the stroke numbed his whole arm, all but penetrating the heavy leather guard.

Bettini now had the advantage, for he was able to parry Hugo's trident thrusts with his shield, without having to worry about the net. They were wearing each other out. Hugo's chest wound had begun to bleed. Bettini had Hugo on the run. As they circled the arena Hugo managed to retrieve his net, but used up much of the energy he had left.

Like a dogfight in slow motion, Hugo thought vaguely, as he saw 37mm flak gently rising to meet him. With renewed energy Hugo moved away from Bettini as he spread the net into its throwing position, then slowed to let Bettini close the gap. Hugo banked left across the centre of the cavern, jumped up onto the steps leading to the cross, and dove down the other side. Bettini was on his tail. Hugo went into a stall turn, twirling the net above his head. Bettini dove down the steps after him. Hugo threw the net. It arched over the Cardinal's rushing body and began to fall on him when an edge caught on the crucifix and the net fell sideways to the right. Bettini veered out of danger. Saved by the cross.

Hugo yanked on the net, but it was caught fast.

The Cardinal hurried across the steps, his broad sword poised to strike. Hugo braced himself, his trident thrust forward. The two weapons met with a metallic clash that echoed off the walls of the amphitheatre. The shield flew from Bettini's grasp; Hugo's trident fell to the arena floor. Hugo threw up his armour-protected left forearm to ward off another blow. Bettini swivelled his hips, dropped his shoulder, and thrust under Hugo's guard.

The blade entered Hugo's side just above his protective belt and below the bullet wound. As Hugo fell, the Cardinal, an evil glint in his eye, delivered a sharp kick to Hugo's groin. Hugo tumbled backward down the dais onto the cavern's sandy floor.

The sword still in his side, Hugo lay writhing in pain at the bottom of the steps. The outstretched arms of the cross seemed to gather him in. Bettini, several steps above Hugo and nearing exhaustion himself, fumbled for the dagger in his belt. Enraged now, all vestiges of sportsmanship gone, Bettini savoured victory. His shadow enveloped the prostrate form below him.

Lying on his good side, Hugo had a view of the Resurrection scene. He saw with great clarity the face of Jesus Christ, although the lights were as dim as Hugo's prospects of survival. But two quirks of fate conspired to give him one slim chance.

Jesus appeared to him as if illuminated by a bright light. The newly resurrected Christ urged Hugo to his feet with upturned hands. Hugo heard Bettini cry, "*Christus vincit, Christus regnat, Christus imperat!*"—Christ conquers, Christ reigns, Christ rules!

Hugo's right hand found the butt of the trident and he struggled to his knees. Grasping the shaft with his other hand, he swung the sharp-pointed trident toward the ceiling just as Cardinal Angostura Bettini rushed down the steps with the dagger before him. Too late, Bettini saw the three sharp prongs swing up to meet his forward momentum. As Angostura felt the pressure against his chest, Hugo, with every bit of strength he could muster, dove forward and upward, crying, "Begone! I Conceal the Secrets of God!" The Priory of Sion had struck in earnest.

Borne up and backward by the surging Hugo Payne, Bettini slammed into the upright portion of the cross, the trident points coming to rest deep in the old wood.

His head flung back, the last thing Bettini saw was the scene of the Last Judgment on the ceiling of the cavern, the Apostles gazing down. In his final moment, he might have hoped to see their thumbs raised and a waving of handkerchiefs, but Romans had always been hard on a gladiator who valued his life too highly: *No quarter for the fallen, whoever he may be.*

His Eminence hung like a skewered vulture, his faith fallen about him in ruin.

Only Hugo could hear Cardinal Bettini's last muttered words: "The law of God is abased and the Devil exalted. So help me God and his Saints."

Hugo, barely alive, was sitting at the foot of the cross. Blood oozed from his side and trickled down the steps. A poem by Charles Peguy, part of the Priory's arcane legend, popped into his head.

The arms of Jesus are the Cross of Lorraine,
Both the blood in the artery and the blood in the vein,
Both the source of grace and the clear fountain . . .

He struggled to look around the chamber of worship and death, Bettini's blood running down the cross to mix with his own. As Mitch and Nestor came quickly to his aid, the next verse played out in his mind.

The arms of Satan are the Cross of Lorraine,
And the same artery and the same vein,
And the same blood and the troubled fountain. . . .

CHAPTER TWENTY-EIGHT

CAMILLE NAVONA

NESTOR RUSHED FROM ONE SIDE of the arena, Mitch from the other. Hugo lay at the foot of the cross.

"We're going to have to pull out that sword," Mitch said.

"Let's loosen this harness and belt," Nestor suggested.

"Hold it," gasped Hugo through clenched teeth. "That might not be a good idea. The harness may be holding my guts in place."

"Right . . . we'll leave the harness on," said Mitch. "I'll get the first-aid equipment," and he took off across the cavern.

"What about Bettini?" asked Hugo.

Nestor felt for the Cardinal's pulse. "He won't be bothering anyone any more," he said, turning back to Hugo, shaking his head. "That was quite a fight, but I wouldn't have given a plugged nickel for your chances." Nestor slowly took in the scene: a man dying at his feet and a Cardinal pinned to a cross with a gladiator's trident. He turned as pale as the death all around him and slumped to the steps. This was *his* doing, he realized—all because of Naturcept.

"A deal's a deal, Nestor," Hugo whispered. "He would have done the same thing to you, I assure you."

Mitch came back with a first-aid kit. "Bite on this to ease the pain," he urged, handing Hugo a piece of leather, "because when I pull out this sword it is going to hurt like hell." Hugo's face twisted into a grimace as the steel slid out of the wound. After raising Hugo to a sitting position, Nestor and Mitch wadded squares of gauze into the wound and bound him tight around the middle.

"You two make a fireman's chair with your hands and wrists," Mitch pointed to Nestor and the guard. Mitch helped Hugo settle into position as gently as he could. "Now let's get going. I've got the flashlight and the money; let's get out of here."

"I could carry the money and the light, señor, and you could carry your friend," the Gypsy guard said.

"No dice, Vito. You'll get paid off at the top as we planned. Once we get an hour's head start you can do a bunco too. All that Bettini's hoods will be looking for is the Cardinal, and that's all they'll find. Eventually, if ever," said Mitch.

"When they find the cavern," Hugo spoke slowly, "they'll be looking for a murderer, too."

"Yes," replied Mitch, "but we'll be far away by then."

As they carried Hugo along the dark passages, Nestor said, "You need a doctor. And soon."

"I know," Hugo muttered. "Take me to the hospital at St. Bartholomew's on the Isola Tiberna."

"Why there?" asked Nestor.

"The brothers helped me before. . . ." Hugo said, his voice fading.

As they passed the small empty chamber where one lone candle still burned, Mitch said, "It's only another fifty yards." He pushed them as fast as they could travel. At a short flight of stairs only wide enough for two, Mitch went first, opening the trap door into the farmhouse. The Italian in the kitchen helped carry Hugo into the pantry. Mitch kept right on going, urging the others to do the same. It was dark outside as he guided them to the van silhouetted against the night sky.

Finn jumped out of the van and helped Nestor and Mitch load Hugo into the back. With Charlotte's help, they settled him onto a mattress, where he lay, pale and gasping. Finn propped some old blankets under his head. "See if he can stand a shot from that brandy bottle," he said to Charlotte, "and then give him some water." He handed her a canteen.

Mitch and Finn hurried back into the farmhouse. They paid off the Gypsies, less Finn's ten percent commission. Back at the van, Mitch jumped behind the wheel, Charlotte got into the passenger seat, and Nestor and Finn climbed into the back with Hugo. "Hang on, here we go," Mitch called loudly into the night air as they started down a rutted track in the steep hillside.

When they reached the rough but flat back roads, Hugo groaned. Forgive the pilot, thought Hugo, as he lay in the back of the van, for he knows not what he does. He was thankful for the smoother ride when the vehicle got onto the paved road that led into Rome.

They drove along the Lungotevere, eventually coming to the Ponte Cestio and crossing onto Isola Tiberna and the church and hospital complex of St. Bartholomew.

"You know the flight plan; you'll do your best to see that this bombing run gets finished?" Hugo asked Finn, who was supporting his head and shoulders in the back of the van.

"You were going to be part of it. That's what we figured. But you're in no shape. Fighting Bettini wasn't necessary."

"Maybe I just wanted one more dogfight. Something about do unto others, but give 'em a fair chance," Hugo said hoarsely.

"You gobshite. Look, there's going to be some questions asked. Nobody can connect Azusipa with this, except Nestor, and he won't say anything. If his pitch to the Pope doesn't work, he and I have worked out a very good deal. But we have to keep a low profile for the present. And I've got to tell you, I hope you make it."

"I can't trust you, Finn, but I know I have to."

"You just said the magic words. I hate nice things said about me. Gives people the wrong impression."

"My contact at St. Bart's," said Hugo, "is Friar Ambrose, who works in the hospital administration. Don't involve him in anything. He saved my life twice before."

"Got it," replied Finn, "and we'll get Nestor to the Pope, like we planned. Don't sweat it, I've still got one ace up my sleeve, boyo."

Hugo looked at Finn, but had no energy left to speak. Mitch pulled the van as close to the service entrance of the hospital as possible. Finn opened the back doors and Hugo slid gingerly through, placed his feet on the ground and slowly stood. He began to shuffle toward the entrance he had left not so long ago. He wondered if he could make it to Friar Ambrose's office. He wondered if he could make it at all.

After getting through the door he knew he wasn't going to last. It's a gut feeling, he thought, and smiled to himself. In his gladiator's tunic and heavy bandaging and supporting himself against the wall, he moved down the hallway. A string of ruby drops marked his progress along the white marble, leading toward the room of Camille Navona. She was still there, repeating her plaintive cry, "Come back, please come back."

Hugo entered her room and leaned against the foot of the bed. "I'm back, love," he said, his voice husky with strain and emotion. "I'm back for good this time. You can stop crying now. You know I always loved you."

Her cries ceased. Recognition lit her eyes as she feebly raised her emaciated arms. "Take me out of here, Antonio. Take me with you, please."

"I will, Camille." Her words seemed to infuse him with strength. Hugo moved to her side. Removing one of her pillows, he bent down and kissed her on the forehead. For a fleeting moment, he saw his grandmother's gentle, smiling face.

"Thank you, Tony," she murmured.

As Hugo pulled back from her embrace he pressed the pillow down over her face. He held it there for what seemed like an eternity until he fell across her, the pillow still in place.

When Guiseppe followed the drops of blood down the hallway into Camille Navona's room, he found a Roman gladiator lying across her body. He recognized Hugo's features and ran to find Friar Ambrose.

CHAPTER TWENTY-NINE

UPON A MIDNIGHT DREARY

MITCH CONTINUED ALONG the Tiber until he reached the Via della Conciliazione, the graceful boulevard which led to the Piazza St. Pietra and the Citto del Vaticano. He skirted the square, looking for the Gate of St. Anne to the north of St. Peter's Square, the tradesmen's entrance to the Papal State. Charlotte, Finn, and Nestor would enter on foot. If challenged at the administration office, Charlotte, who was known there, would vouch for Finn and Nestor.

Charlotte was sure they wouldn't run into any serious obstacles once past the outer office. After all, she had brought Nestor to see the Pope. That is what Cardinal Bettini of Opus Dei had implied was the reason for the trip. If Cardinal Bettini or Opus Dei had been lying, that was their problem. It was time, she knew, to think for herself. If there were faults in her Church, she would try to change them. The odds were against her, she knew, because the Church had always been against the voice of women. Opus Dei was even worse.

Hugo had explained to Finn how to get in and out of Vatican City and the Apostolic Palace. Not many knew the myriad of convoluted passages in the rambling edifice. The Priory of Sion kept close watch on the Vatican, its environs, its denizens, and its security system. This came in handy now. The plan called for a confidential visit with Monsignor Brian Kelleher, private secretary to the recently deceased Secretary of State of the Vatican.

Having successfully entered by St. Anne's Gate and negotiated a few of the intricacies of the Vatican, Finn, Nestor, and Charlotte waited quietly in a wild patch of garden within the Vatican grounds near the Apostolic Palace. In the daytime the garden was noisy with the sound of birds, a sanctuary for sparrows and warblers in the midst of a metropolis; at night it was the habitat of prowling Vatican cats in search of avian prey.

They watched for the Swiss security guards who patrolled the grounds, waiting until they met, talked, and turned again to their assigned routes. Immediately the three slipped through the gap left by the guard's departure, and into the precincts of the Palace. They quietly traversed back stairwells and vacant night-time areas to the offices recently occupied by the late Cardinal Bettini.

The rap at the door gave Brian Kelleher quite a start. At first he thought of the Cardinal, but realized the Cardinal would never knock. Kelleher approached the door with caution. When the gentle tapping was repeated, he flung open the door. Charlotte, in a disheveled raincoat, stood facing him squarely, hands in her pockets. Behind her stood Nestor LaPretre and a pudgy man with a round, smooth, smiling face and a sardonic look in his eyes. He seemed vaguely familiar to Brian.

"May we enter your sanctum sanctorum, Brian?" the man asked.

"We have much to tell you," Charlotte interjected. "May we come in?"

"Where is Cardinal Bettini?" Kelleher wanted to know.

"He is dead in the catacombs, Father Brian," Nestor said.

There was a long silence. Kelleher squeezed his eyes shut in disbelief. Dead in the catacombs? Dear Holy Mother of God, how could that be? he thought as he ushered the three in and closed the door behind them.

"And one of the kidnappers may be dead, too. The rest are gone," Charlotte continued. "It's been a terrible night."

Stumbling towards his desk, Kelleher tried to make sense of what he'd heard. "In the catacombs? What . . . why? . . ." He clutched his way around the desk and sank into the chair.

"Yes . . . the catacombs. We can talk about them later," said Charlotte.

The Cardinal was dead. What was he to do now, Father Kelleher wondered. He felt lost, unnerved. LaPretre was here, but they had lost Bettini.

"May I make a suggestion, Brian?" the stranger asked.

Kelleher's head jerked up. The stranger's familiarity angered him momentarily—there hadn't yet been time for introductions. "How do you know my name?" he snapped.

"Because that's what I used to call you."

"This is Finn Mahoney, Monsignor Kelleher," said Nestor, making the introduction. "He helped me escape from the kidnappers."

The name pierced his brain like a driven nail. His mind flashed back to Dublin, the Parochial School of St. James Gate, where the River Liffey flows.

"Faith and bejasus," Finn boomed, grinning widely, "and don't you recognize me, Brian? I don't blame you a-tall, a-tall. I've let myself go entirely." Finn stretched out a hand across the desk.

Brian took it, dazed, staring intently at Finn. "I see it now, yes, I see it now. . . . It's been a long time, Finn, and a couple of oceans. You went to America, I remember."

"Yes, that *was* a long time ago," said Finn. "When Ms. Lockwood mentioned your name, I knew it had to be you." Finn turned to the others. "We were schoolmates in Ireland. Never thought we'd meet here. I guess every hair on your head did turn into a candle, Brian, to light your way to heaven."

"Same old Finn. I see you've never stopped talking warm words on a cold evening. It is good to see you, but we have serious business before us. What is your suggestion?"

"We must see the Pope. Soon. Get us an audience." Finn watched Kelleher's face.

The Monsignor nodded absently as he gathered his thoughts. The Pope was in charge, was he not, by divine authority? Indeed, now that Cardinal Bettini, the Secretary of State and second-in-command, was gone, there appeared to be no other course of action. Cesare Romereo was certainly in charge of Vatican business until he appointed a new Secretary of State.

"Are you still a religious man, Finn?" Kelleher asked.

"Ah, well . . . we can leave that for another time. Right now we must tell the Pope about Bettini. And we have other business to discuss with him."

"Oh?" Brian was pretty sure he knew what that business might be, but he wanted them to spell it out for him.

"As you know," Nestor began as Finn nodded to him, "I came at the Cardinal's request to talk about Naturcept. With the Cardinal gone, that is up to you."

Brian knew that it was, but he also knew now that Bettini had never intended LaPretre to see the Pope. He walked to the window and gazed out into the blackness. The role of leader was being thrust upon him by unavoidable circumstances.

"I see you have a file on your desk with my name and that of Naturcept," Nestor continued.

"I was about to go over it while I waited for Cardinal Bettini," said Kelleher, who was still trying to absorb the reality of Bettini's death, "but I know what is there. The most recent material is what Sister Charlotte brought." Brian glanced at Charlotte, and turned back to Nestor.

"The file also contains whatever background history the Curia could find on you, as well as the correspondence between you and the Cardinal," the Monsignor said. "There were some private instructions to Charlotte Lockwood and to the administration in Montreal; but that would be in an Opus Dei file."

Charlotte cleared her throat. "His Eminence wanted to help Nestor," she said. "Why else would the Cardinal have risked his own life to rescue him?" She looked around at the three men. None of them met her gaze. "Certainly he would want Nestor to see the Pope without him. I know you can arrange it, Brian." She smiled confidently at him.

"It's true then, that Bettini indicated to LaPretre that the Vatican might endorse a method of birth control comprised of natural substances?" asked Finn, pressing the matter.

Brian paused. Privately he had grave doubts, but that was the implication in Bettini's letter. "That is true," he said. "It seemed a big step, but apparently that is what they were going to do. So, yes, I can set up a papal audience. I'll see Pope Cesare's Chamberlain immediately and arrange a time for an audience and discussion that I'm sure the Cardinal must have planned. The whole matter has to be placed before Pope Cesare. But Cardinal Bettini's death must be dealt with first and that I must do alone. I'll see you all tomorrow." Monsignor Kelleher, now in control, ushered them out of the office and closed the door.

CHAPTER THIRTY

ILLS THAT FLESH IS HEIR TO . . .

A CALVACADE OF FIVE SECURITY vehicles, marked with the insignia of the State della Cittia de Vaticano, proceeded out of the Vatican, through St. Peter's Square, past the Villa Doria Pamphili, and down the Via Aurelia Antica. The vehicles were carrying Kelleher, Finn, Nestor, Charlotte, the Chief of the Papal State Security Police, and the Pope himself.

They parked in a deserted rock quarry. Finn, Nestor, and Charlotte led Kelleher, the Chief, and several officers into the catacomb. A short time later, wide-eyed with bafflement and wonder, the Chief returned to inform the Pope that the Rome police would have to be called in. The Vatican's top Cardinal had been crucified in a previously undiscovered catacomb by an unknown assailant. As if that wasn't bad enough, the Cardinal had been wearing the uniform of a Roman gladiator.

There was time for His Holiness to view the scene before the crowd of officers, reporters, and curious onlookers arrived. The Pope could do nothing for Cardinal Bettini now, but he insisted on going into the cavern to minister to the Cardinal personally. Cesare was solicitously ushered through the labyrinthine corridors of the catacomb to the great chamber. The Pope looked around with astonished reverence at the vast cavern and its elaborate adornments.

From the cross, Bettini stared down on Pope Cesare and his Chief Constable. The Cardinal's lips were drawn back over his teeth in what could best be described as a snarl.

Cesare moved to take Bettini's body from the cross, but the Chief stopped him. The Italian police would need to examine everything; nothing should be touched. But what good could come of them finding the Cardinal, the Pope's right-hand man, like this, the Chief wondered. Nothing that he could see. They could only examine what they found when they arrived. Fortuitously, the Chief thought, we got here first, and in Italy that means you call the shots.

LaPretre had told him in the car that Bettini had come to the catacomb to rescue him from some kidnappers, who had then taken the money and fled. Then why was Bettini dressed as a gladiator and crucified by means of a trident? There were ample signs that a fight had taken place: gladiatorial weaponry, lots of blood on the dais, some strips of bandage, and fresh footprints and scuff marks on the sandy floor of the arena, many of them leading to another passage in the wall of the cavern. Had there been some kind of cult ritual or devil worship? the Chief pondered. Obviously discretion was advisable, since a high churchman was involved.

The Chief decided to played his hunch. He trusted his own men, and what he'd heard from Mahoney, LaPretre, and Lockwood indicated that they'd rather not be overly involved in an investigation. Let the Pope be able to say he had personally tended to the dead body of his Secretary of State when he found him on the cross like Lord Jesus.

"All right, Your Holiness, let's do it," he said. "I'll help you."

They took Bettini's body down and laid him out on the ground. Too late for last rites, Cesare made the sign of the Cross, blessed the Cardinal, and hurriedly uttered a prayer for him. As he placed his cloak over the body, Cesare forced himself to look away from the face, whose hawklike features held a suggestion of the demimonde, and whose dead staring eyes seemed to be watching him closely, as they had always done in life.

Cesare left the Chief to his police chores and walked to the perimeter of the cavern. He took the time to closely examine each painting and artifact. Extremely impressed, he decided he would hold a memorial service for the Cardinal right here where he had died. Perhaps it would be fitting if he never left this sacred place and was buried here. The Cardinal would have liked that, the Pope thought.

During this preliminary investigation, Finn Mahoney stayed in the background. He remarked that in the long run, humanity is only capable of mistakes; rejecting truth, believing falsehoods. Nestor nodded in agreement.

The next day, news of Bettini's death swamped newpapers, radio, and television around the world. Each story was filled with conjecture as to what had really happened in the dark cavern of the cross. Police reports and interviews ran beside articles on the history of the catacomb and the remains of the priceless artwork.

Finn Mahoney read and listened to most of the media reports. Apart from describing the facts of the situation as the police had found it and attempting to exploit those facts, no one came close to the real story. Nor did anyone have any idea who had kidnapped LaPretre, whom Bettini had allegedly been trying rescue. The Gypsies were easy targets to blame, but every grisly rumour was raised, from the return of the Borgias to the poisoning of Popes. Some tried to implicate the CIA, the PLO, or the Libyans; one reporter speculated that the Red Brigade and the Aldo Moro killers might be involved.

Although Finn refused to be interviewed, he did speculate to *La Sola* that the cross in the cavern may indeed be the one upon which Christ was crucified, if records showing how it had been brought to Rome could be found. Being who he was, Finn like to contribute to the mythology of religion whenever he could.

Charlotte Lockwood *was* willing to talk. Too much, in Finn's opinion, but she had been the intermediary between Bettini and the kidnappers, whom she could not identify because they had been masked. Nor could she give a good description of the man presumed to have killed the Cardinal. Charlotte had nothing but praise for Nestor, who was reported as being a leading figure in the world's scientific community.

The Vatican's own radio services, including *L'Osservatore Romano*, reported that Cardinal Angostura Bettini, Secretary of the Vatican State, had been found dead, believed to have been murdered by persons unknown, in a newly discovered catacomb off the Via Aurelia Antica near Rome. His Eminence had apparently been lured to the site by criminals who had kidnapped one Nestor LaPretre, a Canadian Catholic scientist who had come to Rome for consultations with Cardinal Bettini. The news anchor went on to say that the brave Cardinal had gone to rescue his friend, bearing ransom money. In the ensuing events, currently under investigation, Cardinal Bettini had been killed in a brutal fashion—pinned to a large wooden cross of the type used in crucifixions. The criminals had escaped, but Mr. LaPretre was safe.

The report concluded with the statement that Cardinal Bettini was undoubtedly in the same category as the early Christian martyrs, and according to Pope Cesare, was likely to be considered for sainthood.

The Vatican media closed ranks and said little more, leaving sensationalism to the civilian press. When that died down, as it eventually would, then a more rational explanation could be constructed by the Vatican public relations machine.

The long awaited conference with the Pope finally took place a week later. After solicitously welcoming his guests and pouring tea, Pope Cesare turned to Nestor and asked him to begin.

Nestor began with a description of Naturcept and its plant base, but soon realized that the technical terminology he was using was incomprehensible to his audience. His presentation was foundering. The Pope smiled at Nestor's embarrassment. "My son," the Pope said calmly, "perhaps it would be better if you simply tell me a story—from beginning to end. Then I'll ask questions. Are you comfortable with that?"

"Yes, Your Holiness," Nestor answered, relieved. "Thank you."

Nestor began again, describing briefly his early life and what motivated him to study plant genetics. He told of his years of discovery, research, and experimentation, his voice rising as he went along. Finally, Nestor spoke of the rare plants he had found in the rainforest of South America, and the many combinations he had tested before he was certain he had an ideal, natural, form of birth control.

At this point, Cesare slowly raised his hand. Nestor stopped in mid-sentence. "I apologize, Your Holiness," he said, clasping his hands in his lap, "for my obsession. I. . . ."

"It's all right," the Pope interjected. "You are one of the few who have been fortunate enough to experience the Eureka Effect. You *have* been blessed, Nestor, but now I'd like to hear from Mr. Mahoney."

Less forthright than Nestor, Finn explained the role his company wanted to play in the development, promotion, and distribution of Naturcept. And although he couldn't decipher this new Pope as clearly as he'd have liked, Finn threw in some financial figures that would impress even the most dedicated ascetic. Privately, he wondered again if maybe he shouldn't skip to Switzerland to join Mitch Peden while he still had the chance.

Monsignor Kelleher was next, pointing out to the Pope that the Roman Catholic Church was virtually alone in rejecting contraception. He summarized arguments pertaining to overpopulation, poverty, and the suffering of women and children. "We must search our consciences in this matter as well as trusting our faith, Your Holiness," Brian said, "and know that we will forever have to live with our decision. There will always be opposition to change, but at what cost? The man who makes such a decision will not only show great courage, but also a deep and abiding faith in humankind. We are, after all, God's children."

Silence hung heavy in the air while the Pope stared at his desktop. Finally, he said, "Eloquently put, Monsignor, although not quite what I'd expected from you."

Then Cesare turned to Charlotte. "I'm very pleased that we meet once again, Sister Charlotte. I understand that you have become quite the honoured lecturer back in North America?"

"Not at all, Your Holiness—an exaggeration."

"Don't be so modest, my dear. I expect you're well-qualified to speak for women in the Church. And I assume, since you're here, that you have something to say?"

Charlotte hesitated, somewhat overwhelmed. She couldn't remember a time when she felt more nervous. She had to remind herself that he was, after all, just a man. "I am not noted for being a critic of Church teachings. In fact, the opposite is true. Some women devote their lives to virginity, and even after a life of chastity regard it as a special grace from God. But these are few. The majority of Catholic women, as well as all others, are very much concerned about sexual matters and more specifically, the problems of caring for children born into unfortunate circumstances."

Charlotte swallowed hard and continued. "There is a strong desire on the part of women to control their own lives, especially their reproductive lives. Although I have tried, I cannot understand why using a diaphragm is against God's will, yet inserting a thermometer in order to use the rhythm method to prevent conception is approved as being in accordance with natural law. They are both simply methods of trying to prevent conception; once you say prevention of any kind is acceptable, what is the point in arguing about which method is used? In any case, Naturcept seems to fit the requirements of natural law. Reason tells me that intellectual arguments on the matter are posturing which only serves to intensify the unvarying Church fear of all forms of sex, and of women. I've only recently come to these opinions and I hope, Your Holiness, that you will hear me out."

"Certainly, Sister. All sides must be heard in order to make an informed decision."

"My present view, and that of many other women, is that we are subjugated by the will of men. One of the factors contributing to this is the continuing ban on birth control. This has life-threatening consequences for women and children and detracts from the quality of all our lives. The practice and the teachings on sex are in a state of confusion which does no credit to the Church."

Emboldened by the sound of her own voice, Charlotte went on. "As I see it, my views are about saving our species, that is, surviving in the healthiest way possible. Birth control does not negate or diminish faith; rather, the healthier we are, the more able we are to promote the Glory of God, the Virgin Mary, and Jesus. My early Catholic experiences led me to a faith for which I am profoundly thankful, but life experience has led me toward what I hope is a more reasoned and fair religious attitude." Charlotte looked into the Pope's eyes. "I am grateful to Your Holiness for the opportunity to express my views."

"By all means. They are appreciated," the Pope replied.

Charlotte took a deep breath. "There is another matter I'd like to discuss with you, Your Holiness, of a more personal nature."

Cesare raised his eyebrows. "Yes?"

"I'm currently working on a thesis entitled The Genealogy and History of Christianity. I've recently uncovered information that indicates there are. . . ."

"Does it bear upon the matters at hand?" the Pope interrupted.

"Indirectly, perhaps, although I believe. . . . If you'd be kind enough to grant me a private audience at some time in the future. . ." she glanced at Brian, Nestor and Finn, "I would be grateful, Your Holiness."

The hopefulness in Charlotte's voice wasn't lost on Pope Cesare. "Certainly, Sister. I'll arrange a meeting in a few days." The Pontiff smiled broadly at the unlikely foursome sitting opposite him.

Nestor, Charlotte, Brian, and Finn left the papal audience together. They had been duly impressed by the sensitivity and respect the Pontiff had shown them. But in the end, Pope Cesare Romereo I would make the final decision alone.

CHAPTER THIRTY-ONE

L' EAU VIVE

I'M BUYING, BRIAN," Finn said. "Let's go find a bistro that will sell us a jar of Guinness."

Brian shook his head. "It's too early, Finn."

"Nonsense. There's no better time than the present, boyo. We haven't celebrated our reunion yet. We'll talk about old times in Dublin over a pint."

"I have duties, you know. Things are a little hectic here."

"It's not a sin, Brian, not even a venial one. It's a necessity. You've got clout in this quango. Order us one of those chauffeur-driven popemobiles and let's get out of here for a couple of hours. It can only do you good."

Finally Kelleher agreed.

They parked on a side street and Brian asked the driver to wait. He and Finn walked around a corner to a bar in the commercial section of Rome, which stocked beer from around the globe, including bottled triple X Guinness. Well and good, Finn thought as he filled their glasses with the black liquid from the Liffey.

"You don't look happy," Finn said, staring at the priest across the table. "I don't think your yin is in balance with your yang."

"You have strange ways of expressing yourself, but you are right." Brian paused while taking a long pull at the stout. "And it's something I don't like to discuss with other members of the Curia. Come to think of it, I could confess to you. You'd be more likely to give me advice and keep your mouth shut than they would."

"Sure I would. We used to talk when we were at school."

"Yes, we did."

"We were fucked-up then, Brian—by our mums and dads, by the Church, by everybody—maybe we still are. Has this, then, got something to do with sex? That was our main problem back then."

Finn resisted the religion-and-sex jokes that popped into his head. "You know, I've thought about that. Did you notice that although the teachers tried to help us make the right moral choices, they never went as far as trusting us with girls? It was your choice, Brian. Catholicism is deathly afraid of sex in any form. And no one I know of ever said they 'felt the call of celibacy'."

"You took a different route than I, Finn."

"The Church taught that women were either nuns or whores. I came to the conclusion that girls were far better than the solitary pleasures of wanking." Try as he might, Finn could seldom remain serious for long.

Brian shook his head. "I still remember when you told me that the reason the priests wanted us to sleep with our arms outstretched in the form of a cross was to discourage masturbation. I thought it was because God would see me as a good Christian boy and not take me up to heaven in the night. You know, 'if I should die before I wake'." Brian took a long pull of his drink, relishing the bitter, burnt-cork taste.

"You won't find wanking mentioned too often in the Bible, but the Vatican has always claimed it knows exactly what Christ and St. Paul thought about anything. They can't blame some of us for figuring that is bullshit."

"Earthy, but to the point. Finn, I haven't been happy for some time. I feel I've missed a great deal. But I have trouble picturing how my life could be any better sometimes. Better what you know. . . ."

"Maybe you think, to put it bluntly, that you are only one piece of tail away from perdition. You've got to get rid of the damn guilt and shame, get rid of that doctrine of inherent sinfulness of the flesh, for Christ's sake," Finn said emphatically. "If it's the job, if this Naturcept thing works out, Azusipa could use a religious front man, in or out of the Church. We pay well." He paused and ran his finger through the drops of Guinness on the table. "But it's not the job, is it?"

"You're still as blasphemous as ever, Finn. But you're right; it's not just the job. I've struggled for many long hours because I thought I may be having doubts about my faith. But it's not that either."

"We go a long way back, you and I," Finn said calmly. "Remember, we both went out into the world in search of knowledge, some kind of meaning to life. We can express our opinions and discuss our feelings, but in the end we both have to figure it out for ourselves. We've been banjaxed by sex, and your problem may be as simple or as complex as sex. It does create problems . . . but sexual ignorance can destroy lives. Tell me—why should believers in the Kingdom have to choose between faith in God or a rewarding sex life?"

"It's a basic question, all right. I've often wondered if I am any holier or smarter than a married Anglican priest," Brian said candidly.

"Well, you're not, pal, you're not. You could become an Anglican and get married; they'd be glad to have you. Then you could return to the Catholic fold as a married Anglican priest and the Vatican would take you back. It's been done before."

"It's not an issue we discuss," the Monsignor said with resignation.

"There are three classes of people—those who make it happen, those who watch it happen, and those who say, 'What happened?' Which are you? . . . You know very well that something is rotten in the Papal State. Too many priests are being busted for everything from normal lust to outright perversion. That must make you feel damned uncomfortable."

"Of course it does. And I guess it really is quite obvious where the major problem lies."

"Right you are, Brian. You got it in one. Celibacy doesn't work. It never did and it never will. If you want my opinion, go with your sexuality; don't avoid it, it's unhealthy. And speaking of going, I'm taking a little holiday away from Rome. I'm leaving today for Switzerland."

The Guinness had been refreshing, the conversation food for thought. "The apple has already been eaten. Is that what you are telling me, Finn?"

"Right again, boyo. But you could still get a few bites if you tried."

That evening, Nestor offered to treat Charlotte and Brian to dinner. After all, it would be his first real night in Rome, the time in captivity certainly not counting. They went to the L'Eau Vive in the Via Monterone, a restaurant on a small back street near the Pantheon.

They were escorted to their table by an impeccably dressed matron, who, in different surroundings, could have passed for a Mother Superior. Feeling triumphant after having finally met with the Pope, Nestor ordered a magnum of champagne before the meal. The food, although excellent, could not compare with the quality of service. A tall, strikingly beautiful young woman wearing a dress that emphasized her curves waited on them. That she belonged to a missionary order was only obvious if one noticed the small gold cross around her neck.

Charlotte noted that nearly every diner in the restaurant were clerics of varying rank, and that the waitresses were all very attractive. Was this part of the role of women in the Church? she wondered.

Playfully, she asked, "Do you come here often, Brian?"

"Ah, no, as a matter of fact, I haven't been here before, Charlotte," Brian stammered. "But it certainly is different, very impressive." He looked at Nestor. "This will cost you dearly. We who are about to eat and drink, thank you." Brian raised his glass in salute.

The three friends laughed together in the pleasant glow from the champagne. They were full of enthusiasm, pleased that their lives would now settle into a more normal routine. As the men vied for Charlotte's attention, she realized she was thoroughly enjoying herself.

Much later in his quarters in the Apostolic Palace, Father Brian couldn't sleep. He decided to distract himself by going to the office to handle a few routine matters. It might put him in a sleeping frame of mind. He slipped a dressing gown over his pyjamas and put on his slippers.

He surveyed the room in which he had laboured long in the work of the Lord. He carried on into the late Bettini's inner sanctum, switched on the reading lamp over the Cardinal's desk, and sat in the high-backed chair. He felt that he belonged there. He picked up the top file from a stack on the desk and read, "Levesque, Canonization, Sacred Congregation for the Cause of Saints." The last document in the file was the Curia form designed to indicate the Secretary of State's vote in relation to the granting of sainthood to "Saint Athol." It was not completed or signed. He looked for some indication on the file as to what Bettini might have decided in the matter; his vote might well be the one to clinch the matter of Father Athol Levesque's canonization. Then he found a slip of paper on which the word "no" was written.

Kelleher sat and stared at the memo for several minutes. Suddenly a revelation struck him, a proverbial bolt out of the blue. He saw no need to question his decision, no need to weigh the pros and cons. If the man wants to be a saint, let him be one, he thought. When he was alive he must certainly have known that he wasn't. Brian felt very light-headed, as though he had been touched by the hand of God.

Crumpling the memo into a ball, he threw it into the waste-paper basket. With the Cardinal's pen in hand, he back-dated and marked the form in favour of sainthood, forging Angostura Bettini's signature at the bottom of the page. It was later said to be the Cardinal's last official act before he died a martyr.

Nestor couldn't sleep either. Thoughts about his theory of probability competed for attention with the throbbing pain in his left buttock and leg. Had it worked for him again as it had done when he applied statistical methods and produced Naturcept against all odds? That had called for judgment and knowledge plus a recognition of the balance of probabilities which, ultimately, begat success.

Nestor tried to determine which theory he had used when he decided to play along with Finn Mahoney and Hugo Payne—an unlikely combination to be sure. It hadn't been the law of averages, which Nestor knew was superstition. Therefore, he reasoned, he had probably used the improbability theory. Perhaps there was some other force at work he hadn't yet uncovered. He shifted positions for several hours, finally propping the pillows under his knees before falling asleep.

Charlotte Lockwood lay in her hard bed at the Pilgrims' Hospice in Vatican City, thinking about her life. She knew that she had changed radically in recent days and weeks, that her blind obedience to the teachings of the Catholic Church could never be regained. Her life must take a different form, but what would it be? She was looking forward to her private audience with Pope Cesare. Charlotte's mind wandered through the possibilities as sleep carried her away.

"No doubt I'll be finding something else to worry about before long," Finn said to his companion, "the human condition being what it is and all. Sin is the willful breaking of religious law. Religions teach sin at as early an age as possible. Over a lifetime I've gradually analyzed the nature of the sins and heresies promulgated by the Church. I've replaced their fixed dogma, substituted my personal experience, knowledge and interpretation, and I've used logic as a criterion when it comes to what constitutes sin. So, I've eliminated the guilt which Christianity attempts to instill in those who still adhere to the Faith. And maybe that's just what Jesus really wants you to do!"

Then Finn rolled over and fell instantly asleep in a Zurich bed, his state and peace of mind, and that of his female companion, greatly aided by the use of Naturcept.

Before Pope Cesare Romereo fell asleep that night, listening to a Brazilian salsa band on his stereo, he suddenly wished he was home, and not here in Rome. There were too many problems to solve in God's world today. Why, Cesare wondered, must it so often be left up to him to be the final judge? Of course he knew why, and he also knew that this time he'd need a little extra help from the Father, the Son, and the Holy Ghost. His final thought before a fitful sleep was that he would have to call on all three before making one of the gravest decisions of his life.

EPILOGUE

Vatican City, Christmas Day, 1999 A.D.

POPE CESARE ROMEREO I looked down on the assembled throng in St. Peter's Square, a vast wholesale supermarket where sellers and buyers of theological ideas had long met in the gulf-stream of Roman Catholic religious fervour.

Cesare began to speak, opening by paraphrasing the words of Pope Innocent VIII in the Papal Bull of December 5th, 1484, the one which initiated the persecution of so-called witches:

"'Desiring with supreme ardour, as pastoral solicitude requires, that the Catholic faith in our days everywhere grow and flourish as much as possible, we freely declare and anew decree this by which our pious desire may be fulfilled—that all errors in our faith may be rooted out by our toil, as with the hoe of a wise labourer, and with zeal and devotion to this faith, may it take a deeper hold on the hearts of the faithful themselves.'

"This is a day of fraternal union and joy, so let us be guided by Him. What does Jesus the Good Shepherd and Light of the World have to say to us on this, his birthday? His words have guided me in the past and continue to guide me as I announce a decision of great import to our world. . . ."